Rhonda The Rubber Woman

Rhonda The Rubber Woman

by

Norma Peterson

THE PERMANENT PRESS
SAG HARBOR, NY 11963

Library of Congress Cataloging-in-Publication Data

Peterson, Norma.
    Rhonda the Rubber Woman/by Norma Peterson.
        p.   cm.
    ISBN 1-57962-003-5
    I. Title.
    IN PROCESS PS3566.E   R
    813'.54--DC21   97-21535

THE PERMANENT PRESS
4170 Noyac Road
Sag Harbor, NY 11963

PROLOGUE

Until lately a problem with my mom, besides being the town hussy, was the way she thought about life. The way she used to see it, life was like a giant jigsaw puzzle, and you had your place in the puzzle, and that was the end of it. There were the hotshots whose pieces were a part of the real picture, like the blue lake or the gleaming castle in the center. Then there were the others whose pieces made up the clouds in the distance or the trunk of a tree alongside the castle. The way my mom saw it, if that was your place, no matter how hard you tried to fit into the lake or the castle, tough luck. The only place you'd ever fit would be the tree trunk or the cloud.

Me, I like to think life is more like a poem. You can keep working at it and make it better. I want to go places and do things. Right now Bobby Felker wants me to run off with him, and I want to, but if I go it'll mean a life of crime, and I'll have my mom to thank for that, too.

I'm heading back to Philadelphia to write everything down and try to make sense of it, waking up a hundred times a night, thinking of the afternoon with Bobby when Artie Shaw played "Begin the Beguine," trying to feel like a normal human being. I don't know. Life is getting spooky. Sometimes I think I should go back to being Rhonda the Rubber Woman.

Nancy Sayers, age 17, 1947

Georgia's Girl

Part One

1
GEORGIA SAYERS, 1930

I lived for when Carl came to Marysville. The home office sent him around every three weeks and we'd go off in his Packard, Carl driving like a house afire, and park on Wind Gap Junction Road and do it. Afterwards he'd laugh and call me his little sex fiend and I'd laugh, too.

I was surprised doing it was so noisy. Carl moaned and groaned so much at first I was embarrassed, but later I started to moan and groan back a little to be polite. It was like in church when some folks sing the hymns real loud and you don't know the tune, but you try to put in your two cents' worth anyway.

Afterwards we'd smoke cigarettes and look out at the cornfields in the moonlight and listen to the katydids. Carl usually talked about goings-on at the stocking factory but I only listened out of the corner of one ear, feeling sticky and uncomfortable, wishing I could change my underwear.

I liked doing it with Carl, though. I thought about it even when we weren't together. Sometimes feelings welled up in my throat as though they were too much for a little five-foot two-inch person to bear. I pictured us married like my sister Cora and her husband Walt, nestled together in a cute apartment over in Clinton. I was so happy, I called Carl my honey and I wanted to tell the world about us but he said I shouldn't. He said the company frowned on employees getting sweet with one another.

I thought of saying Marian Uhler from finishing went out with Clarence Bobst over in supplies, and nobody seemed to mind, but I didn't. I figured Carl's job was probably more important, being sent around to fix machines at plants like ours all over Pennsylvania. Plus I was lucky to have a job at all. They only hired so many girls.

We had this system. When he wanted to see me, he'd come into the lunch room at noon whistling "Anything Goes." That's what was playing the day we met; I still remember.

Carl is at the counter eating a ham sandwich and I'm

sitting at a formica table drinking a cup of coffee with cream. Carl looks down at me. "I'm Carl Markell. Don't you work at the stocking factory?" I jerk as if somebody'd poked me. "Yeah, over in seams," I whisper. Carl picks up his plate and brings it over and sits down with me. He's handsome, with dark eyes, brown hair, and eyebrows big as brushes. "So you have an advantage over me." He squints and lights a cigarette. "You know my name but I don't know yours." I laugh. "Georgia Sayers."

"*In olden days a glimpse of stocking was looked on as something shocking*," Ethel Merman sings from the jukebox. "So, Georgia," Carl leans toward me, "how about we go out for a ride tonight? Maybe stop at a speakeasy." A speakeasy! I shiver just thinking about it. "Oh, I'd love to," I whisper. "*. . . heaven knows, anything goes*," Ethel sings. "Good." Carl glances at his watch. "Well, back to the salt mines." He gets up. "Yeah." I stub out my Raleigh. "No rest for the idle, huh?" I give him a sunny smile and walk back to work with a belly warm as pancakes.

Carl had said to meet him at Marysville Park so that night and then all the other nights I told Mama I was going to meet some girls from work, but instead I'd walk over to the football stadium behind the park where Carl would pick me up. Mama would just nod and smile as she folded clothes or darned socks, waiting for *Fibber McGee and Molly* or *Easy Aces*, her gray hair pulled back in a bun that hung loose on her neck like a bird's nest. Mama was getting old so she didn't ask questions like she used to. I was glad. I don't know why but Mama always worried about me. Cora used to tease me saying it was because I was so slaphappy. Cora was only nineteen, a year younger than me, but smarter.

Anyway, I kept things to myself like Carl said to until they started going bad, and then I had to tell someone about of my fist. I felt like my nerves were going to jump out of my skin. A clock ticked from somewhere in the dark behind his desk.

"And I got . . . pregnant," I blurted out. There. I'd said it, half expecting a bolt of lightening to hit me, but there was just the ticking of the clock.

"Pregnant!" The reverend's voice sounded like a gun crack. For a minute I felt peeved at him saying it out so loudly. His smile faded, his hands lifted, and he stiffened as he got up and looked out the paneled window at the night. "It's the times. The music. The drink. Women going to work." He turned back toward me. "That's where you met him, isn't it? At work."

I could feel the blood banging in my fingertips. I fidgeted in my chair, wishing he would just give me some prayers to say and get it over with.

"Who is the man, Georgia?" the reverend said in a kind voice, but he had a stern look on his face, like a school teacher. He walked toward me and sat down again.

I hadn't expected this. My knees knocked together and I thought I shouldn't say Carl's name, that somehow it would cause more trouble. "He's moving somewhere else," I muttered. "He's not coming back to Marysville."

The reverend's eyes softened. "Georgia," he said, "the Lord must know the man's name. You can't tease the Lord telling Him just a little." He leaned closer.

I was afraid to say but more afraid not to, so I told him Carl's name. Then he asked me how many times we'd done it and where. His eyes got shiny as I mumbled, looking up at him in shaky jerks.

My voice was small and breathless, but I kept going, scared of what would happen if I didn't. "My . . . uh . . . girlfriend from work, Mildred . . . she found out he's married. He has . . . uh . . . three children. Boys," I stuttered.

The reverend jumped up. "Lord, help us. A wife and three innocent children."

The reverend looked sad for a minute, then sat down again and put his hand over my trembling fingers. "Now now, Georgia," he said. "The Lord understands." He took off his glasses. The skin around his eyes looked like raw meat.

"Pray for forgiveness. Ask the Lord for help in turning away from the Devil's wicked ways."

"Oh, I will," I whispered.

"The child will be your penance. The price of your sin."

I dipped my head and looked ashamed.

Reverend Mackey shifted in his creaky chair. "Would you like me to tell your Mama?"

I nodded.

"Poor Catherine." That made me feel the worst of all. "Is she still feeling poorly?"

"Oh, no." I crossed my fingers behind my back. "They gave her different kinds of medicine. She's better now."

"Good." The rReverend patted my arm. "Well, what's done is done, isn't it?" he said. "I will tell Catherine that sometimes sin just gets ahold of a person. I will tell her to be forgiving."

"Thank you, Reverend Mackey," I said, grateful he was finished.

As he opened the rectory door, he leaned close. "Come and talk to me again any time, Georgia. I understand that the flesh is weak."

"Oh, I will. Thank you."

Then he gave me a hug and I noticed his glasses were thick and dirty; his head just seemed to grow out of his shoulders. In fact, there was hardly any neck at all.

The next church bulletin had a tip for morning sickness. "Keep a tin of soda crackers by your bed and eat two first thing when you wake up, before you even lift your head," it said. "Don't worry about crumbs on the sheet."

But Mama didn't say a word. She was up and around again except she moved slow and still coughed like her insides were rattling around in a bag.

Then one Tuesday morning just after I'd put the sign in the window for fifty pounds of ice, she sat down at the kitchen table and said, "Well, Reverend Mackey came to see me. He said you'd gone and got yourself pregnant."

"I'm sorry, Mama," I whispered, standing by the window. I could feel the wind from outside through the glass. She had a stern look. "He said it was our cross to bear, but I don't like that kind of talk. So I've thought about it, and I don't see why I can't raise another baby. I raised two. I had to bury one. Poor Carol." Mama looked down, blinked and got up for a cup of tea. Her housedress hung on her like a sack. She sat down again and I worked up the nerve to walk to the table and sit across from her.

She looked at me. "Maybe the Lord is giving me another chance." Her voice sounded strong but her eyes looked pale as rinse water.

"Whatever you want to do, Mama." I hung my head.

Mama reached her hand across the table and touched mine. "Georgia," she said, "some folks grow up sooner than others." Her round face looked pale and heavy, like dough. "I always told your daddy, bless his soul, I figured you'd be a late bloomer, but this baby is going to hurry you along."

"I know," I mumbled, but I felt irked. I didn't want to be hurried along. I never hated a person in my life but I had a bad feeling about that baby.

"Folks will gossip," Mama said. "We'll just ignore them. It's not their concern." Her blue-gray eyes widened; she meant business.

I nodded, ashamed.

"Georgia . . ." Mama sounded peeved and her voice rose. "I don't want you hanging your head about this. You're going to have to show some gumption. One thing about the Sayers women, we've always had gumption." She slapped her hand on the oilcloth. "And if anything happens to me, you need to be ready."

"Don't talk that way." My voice came out so loud it surprised us both. "Nothing's going to happen to you." My fingers started twitching. "You'll get better when summer comes."

Mama sighed and looked toward the window. It was drizzling now, and a wet leaf had blown up against the window like a hand. She turned back and gave me a small smile. "Maybe you're right," she said and squeezed my fingers.

After that we hardly talked about the baby except to make arrangements, and Mama and Cora did most of that. I was glad. I couldn't get Reverend Mackey's warning out of my mind, that it would be my penance. Later when it began to kick, I got scared it would be born with horns. I kept acting like my usual cheerful self but at night in my room I whacked pillows against the headboard of my bed my until my shoulders ached. Every time I thought about Mama saying to have more gumption, I whacked harder. At work I did more seams in a day than you could shake a stick at. I wished I could do seams all night, too. Doing seams kept me from going loco.

Cora found me a doctor in Allensville, a town twenty miles away, and he delivered the baby when it was time—a little girl. It didn't have horns, it was just an ordinary baby with dark hair and brown eyes. It was kind of cute except when it cried. Then it got on my nerves, but Mama pretty much took care of it. She'd sit on her squeaky old rocking chair hugging the baby against her chest and she'd cough and its tiny backside would jiggle. I'd tickle its little chin once in a while but the truth was I wanted to crawl up on Mama's lap myself.

I knew people were gossiping. I'd see the women gather in circles downtown and watch their cloche hats tilt together as I walked by sticking out like a sore throat. I just tried to ignore them. To tell the truth, I missed Carl more than I worried about being a sinner or repenting. I missed our nights on Wind Gap Junction Road.

One Saturday when she came to visit, Cora said I should help out more with little Nancy, she was afraid Mama wasn't long for this world, but I told her to shush up, Mama would get better when summer came. I remember we were out in the yard airing out Mama's mattress and beating the germs out of the rugs. It was a warm spring day. Cora had jerked and pursed her lips at me talking back to her. She wasn't used to it and I had to smile a little as I pounded away on the rugs.

I couldn't help being edgy and irritable, though. Summer came and Mama stayed the same. One night I dreamed she coughed all her insides up on the kitchen floor.

it so I told Cora, then I told the reverend, and eventually the whole town found out. What happened was that the chickens came home to roost, and I got caught. Pregnant. One night in September I tried to tell Carl I'd missed a period. I was scared and not so sure we should keep on doing it, but he wouldn't listen. He never liked me talking beforehand. If I ever tried to say anything beforehand, he'd put his fingers over my mouth and say "Sh sh sh sh. It's better if you don't talk."

So I told him afterwards. He looked peeved. He lit a Camel and stared out the car window for a long time. It was drizzling; everything seemed to smell damp and dreary, and you could hear the rustling of wet leaves.

Finally he said, "It's probably just your nerves." He flicked his cigarette out the window and looked at me, his mouth curving way down on one side.

"Do you think so?" I wondered. I always did have bad nerves. Bugs. Thunder. Just someone walking up from behind could scare the daylights out of me. Cora called me Jittery Georgia.

"Try to relax," Carl said. He ran his fingers down my cheeks and across my neck and squeezing my shoulders. "That's all you need to do, relax."

But I couldn't relax. I missed another period and I started feeling queasy. I had to tell everybody I had the stomach flu. Then one night when we were parked on Wind Gap Junction Road, Carl told me the bosses in Paoli reassigned him to work in another region and he'd be moving away from where he lived out in the R.D. He wouldn't be coming to Marysville anymore.

"I'll miss you, Georgia." He took off his fedora and ran his fingers around the brim of it instead of looking at me. "You're really sweet. But I bet some nice guy will come along before you know it, some nice guy who'll take care of you."

I twisted a button on my sweater, so scared my heart started beating a mile a minute. I wondered if this is what happens when a body is heartbroken. Your heart starts beating so fast it goes all helter skelter and so do you.

Carl reached into my purse, pulled out a Raleigh and lit it for me. When I took it, our hands touched, and I shivered. He lit another Camel for himself and rolled down the window of the Packard. The night air, with its scent of sweet corn and fertilizer, slapped against my face.

I started to cry.

"Come on, Georgia, you're a big girl," Carl said. He leaned over and kissed my throat.

I wasn't even worrying anymore about getting pregnant.

"I'll miss you so much," I whispered.

"Oh, Georgia, I'll miss you, too," he said.

My Raleigh was wet from tears and my nose started running. Carl gave me a hanky, and put his fingers over my eyes and mouth, saying, "Sh sh sh sh," to stop the crying. Then before you know it, he whispered, "How about one more time, Georgia? One for the road."

"You got knocked up?" Cora's mouth fell open when I told her. We were in Mama's kitchen having coffee. Cora came to visit once a week from over in Clinton. She and Walt had moved there after they got married. "A big city is more debonair," Cora had said. Now she was sitting on a wooden chair tightening her garters, her silky blond hair hanging over her face on one side. But when I told her what had happened she jerked her head up fast and stared at me, her eyebrows arching like two pyramids.

"Jesus, Georgia," she said. "Sometimes I think when they gave out brains, you were in Toledo."

"Don't say that, Cora." My chin began to tremble.

She clutched her garters, her legs milky white above her rolled stockings. "Didn't you make the jerk use anything? Don't you know about rubbers? These days everyone uses them."

I had heard about rubbers but I blushed at Cora saying the word out loud, and I wouldn't in a million years have been able to say it to Carl. I figured he knew what he was doing. Anyway I was always too busy thinking how romantic it was, Carl on my mind all the time, then the two of us being so warm and close when he came to Marysville—as warm and close as two people ever can be. Plus there'd been something else. A part of me had wanted to show Cora I could get a little something out of life, too. Cora always had all the luck. I wanted some of it, too.

By now I wasn't feeling very lucky, though. I was feeling miserable and sinful. I started to cry and reached in my blouse pocket for a hanky.

Cora got up and walked over to where I was sitting on the other side of the table, alongside the coal stove. "What are you going to do?" she asked, perching on the edge of the table and putting her arm around me. Her left hand hung down over my shoulder. The tiny diamond on her engagement ring snuggled next to the wedding band sparkled like a sunburst through my tears.

I wanted to push her hand away, but I turned my head instead. "I don't know," I sobbed. "My friend from work, Mildred, found out he's married," I sputtered through the hanky. "He has three children. Boys. They live out in the R.D. But they're gonna move."

"Jesus," Cora whispered. "What a bastard!" Then after a minute she said, "There are places you can go to have it. Homes for wayward girls. I heard about one up in Boston."

"Boston?" She might as well have said the moon. I hadn't ever even been to Philadelphia or even Hershey, someplace I'd always wanted to go because I loved their chocolate—places right here in Pennsylvania. How would I ever get to Boston?

I cried harder and she patted my shoulder. "Well, there are probably places closer by," she said. She started naming towns that might have homes for wayward girls, but then decided they were probably expensive, wherever they were, and I only made $15.00 a week at the factory and I gave $7.50 of it to Mama for room and board.

Cora pulled a chair up and we sat quietly. She hugged me again. I felt sick to my stomach and wished I had a saltine. Looking down at my lap, I twisted my hanky into a tight knot.

After a while Cora lit a cigarette and said, "Do you want me to tell Mama for you?"

I looked at her through the cloud of smoke, afraid she wouldn't tell it right.

"No. I'll do it."

But I put it off and the next thing I knew, Mama got a bad cough that came from way down inside her and cracked like sheets snapping in the wind. The doctor said pneumonia, gave her pills and put her to bed for a month. I decided to go see Reverend Mackey, who I knew liked Cora and me. He'd tell us we had the nicest peaches and cream complexion of any girls in the congregation, and sometimes he'd give us an extra pat or a hug.

I hadn't ever been in the rectory before. When I knocked on the heavy wood door, Reverend Mackey opened it right away, his head big and round as a red cabbage. He gave me a smile and said, "Here, Georgia, have a seat," putting his stocky hand on a chair in front of a huge desk.

I sat down, my heart thumping to beat the band. The desk lamp had a papery orange shade that made the light dim but I could see the reverend had on a dark jacket and a sweater vest underneath. When he bent down to pull another chair up closer to mine, I noticed that his thin black hair was combed straight back so neatly the teeth marks of the comb still showed.

"Well, Georgia," he said, putting his hands palm down on his legs, "you say you have a problem."

"Yes," I whispered.

"Well, now, you don't need to be embarrassed here." The reverend smiled wider. "This is the house of the Lord." He put one of his hands on mine, which were clenched in my lap. I noticed there was a copy of the church bulletin on his desk with a note clipped to it that said "Castor Oil for Corns." The reverend was an expert on home remedies for everything from pinkeye to phlegm in the throat. He liked to print little tips for the ladies in the church bulletin.

"Just tell me what's bothering you as though you were praying to the Lord, Georgia," he said.

"Well . . . " I began, so scared, my heart pounding, "I . . . uh . . . have been seeing a man."

"Yes, yes," Reverend Mackey put his other hand on top

3
NANCY, 1942

I knew my mom had boyfriends but at least she never brought anyone around to the apartment when I was little. I was glad. I hated how the kids teased, "Hey, it's Harry, Dick, and Tom, havin' fun with Nancy's mom." I hated thinking of my mother doing anything funny with men. When I was eleven, I decided I was a virgin birth. My dad visited my mom in a dream, and the next thing she knew she was pregnant. I decided I was supposed to be a savior, like Jesus. I liked the idea of being a savior, but then I'd get to school and want some attention so I'd do my Carmen Miranda imitation where I'd hold a banana over my head, roll my eyes, and sing "Ay Ay Ay Ay." Later I'd go home and feel let down, realizing I probably wasn't a savior after all. The only good thing I ever did was let kids copy my homework, but that was to make them like me.

Anyway, things got worse when I was eleven and my mom met Eddie Jeffers.

Out of the blue, she came home from work one day and said, "I'm . . . uh . . . having a guest tomorrow night, and when he gets here, you should . . . uh . . . well, after dinner, you should go right into your bedroom and do your home-work." We were in the kitchen, where I was doing frac-tions.

I felt my chest go weak. "A man?"

She giggled and put her purse on the counter, her blond hair fresh and fluffy. "Now, Nancy, you know children are supposed to be seen and not heard."

She lit a cigarette, shook the match out and dropped it into a green glass ashtray on the kitchen table, then flicked on the radio and walked into the bathroom. I drew a baby with a deformed arm on my math paper. I drew a girl with missing ears.

"Rosie the Riveter" started playing; an announcer came on and said, "Young ladies, if your brothers or boyfriends are off defending democracy, do your part, as well. Take a war job. Be the woman behind the man behind the gun."

"Nancy," my mom called out, "did you get these water spots on the spigot? Haven't I told you a thousand times to wipe off the spigot? What would a guest think?"

"I'm sorry," I mumbled. We had a lot of neatness rules since Grandma died and we moved into an apartment above Doc Gummerman's drugstore. No finger prints. No scuff marks. My mom waxed the old cracked linoleum every other week and we walked on hankies for two days until it settled. And she cancelled the newspaper. She said it smudged things too much.

"I'll wipe it off," I said, heading for the bathroom. The radio went staticky as I walked away.

"No, never mind, I'll do it myself." My mother had taken her dress off and was standing at the sink in her slip wiping the chrome, her bosom jiggling underneath the lace as she rubbed. "I want it done right." Her cigarette crackled in a tin ashtray on top of the toilet tank.

I stopped. The sound from the radio was almost all static now. I slouched into the living room and stood staring at a ceramic wall decoration my mother had bought at a church bazaar of a devil sitting on a swing in the middle of a bunch of green grapes. He was dressed all in red. Red pointed hat, red suit, red boots, and he had a smile on his face. I'd always thought he looked too cute to be a devil, but somehow he scared me all the more for it. He reminded me of Reverend Mackey. The reverend came around once a week saying the Lord wanted him to help his Baptist families in distress. I didn't like being a family in distress, and I especially didn't like Reverend Mackey. His skin was too oily, like cheese in the sun, and he smiled as though he had gas pains. I always had to stay in my room when he came.

Sometimes I tried to listen to them through the wall. I'd hear Reverend Mackey preach about sins of the flesh and ask my mother questions, then I'd hear her little-girl voice quiet as whispers, but I could never make out what she said. Before he left, he always gave her a health tip, loud enough so I could hear it. Try some potato water for that chapped skin. Remember, honey for the tummy, world's best pick-me-up for low energy. Once he brought around a gizmo he said he'd invented. You hooked up some wires around your ears and ankles and it was supposed to suck the poisons out of you. My mom tried it a couple of times but Aunt Cora busted out laughing when she saw it. Now my mom came into the living room. She'd turned off the radio and looked friendlier. She had her purse. "Uh, look, why don't you go get some hot dogs and I'll boil them for dinner." The butcher had started staying open late for war workers. "Here." She pulled out a dollar and gave me two meat coupons. "Go get some hot dogs and buns." She tugged out another dollar and smoothed a wrinkle in it. "And stop at the bakery and buy some cream puffs. We'll have a nice meal."

The next night Eddie came to dinner. My mom took off early from work and cleaned as if the King of Siam was visiting. She sent me out to buy beef pasties from the church. The Methodist ladies held bake sales twice a week. On Wednesdays they made pasties. Friday was doughnut day.

"Stop at Doc's and get three nice slices of Boston cream pie," she said. One good thing about living above Doc's, we spent a lot of time there. My mom hated to cook. "All that work, peeling and chopping and measuring, and then you eat it in five minutes," she complained. "It's easier to go downstairs for a melted cheese sandwich." I loved the people at Doc's, Ben Kleeber, who worked at the bank and looked like Tyrone Power, and Bob Bruch, who was an usher at the movies and always good for a laugh. They'd come in for Cokes and joke around with us and I'd feel proud of my mom for a while, with her sunbeam yellow hair and her hourglass figure. I'd feel sorry for kids whose moms had backsides that heaved when they walked and you couldn't find their waists anywhere, like the President's wife, Mrs. Roosevelt.

Sundays were special. We'd get all dressed up. "It's important to put your best face forward," my mom would say. On Sundays we'd order something extra to go with our sandwiches. Potato salad with sliced egg on top or jello cubes with whipped cream for dessert. But then later when we went back upstairs, my mom would stop trying to put her best face forward. She'd chain-smoke, stare at the linoleum, and talk to me in a voice like a kid giving a boring geography report. Sometimes if a love song came on the radio, she'd look up at me as if I hurt her eyes and go into the bathroom.

At 5:30 p.m., the doorbell downstairs rang. I heard my mom giggle as she answered, then footsteps on the stairs. Eddie sounded like he was purposely thumping his foot every other step. I held my breath as they walked in. He was small and skinny, sort of like Fred Astaire. He had creamy skin for a man, with dark hair and a mustache. Then I realized why he had thumped on the stairs. One of his legs was shorter than the other one so his right shoe had a big sole on it thick as a brick. "So this is Nancy," my mom said, a look of desperation in her eyes, as though she wished I was a bunch of daisies she could plunk into a vase of cold water and forget about.

"How do." Eddie smiled at me. A lock of his hair sprang out of place and fell down over his forehead.

I mumbled, "Hello."

"I brought ya little sumthin'," Eddie said, still smiling. He reached into his pants pocket and pulled out a small package wrapped in wrinkled blue and yellow striped paper. I didn't want to touch it after it had been in his pocket. I looked at my mom, who was bouncing a little.

I took the present and opened it. It was one of those straw thingamajigs you get at carnivals where you stick your fingers in and pull, and the next thing you know, you can't get your fingers out again.

"So if ya like it, there's plenty more where it came from," Eddie said with a laugh. Eddie sold carnival novelties—plastic dolls and wax teeth and combs shaped like fish. Marysville was on his route.

My mother and I were stiff at dinner, but Eddie didn't seem to mind. He rattled on and on with circus stories in a voice like Popeye. My mom beamed and laughed and said a million times, "Isn't that something?" I pushed pieces of meat and potatoes around on the green plate with the ribbed edging as though they might form the words that would answer my prayers.

Eddie laughed at his own jokes. His laugh sounded like he was sniffing, and once it looked like there was a piece of snot underneath his nostril, but it could have been cooked onion. My mom pretended not to notice.

After dinner, I went into my bedroom and stared at the swirly purple and green wallpaper and daydreamed about the places I was going to run off to someday. Decatur, Illinois. Fargo, North Dakota. Pierre, Wisconsin.

I decided to become a Catholic. I'd prayed to God a zillion times to change things, and it never worked, so I figured being a Baptist wasn't good enough. I knew about Catholics because a lot of Italian kids at school went to the Catholic church, and I listened to them. I was a pretty good snoop.

I pictured myself rubbing my hands on the blood-stained legs of a statue of poor Jesus on the cross and kissing his feet and eating wafers and drinking wine. I'd put statues of saints in the bedroom, wear a necklace of glass beads, and say Hail Marys, so the Lord would finally hear me. A letter would come or the phone would ring and someone would say there had been a mix-up when I was born. I really belonged to a family in Tallahassee, Florida, and they would come and hug me and say "Our baby," and take me home with them and buy me a red velvet dress like the one in Reddick's Fashion Center window to make up for all the misery I'd been through.

The problem was I didn't know whether you could just become a Catholic or if you had to be born one like you were born German or Welsh or Polish. Most of the Catholics at school were Italians and hung out together like the rich kids and the future farmers.

Then in fourth period math class I got my chance. A new girl, Eva Giacometti, had just transferred to Marysville from Carpenter's Corner. She sat by me and had trouble with math, so I helped her out.

It took me a while to work up my nerve. I could be a bigmouth when I clowned around, but I usually went tongue-tied if I had be serious. Finally one day at recess I plunked down next to Eva on a bench alongside a group of boys playing basketball and just blurted it out. "Uh, Eva, do . . . uh . . . they allow visitors at your church? I . . . uh . . . thought it would be fun to go to church with you some Sunday." I looked away, nervous. Leroy Burnham kicked at a ball but stepped on it and fell forward on his knees. I winced.

"Well, sure," Eva said. I looked back at her. "We go to meetings at the Carpenter's Corner Kingdom Hall. My older brother Daniel drives a bunch of us over every Sunday."

Carpenter's Corner Kingdom Hall?

I gasped. Eva wasn't Catholic. She was a Holy Roller. Leave it to me. I picked the only Italian Holy Roller in town.

I thought fast. "But . . . uh . . . I have to ask my mom first. I mean, I really want to come to your . . . uh . . . church, but I have to ask my mom. I'll ask her tonight and let you know if she says I can go, okay?" I started backing away, bumped into a water fountain, felt myself go red, and rushed in to Mr. Pennymacher's science class.

"Well, sure," Eva called after me, and practically as soon as I got home from school, she came around with a pile of pamphlets telling how wonderful it was to be a Holy Roller.

"Gee, thanks," I said, standing at the door, holding the papers out as though they were old socks.

"Oh, that's okay," Eva said. "I thought you might want to read this." She slipped a pamphlet out of the pack, look-ing down. She had the thickest eyelashes I'd ever seen and her black hair grew down on her cheeks, like sideburns. "This one is good because it's not too long."

"Thanks a lot." I started closing the door. Eva sighed, but smiled as she turned around. I felt bad for a minute, but the last thing I wanted was to get in with a Holy Roller. Holy Rollers were even lower on the totem poll than I was.

I sat on a stuffed chair in the living room, flipped my legs over the arm, and read the pamphlet anyway. It said Jehovah's Witnesses were preparing for Armageddon. It said we were living in the last days of the world but a new and better world was coming. It said Jehovah's Witnesses were more moral than other people. Some of them even lived as husband and wife without sex.

I perked up. This was just what I wanted. A better world. A life without sex. The nap of the chair started scratching the backs of my legs so I swung them off and stood, staring out the window. Maybe it wouldn't hurt to go to church with Eva just one time. One little visit couldn't hurt.

"So Eva, a new kid at school, asked me to go to church with her tomorrow," I lied to my mom. "It seems like the friendly thing to do, don't you think? She's new in town and all." It was Saturday morning. My mom was in the bedroom getting dressed to go out with Eddie.

"Well, yeah, that would be friendly." My mother gave me a sunny smile. She reached into the sleeve of her eyelet blouse and tugged on her dress shields as she studied herself in the mirror. "You can wear your blue straw hat. It'll look cute."

"Yeah."

She didn't ask what church Eva went to. She was too anxious to try out some new leg makeup she'd just bought. Since the war, she couldn't get any stockings. The Rutt Ridge Silk Factory, where she worked, didn't even make them anymore.

They made parachutes and camouflage material instead. She and the other girls she worked with put tan makeup on their legs to look like stockings, then drew seams up the back with eyebrow pencil. It never looked like they were really wearing stockings. It looked like they were wearing leg makeup with seams drawn up the back. But you could tell they were proud of themselves for finding a way to make do.

I stood in the doorway for a minute and watched my mom rub the thick tan liquid on her right instep, ankle, shin, and knee, her fingers working carefully and slowly up toward her thighs. I slipped outside and headed for the empty lot behind Doc's to practice some of my double-jointed tricks. I could bend down in front and touch my nose to the ground. I could curl up into a tight ball and roll.

My mom had a conniption fit whenever she caught me. "That's so unladylike," she'd scold. But later a kid at school would say, "Hey, Nancy, show Horse Uhler how you can twist yourself," and that would be all I needed.

On Sunday Eva and Daniel picked me up with a car full of yokels wearing plain cotton dresses and no hats or gloves. At the Kingdom Hall, Eva said she had to sit with her family but Virginia, one of the kids from the car, would take me in to the meeting.

Virginia was ugly and wore huge thick glasses. "So, do you have any questions?" she asked.

"Well, uh, yeah, I do. I was wondering if Jehovah's Witnesses have a special way of praying?" Aunt Cora had once told me they cried out and talked in words that weren't really theirs but came from the spirit world. She said they sometimes rolled in the aisles.

Virginia narrowed her eyes. "That's not a good question. You should ask how you can be saved when the world comes to an end."

I wanted to say, "Well, isn't praying a part of it?" But I decided not to argue and I touched the fingertips of my white gloves together. "Okay. How can I?"

She started spouting off the same stuff I'd read in the brochure except more boring. The only interesting thing was I could see my reflection in her glasses. The sun fell on them in a way that made my face look curved and out of shape, like in the funhouse mirrors at Dorney Park. My straw hat looked like a bright blue halo around my head with glimmers dancing at the edges. I kept staring at my reflection and Virginia seemed to think I was fascinated with what she was saying. It seemed like a trick worth knowing.

Finally she shut up and took me inside. There were no statues of Jesus. No beads or stained glass or lighted candles. Just bare cement walls and a wood table with a pile of *Watchtower* magazines. We sang a hymn "Here he is who comes from Eden, all his raiments stained with blood." Then a man with red hair and short arms got up and preached.

"Never forget, we are imperfect beings, descended from the wretched sinner, Eve," he said.

"Remember," he said, "we offend Jehovah twenty-seven times a day. Every one of us." I looked around. Kids stared at their shoes. Grown-ups shook their heads, and I wondered what sins they hid behind their frowns. Little things, I was sure. Gossip, maybe. Backbiting. Coveting a neighbor's something or other once in a while. At least they knew enough to frown and repent. My mom always sat in church smiling and staring straight ahead, looking innocent as a baby.

The red-headed man rambled on about the millennium. I would rather have seen people talk in a weird language and roll in the aisles. But at the end he said, "Remember, it is better to be persecuted than to be popular," and I perked up. Maybe I fit in with the Holy Rollers after all.

On the way home we stopped at one of the girls' houses for milk and cookies. She lived in the sticks, but her house was like a normal one you'd see in Marysville, with windows and a roof and a kitchen. I was surprised. I thought people from the sticks lived in shacks, like Charlie Chaplin.

As she handed me a glass of milk, the girl asked me, "So whose kid are you?" The old panicky feeling rushed through me, but I was getting older and smarter. I came up with a story Mrs. Stiles would have been proud of. Mrs. Stiles often wrote on my compositions, "Such a lively imagination."

"Uh, well, the truth is I live with a woman named Georgia Sayers," I said, "but she isn't my real mom. My real parents were the Foul Rift Lovers. Uh . . . have any of you ever heard of the Foul Rift lovers?"

They shook their heads.

"Well," I explained, "they lived on two different sides of the Delaware River at Foul Rift. Foul Rift is the most dangerous part of the river. The current is so strong boats get sunk and people crack their heads on the rocks and die."

I took a sip of my milk. It tasted terrible, as though the glass had been washed with Bon Ami.

"Well, once a beautiful girl named Carrie who lived on the Pennsylvania side fell in love with a handsome man named Keith from the New Jersey shore, and he would swim over to meet her. Their love was so strong he was the only person ever able to swim across Foul Rift and live."

I liked them staring at me.

"Eventually Carrie and Keith got married and he moved in with her family. It was like a movie, they were so happy. Then to celebrate their first anniversary, they took a boat out together and the Foul Rift current got stronger than it ever had before and their boat sank. They were never found."

"Oh, no," Eva said. I was quiet for a minute. You could hear the crunch of cookies between teeth.

"Sometimes on moonlit nights folks say you can see them out on the water," I said.

"Wow. That's so sad. But so romantic," Eva sighed, her mouth hanging open like a little pink tunnel. Virginia gave her a dirty look.

"What nobody knew," I finished, "was that Carrie had a baby before she died. That was me. Her parents were too old to take care of me so they gave me to Georgia Sayers. That's why I don't look anything like Georgia." I loved calling my mom by her first name.

"So how did Carrie know Georgia?" Virginia asked. I stared at the stringy brown hair and glasses. People who were so ugly shouldn't talk so much, I thought.

"She just did," I snapped. "I don't know every little thing."

Virginia scrunched up her face and my heart started racing. I remembered people from Carpenter's Corner worked at the Rutt Ridge Silk Factory. Suppose one of their moms or dads knew my mother. So I quickly added, "Some people tell other stories about Georgia, but they're not true. This is the real truth. But you have to promise not to tell because Georgia wouldn't like it. She promised she wouldn't let people make a fuss over me."

"Oh, we won't tell," Eva gushed. I believed her. After all, their pamphlets said the Jehovah's Witnesses were moral and trustworthy. Plus Eva depended on me to help her get through math.

Besides, I was so thrilled with how smoothly the story had all come together, I could hardly sit still. I liked the

Holy Rollers better all the time. Maybe God really was beginning to hear my prayers.

Daniel drove us back to his and Eva's house, and I strutted home from there feeling light as air. I passed Bobby Felker, a cute kid from school, and his father, Barney, putting tin cans in the scrap metal bin outside the five and dime. I gave them a sunny smile. They smiled back and I got chills across my neck. I crossed Broadway daydreaming I was standing at the door of a wooden riverside house waving to Bobby as he rowed across Foul Rift smiling at me.

"Well, I guess you had a good time with Eva," my mom said. She'd taken off her church dress and sat at the kitchen table in her slip drinking a cup of coffee and smoking. She'd put her spectator pumps out on the fire escape to air.

"Yeah. I sure did."

"Well, I guess it's nice to go to church with someone your own age," she said. She leaned over the table to stub out her cigarette and I could see inside her brassiere. I turned away.

"Yeah," I said, staring at the linoleum. I decided I didn't care if the Jehovah's Witnesses did have boring meetings. I didn't care if people did make fun of them. I was going to become one. I wanted to make up for the sins of the wretched sinner Eve and the wretched sinner Georgia. I wanted to be saved before the world came to an end. I wanted to live in paradise on earth.

But Virginia ruined everything. I found out on Wednesday after book hour at the library.

My mom was sitting on the sofa with red eyes and droopy shoulders. Aunt Cora was there. "I want to talk to you," she said. "Your mom is too upset."

In the kitchen Aunt Cora sat me down next to her and told me what had happened. Virginia had blabbed everything to her mother, and her mother told Mrs. Mackey at the beauty parlor. Mrs. Mackey told Reverend Mackey, and he called my mom. He'd offered to talk to me, but she'd said no, Cora would come up from Clinton and do it. I was grateful for that. I loved Aunt Cora. I had once overheard Uncle Walt gripe about her driving up to Marysville so

31

often but she told him Grandma had made her promise to keep an eye on Georgia. Uncle Walt had said, "Jesus P. Christ, that's gonna do a lot of good, isn't it? She's already a slut," and I heard him slam a fist into the palm of his hand. But Aunt Cora was used to my uncle's temper. She had just said, "Oh, shush, Walt," and kept on coming anyway. Aunt Cora cheered me up with stories about her job at a music store and her jokes and big-city smells—spicy, smoky, bittersweet smells that reminded me there was a whole other world somewhere.

"Nancy, I'm sure you know that was a very bad thing to do . . . to lie like that," my aunt said now. Her blue eyes in her perfect face looked straight at me in a way my mother never could. I didn't even mind her scolding me, I was so glad to see her. In fact, I kind of liked it, her face tilted toward me, her breath warming the air between us.

"It was just a joke," I lied, but I had to turn away. I stared for a minute at the Bless This House cross-stitch above the stove, then looked back at my aunt. "We were just some kids sitting around telling jokes. Making up stories."

Aunt Cora's voice got quiet. "Jehovah's Witnesses wouldn't sit around after church making up stories," she said. "And certainly not about their parents."

I jerked in my chair at the word "parents."

My heart jumped. This was the first time anybody in my family had ever said anything about my situation. Suddenly I couldn't look at Aunt Cora. Suddenly the air in the room was pushing against my chest. I felt like I couldn't breathe, as though Aunt Cora had stirred up a voice that was always deep inside me, asking, "Do you think he cares a fig about you?"

"I'm sorry." My mouth felt dry. I clenched my fists until they hurt.

Aunt Cora reached over and put her hand on my shoulder, her eyes watery. "Go in and tell your mother. There's nothing else you can do."

I shuffled into the living room and whispered, "I'm sorry. I thought everybody was just kidding around."

My mom didn't answer. She was so upset she didn't

even bounce, just sat there with empty eyes, smoking and rolling the cellophane wrapper from her Raleighs into a tight little ball.

Watching her, I wasn't sorry at all. I was furious. Why couldn't she say something? Why couldn't she tell me the real story? What was so dark and terrible about having me that she couldn't even say it out loud? I felt rumbles in my stomach like thunderstorms rising.

4
GEORGIA, 1942

I thought we'd have a lot of fun—me and Eddie and Cora and Walt—sort of a double date. Walt's such a card I thought Eddie'd get a kick out of him.

Things started fine. We were at the Tip Top Tap Room over in Richmond Township. It was nicer than the tap rooms in town. It had a ladies' entrance and a polished wood bar with a pyramid of glasses stacked upside down. Walt and Cora were drinking bourbon, Eddie had a beer, and I had a Pink Lady.

Eddie looked good. Even though it was winter, he was wearing a yellow cotton shirt with loose sleeves that got tight at the wrist. He said it had once belonged to one of the Flying Wallendas. Eddie had snappy clothes.

"So, did you hear the one about the insurance man who asked a couple if there was any insanity in the family?" Walt joked.

We shook our heads.

"The wife said, 'Only that my husband thinks he's the head of the household.'"

Everyone hooted.

Walt's eyes went glinty. He was getting started. "Well, if you ask me, I'd tell you the Army has it all wrong to not draft married men."

"How come?" Cora smiled and lit up an Old Gold.

"Because they'd be the only recruits who really know how to take orders."

Cora snorted from laughing and inhaling her cigarette at the same time.

I nudged Eddie. "See, I told you. Isn't Walt a card?"

"Yeah. A real pistol." Eddie'd been tapping the plastic stirrer that came with my drink on the table, and now he tapped it on my fingers, looking down. His hands were almost as small as mine. After he finished all my fingers, he looked up and gave me a wink and a smile. It felt good being part of a couple.

We had another round of drinks. The Andrews Sisters sang "Boogie Woogie Bugle Boy" from the jukebox. Cora and Eddie wiggled in their seats to the music, Cora's shoulder pads bouncing up and down. Walt rolled his eyes but then the glint in them went out. Cora had started doing a patty-cake with Eddie to the music, and you could see Walt didn't like it. His face changed, like in the movie, "Dr. Jekyll and Mr. Hyde." Maybe he'd put down too many. Walt could be a mean drunk.

He looked at Eddie. "So, I don't know about you, little guy, but me, I'm ready to sign myself up. I'm going to go kill me some Krauts." He eyed Eddie's club foot.

Eddie just smiled, but I saw a little tic around the edges of his mouth.

"I guess you can take care of all the gals us GIs are going to leave behind on the homefront." Walt grinned but it was all teeth. There wasn't anything friendly to it.

Cora poked him. "Oh, Walt, with your flat feet you'll probably be right here on the homefront yourself. You can take care of all the gals yourself."

Eddie laughed. He's like me. He ignores insults. I like that about him. He took a swig of his beer and licked his lips. The yellow light in the bar seemed to go orangey and harsh. It made me blink.

We weren't having any fun any more, so we left the Tip Top and went back to the apartment. Walt made a beehive for my room and passed out. Nancy was asleep in the other bedroom.

Eddie and Cora and I sat in the parlor.

Cora flashed Eddie her flirty smile "Tell me, Eddie, being in the circus business, do you ever meet any fortune tellers?"

Eddie leaned back on the blue plush sofa. It had started snowing on the way home, and a lock of his hair was wet, falling over his face. It made him look a little like Clark Gable, I thought as I sat alongside him. Only smaller. "Ah, fortune tellers," he said. "You betcha. You betchur boots. All's you gotta do is name 'em, honey. I've met 'em." Eddie called girls "honey."

"I've always thought I'd like to get my fortune told," Cora said from the easy chair, "but Walt says it's crap. Dirty gypsies peddling superstitious crap." She grinned saying the word "crap." Cora loved to shock people more than ever since she got married. Walt egged her on. "I guess men think they already know everything."

"Not me," Eddie said. "I've had my fortune told probably a hundred times. Madame Rachel. The Omniscient Olga. Bernadette from Bengal. I've been to 'em all. Of course, being in the business, they do me for free." He rearranged himself on the sofa and picked at some of the loose pleats in the sleeve of his shirt. I felt the cushion shift underneath us.

"Is that right? Do they use a crystal ball? Tea leaves or what?" Cora's eyes were as bright as neon signs. Me, I was like Walt. I didn't care for fortune tellers. I didn't like dirty people either, plus I didn't want to worry about the future.

Eddie pushed the hank of hair off his forehead. "They're all different. Some read cards. Some read your palms. Tea leaves. Coffee grounds. All kinds of things. Madame Sharon over in West Virginia felt the bumps there. Told my fortune by feeling the bumps on my head. There's a lot of ways people who have the gift can see the future."

"What did they tell you?" Cora asked.

Eddie smiled. "Well, now, that's for me to know and for you to find out."

He noticed we looked disappointed so he added. "Okay, I'll tell you one thing. They told me I'd meet a gorgeous blond lady who smokes Raleigh cigarettes and we'd live happily ever after." He put his arm around me. We all laughed. Suddenly Walt burped loud from the bedroom. We laughed again. "That's my hero," Cora giggled. "I guess he's really pickled."

"Reminds me of a circus story," Eddie said, and he told us about the Siamese twins who did everything the same except one was a drunk and the other was a teetotaler. "They were real freaks," Eddie said. "They were joined at the side. They got hungry and sleepy at the same time. They smoked at the same time. They even knew what the other one was thinking. The only difference, Chang would drink himself silly and Eng wouldn't feel a thing."

"Isn't that something," I said.

"No kidding," Cora added.

"Chang died one night after a drunk and the next day Eng died, too. There wasn't any alcohol in his body but he died anyway." Eddie made a smacking sound out of the side of his mouth. "Too bad. Good old Chang and Eng. They were real freaks."

"Boy, you never know, do you?" I said.

Cora shook her head and frowned. "So, I guess the moral is don't get connected to a drunk, eh?" She doodled with her finger on the arm of the chair. "I guess it only takes one drunk to kill two people."

Eddie looked at her. "It don't take a drunk. Let me tell you, Cora gal, I seen a lot of characters, here, there, you name it, all kinds of trouble. It don't take a drunk. You get hooked up with someone, it works on you. Everyone's always pulling everyone up or down. You make a connection, ya got pullin."

Cora smiled a little smile and kept doodling.

"Other hand," Eddie pushed his hair back with his fingers, "you don't make a connection, whaddaya got?" The two of them exchanged a look as if they knew something I didn't. I felt left out, crossed my legs and looked at Eddie and smiled. My legs and my smile are my best things. Everyone says so.

Eddie smiled back. Then he jumped up and said, "Hey, time for me to get my beauty sleep."

After Eddie left, Cora laid back on the couch for a minute to rest her eyes while I made hot chocolate.

I put the milk on the burner and turned on the gas and decided to tell Cora that Eddie might move into the apartment. I knew some people would look down their noses at us, but that wouldn't be anything new. I was used to that. When Nancy was born we put up with our share of people jabbing each other when we walked by. I learned to laugh when kids who didn't have any manners yelled, "Hey, is that the bastard baby?" I laughed as loud as I could. And I stayed away from the snooty ladies who looked like they didn't want to touch you with a hot potato.

The milk started to boil. I turned it off, poured it into two cups, and stirred in the Hershey's chocolate.

Cora was asleep in the living room. I tiptoed over and whispered, "Cora, wake up. The hot chocolate is ready."

"Mmmm," she groaned and turned over. Her blue crepe dress got pulled to one side at the neck and I noticed there was a black and blue mark on the little hollow between her shoulder and her collarbone.

"Cora," I said louder. "The hot chocolate is ready. Wake up. I have some news."

"Oh, yeah?" Cora's eyelids fluttered and she peeked up with one eye. "So tell me. You know I hate suspense."

I cleared my throat. "Let's go in the kitchen for our hot chocolate."

We sat at the table. "I . . . uh . . . was thinking of renting Nancy's room to Eddie."

Cora's eyebrows shot up. Her hair was limp from the snow, like a tangle of silk threads.

"Won't that be kind of crowded?" she laughed.

"I mean, uh, Nancy can sleep with me." I gave her a cup of hot chocolate. "Eddie could help out with the rent." Eddie rented a room over in Benbow but it was small and cold and he said it was no decent way for a man to live.

Cora tapped an Old Gold against the outside of the pack. "Well, I think it's a good idea to rent the room. But, gee, Georgia, I don't know about renting it to Eddie. People might talk." She pulled out a pack of matches from the Tip

Top Tap Room, struck one, and lit her cigarette. I took a sip of hot chocolate, then jumped up and grabbed the dishrag to wipe a spot off the woodwork.

"Oh, I don't know," I said. "Lots of people rent out rooms. Mrs. Styles down the street rents out a room to Barney Updegrove."

"But Mrs. Styles is almost seventy," Cora said. "Barney is twenty-six. And that's her house. It's different."

I sighed and felt irked. Cora never used to care what people thought.

"Well, Mildred from work thinks it's a good idea," I said, peeved. Mildred was more open-minded than a lot of people. She grew up in the city. Newark, New Jersey. Mildred knew more about life. She even had a man's job at the factory. Inspector C. Only two girls had ever been promoted to that. If I was going to listen to anyone, it should be Mildred.

"Maybe we'll get married. Me and Eddie. We've been keeping company for a year, at least when he's in town. I know he hasn't asked or anything yet, but he likes me, Cora. What I mean is, he wouldn't want to move in if he didn't like me, would he? And you heard what he said about the fortune teller. About meeting me and us living happily ever after, didn't you?"

"Well, I think he might have been just kidding about that, Georgia. But you're right. I think he likes you."

"Yeah." I got a nice warm feeling thinking Eddie might stick around. I sat down again and stared at the dish rag still in my hand. I didn't feel about Eddie the way I had felt about Carl. Carl had been special. Sometimes I'd hear the song, "Remember," on the radio, and I'd think about how Carl used to look at me when he'd pick me up at the football stadium—sort of out of the side of his eyes and with that little grin—and I'd still get chills. But Eddie treated me good, and it would be nice to have a man around the house.

"Have you said anything to Reverend Mackey?" Cora asked.

The warm feeling scooted away. Reverend Mackey wouldn't like it. Not that he ever scolded me for having boyfriends. That was one thing I liked about Reverend

Mackey. He said he could understand how a woman in my position would need male companionship. He came around and prayed for me to resist temptations of the flesh but said I shouldn't despair if I failed. I should just tell him about it. Who I was with and what we did and all. He said things would be fine if I prayed and repented. He understood that the flesh was weak.

But if Eddie moved in, things would be different. Nancy knew to leave me and Reverend Mackey alone to pray and talk but I wasn't sure Eddie would do that. But then I thought again, well, gee, if Eddie was around, maybe Reverend Mackey wouldn't have to come and pray for me so much. It was confusing.

I felt even more irritated at Cora. "I like to have a man around the same as anyone. It's easy for you to criticize." My fingers felt ice cold. "Everything's fine for you. You're married. Everything always works out just swell for you." My voice came out in quick little gasps and tears started up in my eyes as I twisted the dish rag into a roll.

"Oh, Georgia," Cora said. "That's not true. Everything doesn't work out just swell for me. Let me tell you, kid, marriage isn't always all it's cracked up to be."

Just then Walt walked into the kitchen, his hair all flat on one side and sticking up at the top. There was a pattern from my chenille bedspread on the side of his face. "You won't get any argument from me, Miss Blabbermouth," he said and he gave Cora a look that could kill.

Cora looked scared, then laughed. "We're just joking, Georgia," she said. "I saw Walt coming out of the corner of my eye and said that to tease him."

Walt didn't say anything, but he kept the mean look on his face. My tears stopped and I felt edgy so I laughed loud and said, "Oh, sure, everyone always says you two are real cutups. Always good for a laugh."

"Yeah," Walt said, looking at me with a tiny smile. "Yeah, sure."

"I heard you talking to Aunt Cora last night," Nancy said at breakfast, brown eyes looking at me. She broke off a piece of doughnut, popped it in her mouth, and licked the powder off her fingers. We bought our doughnuts from the Methodist Church Ladies' Auxiliary. They made them fresh every Friday morning, and they were softer on the inside and crunchier on the outside, plus they had more powdered sugar than what you could get store-bought.

"Yeah, we went out together. Me and Eddie and Cora and Walt. We had a good time."

"I heard you say Eddie was gonna move in."

"Well, well, little saucers certainly have big ears, don't they?" I snapped. "You were supposed to be sleeping, young lady."

"I couldn't sleep," she said. I felt annoyed. I never knew such a restless sleeper. My bed was always neat as a bug in the morning and hers looked like a cyclone hit it. I couldn't think what to say so I started to wash out the coffee pot and put on the radio. Don McNeil and the Breakfast Club was just coming on.

"Is he going to?" Nancy took a sip of orange juice, then looked down into the glass. Her face was red and splotchy like from nerves but I figured, a kid, it couldn't be nerves. It must be bad circulation. I wished she looked more like the rest of us Sayers girls.

"Good morning, breakfast clubbers. Good morning to ya," the radio sang.

"Is Eddie going to move in?" Nancy asked louder.

"We got up bright and early just to how-de-do ya."

My stomach felt like it was heaving, like a water wheel. "That's for us grown-ups to decide," I said. I hated it that a kid could make me feel so jittery, always looking at me with those eyes, always asking enough questions to feed an army.

Nancy stared at the linoleum. Her hand was clenched tight around her juice glass.

"Well, you'd better go or you'll be late for school," I said. Then I felt bad that I didn't like her more. "Maybe I'll make some pineapple puff for dinner. We'll have a nice dinner." I dried off the coffee pot, put it back on the burner, and started wiping the counter. Don McNeil announced it was time to march around the breakfast table in his big-voiced cheery way. Behind me Nancy muttered, "Okay," and in a minute I heard her shuffle down the stairs in Cora's old boots. They were too big for her so they made a swooshing sound every step she took. But she'd outgrown her old ones so we'd given them to the scrap rubber drive. Don McNeil laughed, and for a minute I felt disappointed and confused. Why couldn't we start out the morning bright and cheerful like the breakfast clubbers?

Eddie came over Saturday afternoon with a cute little ceramic statue of the See No Evil, Hear No Evil, Speak No Evil monkeys for me. "One of our newest novelties," he explained. "I thought, hey, that's just the thing for Georgia."

"Oh, I love it," I gushed and set it on the end table next to the sofa. I stood back to admire it. "They're so cute. Look at their little shirts. And they have shiny little fingernails and everything." I flashed Eddie a smile and went to make a pot of coffee. Nancy was sledding up at Cemetery Hill.

"Mmmm. Sure hits the spot," Eddie said as we sat on the sofa sipping coffee.

I smiled. I make good strong coffee. I took a sip, too. Eddie put two cigarettes in his mouth—one Lucky Strike and one Raleigh—squinted his eyes, and lit them both. He gave the Raleigh to me.

"So what do you think, doll? What do you think about my moving in?"

"Well, I'd like that," I said. "But I don't know. Cora said people might talk."

Eddie rolled his eyes. He took a drag and lifted his head to blow the smoke up. "Sure, they will," he said. "They'll talk about what a lucky guy I am." He snuggled closer.

I laughed. "Well, gee, let's think about it a little . . . " My chest was tight and I wished I could just do what I wanted in life without having to worry about people looking down their noses at me every minute.

"That's okay by me, doll, but let me give you some free advice. Don't listen to your sister Cora." I was surprised at how sure of himself Eddie sounded.

"Being in the entertainment business, I know about people, and let me tell you, doll, that sister and that husband of hers have problems."

"No," I said. Eddie could sure be outspoken. It made me nervous. I liked people to get along.

"Yeah," Eddie said back. "For one thing, Walt don't like you. Or me. He don't like people who have things wrong with them. I could tell it the minute he opened his mouth. Even before then. Just when I saw him, with that jaw and that pompadour."

"Oh, Eddie," I said, trying not to feel so irritable. "Walt's a good guy. He's a lot of fun. He just gets a little drunk once in a while." I wondered what he meant, people who have things wrong with them. I knew Eddie had a bum foot, but I didn't. I had all normal parts.

Eddie squished his cigarette out and twirled the signet ring on his little finger. A sword-swallowing girl had once given it to him. He shrugged. "Maybe so," he said.

"Anyway, we don't have to decide now," I said. "I still have to ask Mr. Statdler. But I think he'll probably like it that you have a steady job to help pay the rent." I felt myself get flustered. I didn't want to sound like a gold digger. "What I mean is, us Sayers girls are real good workers. But you know landlords. They think men are more reliable."

Eddie smiled. "And you'd like to have me around more permanent like, right, doll?" Eddie said. He ran his fingertip along the tiny beads on the collar of my dress.

I felt myself blush. "Yes, I would," I said. I wished I had the nerve to ask if that meant he wanted to get married. I peeked at the signet ring on his finger and thought about the sword-swallowing girl.

His eyes traveled around the apartment. "Well, I think it would be great, Georgia. Just great. Being around a beautiful doll like you all the time. At least all the time when I'm in eastern P.A."

The doorbell rang and I went down to answer. It was Shirley Hunnicut, one of Doc's waitresses. She looked worried.

"Listen, Georgia, don't get upset," she said, putting her hands out in front with the palms toward me as I opened the door. "Nancy had an accident."

My neck started to hurt and the icy air from outside made me shiver. "Oh, no. Where is she?"

"She's in the back room. I cleaned her up a little and told her to let me talk to you before she came upstairs."

"What . . . uh . . . happ . . . oh . . . "

"She was sledding down Cemetery Hill. You know the part right by the grove where you have to turn left at the bottom or you'll hit the gate?"

"Yes." My knees started knocking together.

"Well, Nancy's sled must have gone out of control. She didn't turn. She hit the gate. Her face is cut bad."

"Oh, no," I cried. I can't stand the sight of blood. Goose bumps started crawling up my arm.

"I knew you would be too upset to see her," Shirley said. I thought I saw some blood on Shirley's wrist and grabbed the wall so I wouldn't faint.

"That's why I took her in the back. Do you want me to call Dr. Di Salvo for you?" she asked.

Eddie came down the steps and asked what happened. Shirley told him.

"No, you don't have to call Dr. Di Salvo," he said and put his arm around me. "We'll call him. Thanks anyway, Shirley. We'll handle it."

That did it. I knew then and there I would definitely let Eddie move in. No questions asked. We needed a man around, me and Nancy.

5
NANCY, 1942

If I live to be a hundred, I won't forget the Saturday Eddie moved in. It was a cold December morning. My mother woke me up at 7:30, wearing her blue flowered housecoat and new blue satin slippers, her hair tied up in rats. She smelled like Palmolive soap. I was supposed to spend the day at my girlfriend Pauline's.

The minute I opened my eyes I felt hot and dizzy. "Mah throde eh zore," I croaked, my voice like chalk on a blackboard. A part of me wanted my mom to sit down and say, "Oh, poor Nancy," and call the whole thing off.

But her face just dropped a mile and she bounced and looked around as though somebody might show up to help. She rubbed her hands together, opened a drawer, then closed it and glanced back at me. "It's probably just a little cold. Just some sniffles. Winnie at work has had the sniffles all week. They're going around."

My throat felt so thick I thought I might choke. "Id erds a lot," I whispered. My mother took a quick step toward the dresser, then another back toward me, looking bewildered. Her housecoat fell open and I saw the patch of blond hair at her crotch and turned away.

"Oh, dear. Well . . . uh . . . I'll see if there's some aspirin." She rushed off with her rats flapping behind her, her housecoat swishing, stirring up a flurry of cold air.

I heard her bang on the bathroom wall, then she came back and said there wasn't any aspirin but she found some pain pills left over from my sledding accident.

"Here, take one of these," she said, poking the bottle at me. "They're . . . uh . . . probably better." Her chin quivered as she unscrewed the cap and she swallowed hard. I wasn't sure I should take a sledding pill. They had made me dizzy before and I was already woozy now. But I could tell my mom was riled up.

"Okay," I wheezed, and she dropped one of the pills into my sweaty palm and gave me a glass of water.

I got dressed in the thin, gray morning light. I watched my mom lean over the bathroom basin, lift a sopping wet hot washcloth to her face and pat. She used to scrub her complexion until it was bright pink because the women's page of the newspaper had said scrubbing would remove old dead skin that causes blemishes. But then later the paper said scrubbing would make your face sag and go lifeless. My mom had sighed and complained it was hard to keep up. I had asked what was so special about peaches and cream complexion anyway and she'd just laughed and said I'd see.

I dragged myself to the window and touched the white dotted Swiss curtains with the pink rickrack at the bottom. They used to be the curtains in Aunt Cora's room at Grandma's house. I started to cry. It didn't seem right to give Eddie the white curtains with the pink rickrack. The tears made my cheeks burn. I wished Grandma was still alive. I wished I was sitting in her lap with her warm breath on my ear as we listened to *Stella Dallas* together and shelled peas.

"Nancy," my mom called from her room.

"Yeah." My voice cracked.

"Make yourself some toast."

"I did," I lied. I peeked into the tarnished mirror above the maple bureau. A tear was stuck on my cheek just above the scar. The doctor had said I was lucky because the biggest gash was on the side of my head, under my hair, where it wouldn't show. It was strange, he said, as though I'd turned my head to avoid the gate but forgot to turn the sled.

"Good. That's good. You know what they say, feed a cold."

"Yeah." I sniffed and tied up a quarter and two nickels in a hanky and stuffed it in my pocket. My arms ached and the air in the apartment seemed too thick. I wondered what the bus to Clinton to visit Aunt Cora would cost.

"So come home from Pauline's about four o'clock. I think Eddie should be all moved in by then."

I moved to the door to my mom's room. She looked beautiful. She'd combed out her hair and put on Jergen's face powder. They sold it at Doc's underneath a sign that said, "Be His Pin-Up Girl. Start His Head A-Whirl . . . Wear the Shade Meant for You." She was laying out a pink sweater and a gray and pink plaid skirt to wear.

"So you want me to move my stuff into your room?" My breath sounded like it was coming through a rusty pipe.

My mom looked at me, confused. She frowned and

rubbed a fingernail, then looked back. "Nah. We can do it later. Bundle up now. Wear your scarf."

I didn't even have time to get my jacket off at Pauline's. "Why, Nancy, your face is red as a beet," her mom said. "I think you have a fever."

"I don't know."

She took my temperature and said it was 103 and I should go home to bed. "You shouldn't be out in this Pennsylvania winter," she announced, stern as a preacher. "You shouldn't be spreading what you have around."

I trudged out and stood on the pavement, shivering. My mother would have a fit if I went home. I wandered over to the schoolyard and sat on a swing trying to imagine Eddie living at the apartment. The way my mom talked, he'd just be a boarder like Barney at Mrs. Styles'. He'd pay for his room to help out with the rent. Plenty of people took in roomers, she said. But then I thought about the sounds I heard my mom and Eddie make in the living room at night after I went to bed, and I knew Eddie wasn't going to be a roomer like Barney.

I tried to put it out of my mind. My shoulders ached, as though pushing the thoughts away was wearing me out. I grabbed the ropes of the swing, slumped down and closed my eyes. The world spun.

Suddenly a voice broke the quiet. "Hey. Nancy Sayers."

I blinked with sticky eyes. It was Bobby Felker. Something fluttered inside my chest. I hadn't expected anyone to be around the school on a Saturday, Bobby Felker of all people. He was so cute. Thirteen, two years older than me.

"So what are you doing here all by yourself?" he asked.

He took me so much by surprise I told the truth. Well, almost. "Oh, I was just at my friend Pauline's and I felt a cold coming on. I'm on my way home."

"Boy, it sounds like you have a cold." He pinched a thumb and a finger to the tip of his nose. "How aboud if I walk with you. I'm taking some war bond posters to Doc's."

I giggled, surprised Bobby knew where I lived. I wondered what else he knew.

"Sure," I said. I was too weak and dizzy to think of a way out of it. Bobby had sandy hair that stuck up in cowlicks. He was thin and had a way of moving that reminded you of a dance. Plus when he smiled, you felt there was a whole other world somewhere.

He unrolled a poster to give me a look. It said, "Autograph a Bomb for Tojo or Hitler," and the picture showed a bomb on a parachute hitting the top of the world. Little orange bursts of fire were knocking Tojo, all teeth and glasses, off the world on one side and Hitler off on the other.

I had wanted to help with the bond drive but you had to pledge to save for a bond yourself. You could buy a 25-cent savings stamp at school every week and paste it in a little book. "Just a $25 bond can buy a fragmentation bomb," I had told my mom. "That's what Miss Sandercock said. We'd only have to buy enough stamps to add up to $18.75, and in 10 years we'd get $25 back. It would be patriotic and a good investment, too. Miss Sandercock said so."

But my mother had said Miss Sandercock must think money grew on trees, so I helped out with the tin can drive instead.

Bobby and I started toward Doc's. The day was warming up. The bright sun made the crusty snowdrifts glisten like meringue. I sneezed and pulled my hanky out of my pocket.

"So are you still playing the triangle?" Bobby asked, his mouth stretching into a grin. We'd been in Mr. Music's class together. Mr. Music came every Thursday after school and anyone could sign up. Bobby had played the trombone. He was real good. I'd played the triangle. I was so-so.

"No, I started junior high this year." I giggled. Walking with Bobby Felker was making me giddy.

"Junior high already?"

"Yeah, I skipped a grade."

"Good for you." Bobby stopped and gave me a smile as if we were a special couple walking together in the snow and the sun, as if we shared a secret. "You like it?"

"Oh yeah." Talking was hard. My throat felt as though

it might close any minute, and my head was spinning. The main thing I liked about junior high was that it took me one year closer to being old enough to kiss Marysville goodbye.

"Me too. There's more to do. And lots of different kinds of people. Someone like you. You're different than a lot of girls. I can see you'd like junior high."

I closed my eyes for a minute against the sun. I felt like it was burning into my brain. What did he mean, "different?" We were almost at Doc's. Suddenly I got a terrible thought. What if Eddie was moving his stuff in when we got there? What if Bobby saw Eddie moving in to our apartment? I'd die of shame.

I stopped. A shudder went down my legs. "I just remembered, my mom isn't hobe. I'm so silly. I forgod. She's at her girlfriend Mildred's."

"Don't you have a key?"

"No." My lips felt dry and cracked.

"Jeez."

"I'll just go back to the school and wade."

"Well, jeez, with that cold, I don't know if you should."

"Oh, it's okay." Then suddenly the world started to spin even more. I grabbed Bobby's arm.

"Whoa," he said. "You better wait in Doc's."

I was too weak to argue. Bobby helped me across the street. Everything was a white, and gray, and yellow swirl, the snow and the pavement, the rays of the sun.

"Let's ring your bell just in case," Bobby said. "Maybe your mom came back early."

I clutched at the door, too limp to even be embarrassed. What did it matter? He'd find out anyhow.

Bobby rang the bell and we waited. There was no answer. Now I sat down on the stoop and dropped my head into my hands.

He rang again. Still no answer. I was surprised. Where was my mother?

"Let's just try it one more time," he said. "You never know. She could be on the phone." He rang again, then he peered through the glass door at the stairs that led up to our apartment.

"Oh, there's someone. There's a leg on the steps. Your mom is home after all," he said, smiling, and giving my shoulder a squeeze. I felt the warmth of his hand through my jacket.

But nobody came down, and when he looked again, he said the leg was gone.

I got up and we both stared through the glass as though we were trying to see into the future. My mom was coming down the steps, after all. She still had her housecoat on and she was hunched over like a monkey with her arms across her chest. Her hair was tousled.

I went stiff and my cheeks felt hot. Bobby looked at me, then we both quick turned away from one another. "Well, I'd better take these posters in to Doc," he said and hurried off.

My mom's face was red and streaky, like she had rubbed off part of the Jergen's face powder.

"Nancy, what are you doing here?" She sounded cranky.

"Pauline's mom took my temperature. It's 103," I said.

"Well, for goodness sake. Why would she do a thing like that?"

"How come you didn't answer the door?"

"Oh, Eddie had his shoes off. I didn't know who it was and he wanted to put his shoes back on." I didn't understand how it could take a person that long to put shoes on, not even Eddie. Plus why was my mom wearing her housecoat? Where was her pink sweater and pink and gray plaid skirt? For a minute I got a terrible thought but I put it out of my mind. Not during the day. People didn't do it during the day except maybe gypsies.

"Who was peeking in the door with you?"

"A kid from school. He lives out in the R.D."

Her eyes widened. "I don't like you running with kids from the R.D."

"I wasn't running with anybody. He walked me home. Anyway, what's wrong with the R.D.?"

"I don't trust R.D. people."

"Why not?" She wasn't making any sense. Some of the best families lived out in the R.D.

49

"Peeking in people's doors."

I was too sick to argue. "I feel real dizzy," I said.

She scrunched her eyebrows and put on a sad look, turned around and started slowly back upstairs. She had a funny smell to her and I trudged behind her, miserable, not just from being sick but because I knew I'd let her down coming home. That's why she was cranky, she just wasn't saying it right. It was Bobby's fault, showing up at the playground with his cute sand-colored cowlick, making me forget I didn't want to come back to the apartment any more than my mother wanted me there. My cheeks became hotter still as I realized I'd made a fool of myself in some way I didn't understand. I clutched the chipped wooden handrail and climbed.

Eddie's shirt was unbuttoned in front and he didn't have an undershirt on. I could see dark curly hairs on his chest, like a scouring pad. They looked sweaty. I hadn't ever seen a man's chest up close before. It gave me the creeps. He grinned at me. I hated him.

"Pauline's mom sent Nancy home. She said she was too sick to play," my mom explained. "I guess maybe her cold got worse." She rubbed one of her hands over her mouth and chin. "She seemed fine when she left."

"Oh, too bad, kid." Eddie's grin faded. "I'd been figuring we could all go over to the firemen's winter carnival at Pembroke Township tonight. I figured we could have a high old time—the three of us. Maybe you'll be feeling better by tonight."

I didn't say anything, just tottered toward my mom's bedroom, but at the door, I got a shock. There was a pile of Eddie's shirts on the chair, enough colors to be a box of Crayolas. A paper bag full of underpants sat on the floor. An old torn suitcase was open on the bed. What was going on? I edged in. Eddie was supposed to move into my room.

He came in behind me. How could he do that? How could he walk right into the bedroom with me with no undershirt? He might as well try to dig underneath my skin. I felt so trapped I dropped to the floor, curled into a ball, and burst out crying.

I heard Eddie walk away, every other footstep slamming. I heard him talk to my mom, but their voices were low, like a portable radio going dead; then they were in the hallway.

"Go on," Eddie said.

"You do it."

"She's your kid."

There was a long silence. I heard matches striking and smoke started to curl around the bedroom door like the devil's finger. My mom began crying. My heart felt like it weighed a ton.

A few minutes later she came in. "Ah, Nancy, Eddie says he can understand you're feeling discombobulated. Having a cold. Having a temperature. He . . . ah . . . he says to tell you he can understand you being discombobulated."

I stared at my fists.

She twisted a piece of her housecoat around her finger. "Why don't you go rest on the sofa. Eddie will take his stuff into your room. He, ah, opened it up in here without thinking. The closet looked bigger here."

I moved my lips but no sound came out.

I slept most of the weekend. I was glad because I didn't have to talk to my mother or Eddie. My mom brought me some aspirin and chicken noodle soup. She rubbed Vicks on my chest and put butcher paper over it so I wouldn't smear the bed. She brought in the portable radio and I listened to the Billboard Chart Hits. "Tangerine." "Moonlight Becomes You." "White Cliffs of Dover." I listened to the news and President Roosevelt came on saying some companies didn't like to hire women in jobs GIs left behind and that was wrong. He said we couldn't afford that kind of prejudice. I thought good for him and wondered how old I had to be to get a job. I wondered which big cities had the most of them.

On Sunday night, Eddie insisted we had to go to the winter carnival. "Hey, it'll be good for you."

His car only sat two inside so I bundled up and climbed into the rumble seat. I scrunched down and thought about ways to get back at my mom as the black night air whipped at my head. I thought about getting pneumonia and dying. I saw people standing over my coffin saying what a terrible thing, my mom taking me out in the night air when I was sick, and now look. I thought about jumping out of the rumble seat in front of a coming car. I pictured my body in the street, broken like an old doll, with my mom standing over me shrieking, "It was my fault; I was a sinful mother. I brought her too much shame." I edged to the driver's side of the rumble seat, and stuck my head out, wondering what it would feel like to jump. Then all of a sudden a car zoomed around a corner toward us and I got so panicky, I threw myself down on the floor of the rumble seat and crouched there quivering as the bare branches of the winter trees raced by.

The fair was inside a giant warehouse fixed up to look like summer, with paintings of trees and birds on sheets tacked up along the walls. There were popcorn and cotton candy stands and carnival games. A lot of the men were in shirt sleeves and vests. Some of the women wore slacks. Aunt Cora had said some big stores were opening slacks departments for women. I liked how they looked.

"Evenin', friend," Eddie said to a man running a pitch penny concession.

"Hey, Eddie, how you doin'?" The guy leaned over the roped-off square and winked. "Lotsa marks tonight. Everyone's dyin' for a carny by December."

"You betcha," Eddie replied. "Hey, this here's Georgia and her girl Nancy. Say hello."

"Well, hello," the guy said, making googly eyes at my mom. "Eddie always did know how to pick 'em."

My mother grinned, but by then Eddie was hot-footing it on to the next stand, calling out, "Hey, Mack, evenin' to you."

"Eddie Jeffers, in the flesh." The guy flashed his teeth.

My mom nudged me. "Eddie's really in his eminent" she said.

"Hey, Georgia, Nance. Looky over here," Eddie called. "Mack here carries my merchandise." He pointed to ceramic dolls, "Only Mack calls it moichandise. He's from

New Joisey," Eddie joked. There was a tooth missing in the corner of his mouth when he laughed wide.

My mom padded behind Eddie, happy as a kid. I grumped along. Suddenly Eddie stopped.

"You gotta see this," he said, jerking his shoulder in the direction of something called the Mouse Game.

We walked over to a flat wooden wheel with small numbered holes around the rim. The guy running the game spun the wheel, brought out a teeny cage, opened the door, and a mouse ran out. The mouse raced around and around until he finally ran into a hole.

"The hole the mouse runs into, that's the number wins," Eddie explained. "Is that sumpthin' or what?" His mustache stretched into a thin furry line across his face as he smiled.

"Oh, isn't that awful," my mom said. "Poor little mouse."

"Nah, that ain't no poor mouse. That's a mouse gets a lot of treats, lotsa pieces of cheese." He curled his hand around one side of his mouth. "I'll let you gals in on a secret if you promise not to tell."

We nodded. I was curious despite myself.

"You'd think there was no way to tell which hole the mouse is gonna run in, right?"

We nodded again.

"Well, you're wrong." Eddie hitched up his pants and stuck out his chest. He nudged us a little bit away from the crowd. "I ain't sayin' it's happenin' here," he whispered, "but I seen it happen. Sometimes the guy running the game puts ammonia on the holes nobody bets on. He rubs his finger around the hole like he's just cleaning the dust off but he's really rubbing ammonia on it. Well, ammonia smells like another mouse to a mouse so the mouse runs in that hole."

"No!" My mom was shocked. So was I. I didn't say peep, but I hated Eddie even more than before.

I had bad dreams. I kept waking up, my heart pounding, my hair follicles feeling like needles in my scalp. Then toward morning I dreamed I was dancing with Bobby

Felker on a stage with shimmering silver curtains. Mr. Music was playing "Let's Face the Music and Dance" and I wasn't all feet like in real life. I was light as dandelion fluff, and I wanted to dance forever.

But when I woke up, it was a cold gray Monday and even though I still felt sick I had to go to school on account of my mom didn't like me in the apartment alone. I gagged at the man smells in the bathroom. Shaving cream. Cologne. Man pee on the underside of the toilet seat.

Miss Sandercock asked us to write essays telling four important things to do in an air raid but I couldn't write a word. I just sat there watching the pieces of dust float around in the sun that was streaming through the window. I remembered what Mr. Schmoyer had told us about how most of the particles that float around in the air are dead skin cells. I figured most of the dead skin cells floating around that day were mine. The sunnier it got, the deader I felt.

At the bell, the kids handed in their papers and left but I just sat there. Miss Sandercock looked at me and asked, "Is there something wrong, Nancy?" The bright white winter sun glimmered on her pearls and her auburn hair.

I couldn't talk. I tore a piece of lined paper out of my Indian Chief tablet and scribbled on it, "Miss Sandercock, I need help. A man has moved in with my mom and I hate it. It's making me sick. Help me, please. Don't talk to me about it. I can't talk about it. Write me back a note, please. Please, Miss Sandercock."

Dancing the Dark

Part Two

6
CORA SAYERS DOWLING, 1943

Cora sat at her usual table by the window, the white winter sun shining in on her like a spotlight. The tavern was quiet, with just Cora, Floyd the bartender, and a couple of afternoon regulars playing dice and griping about the war and the rations and the blackouts, guys who had been deferred, were 4-F or too old to go.

Cora took out a picture of Walt in his uniform and ran a fingertip around his jaw line, wanting to feel his rough strength on her cheeks and thighs and chest. She missed him something awful. Having Nancy come to live with her would help. Would keep her from getting too blue in the evening or from getting too friendly with some of the lonely soldier boys who were always coming into the tavern. It was hard, there were so many of them. Good-looking boys who'd kid around and tell Cora she was as swell a blond as Betty Grable. There'd been temptations, she didn't mind admitting it.

She lit up an Old Gold and sipped a cup of coffee. Cora never drank until 5 p.m. She had her standards. The steam from the coffee and the smoke from the cigarette swirled around her head. Her blue eyes took on a dreamy look and her cherry red lips puckered as she assessed her place in the scheme of things.

"I could have been a movie star," she thought. "I'm pretty enough; I have the figure." Cora didn't mind bragging, never had any patience with the holier-than-thou girls she'd grown up with, girls who'd coo, "Who, me?" anytime anybody paid them a compliment. And what did it ever get them? A lifetime of covered-dish suppers and husbands with potbellies and hemorrhoids.

Cora and Walt had aspirations. After the war, Walt planned to try out for the Secret Service. He knew a guy who had gone all the way to being a bodyguard to the President. Walt would love that. Cora too.

The tavern door opened and Blanche, another war wife, whirled in, waving a letter.

"Jack says he got cigarettes and gum I sent," Blanche gushed, plunking her purse and a newspaper on the table. "He says one boy in his company passed around some pecans from his mother's farm. He says it was like eating a steak dinner, he's so sick of rations."

"Oh, Walt complains too," Cora cut in. "He says when my burnt cookies start tasting good I know how bad things are."

"That Walt, he's something, isn't he?" Blanche laughed. "A real Jack Benny."

"Yeah. As long as those Mama-mias—those Eye-talian women with their big bozooms and their spicy spaghetti don't start looking too good to him."

"Oh, Cora, you don't have to worry. You and Walt are a real team."

Cora looked down and twirled the ashtray. "Well, you never know. I hear things are the worst in the artillery. The boys don't get to change their underwear for weeks. Don't sleep in a bed for months. Who knows? They get a leave, go into some town, get cleaned up. Who knows what mischief they get into?"

Blanche frowned, then smiled as though she decided to put it out of her mind. "Did you get a letter this week?"

Cora stretched her hands out to inspect the cherry red nail polish. "No," she said slowly, "But you know how the V-mail is. You don't get anything for awhile and then it's five letters at once." She lifted her chin and lit another Old Gold.

"Yeah I know." Blanche looked hesitant for a second, then put the letter into her purse and spread the newspaper out on the table. "Hey, good news. Remember the charm school I told you about?"

"Yeah."

"Well, the paper says that if you sign up this week, you get one lesson free. Look."

Cora tilted her head forward to see, her silky yellow hair sliding down over her forehead on one side as she read. "Capricorn Charm School. Be a Model or Look Like One.

February Special. One Free Lesson with the Six-Month Charm Course." The ad went on. "Whether you know it or not, you model every day of your life. Somebody is watching you. Somebody is remembering what you do and say."

Cora leaned toward Blanche, who smelled like Joy cologne. "Are you going to sign up?"

"I might. Not that I'll ever really be a model." Blanche lowered her eyes, her lashes forming a fetching black fringe on her cheeks. "I'm probably not pretty enough."

Cora sighed.

"But if I had more poise—see here, it says the course helps build poise—Jack could be really proud of me when he comes home. I could entertain. We could invite the mucky mucks from the company. You know how important it is for a man, being a gracious hostess for him."

Cora narrowed her eyes at Blanche. She was younger, with her striking violet eyes in a creamy face, but Cora was prettier. If Blanche could go to charm school, damn it, so could she. She could build more poise and help Walt get ahead with the Secret Service. If she helped herself get ahead, too, all the better. Why work in a music store all her life? Cora looked out the window and squinted into the sun.

She pictured President Roosevelt singling Walt out. "That young man there," the President would say. "That's the one I want for a bodyguard. The one with the beautiful blond wife. Who is she anyway? She must be a model."

How much did the course cost? The ad didn't say. Cora had her allotment and her salary from the morning job at the record store. Even a part-time salary added up. She could pass for a lot younger—twenty two or twenty three. Nobody would guess she was already thirty.

Cars sputtered across the street. A clutch ground. The nurses and orderlies from the day shift at the hospital were heading home.

Blanche looked out. "Oh, is it that late? I gotta go. Jack's mom is coming to dinner." She rolled her eyes. "I swear that woman can spot dust two rooms away."

Cora grinned. "I'll hang onto the ad, one less thing to clutter up your place."

She moved to the bar and perched on a stool. "Can you

believe this?" she asked Floyd, pointing to a news story. "An aircraft plant sent home fifty-three girls for wearing sweaters on the job, complained sweaters were too sexy."

Floyd shook his head and told Cora he was glad The Tune Time Record Shop didn't have any such cockamamie rules. "We don't need Ann Sheridan when we got our own sweater girl right here," he kidded.

Cora rubbed her hand down the sleeve of her coral boucle sweater and beamed at Floyd in appreciation. But she felt uneasy, too. It didn't seem right, sending the girls home. Why not send the guys home for ogling the girls when they had war work to do?

She glanced at her watch, looked up and shot Floyd a dazzling smile. "So it's about that time. I'll have the usual."

"You got it." Floyd poured a generous jigger of bourbon into a highball glass decorated with frosted strawberries and topped it off with a bubbly splash of Seven-Up. He worked underneath a four-color poster that showed an American flag and urged, "Zap the Japs Off the Map."

He set the Seven and Seven in front of Cora, who was now hunched over the Capricorn Charm School ad.

"So when is that niece of yours coming to stay?"

Cora looked up. "Oh, this weekend. She's coming this weekend." She sipped her drink and nodded her head. "It'll be good, having company." She smiled again, but thinner. "Nancy's a good kid. She writes poems, you know."

"Is that so?" Floyd rubbed the inside of a shot glass with a stained rag, then carried some glasses to the other end of the bar.

Cora thought back. Things had happened fast after Nancy's English teacher had called a social welfare agency and explained, "The child came to me in a state of trauma." The overburdened social workers had asked if there was a responsible relative the girl could live with until things blew over and that had led to Cora who'd been more than happy to oblige. In fact, she had been feeling a little guilty that she hadn't been looking after Georgia and Nancy as much as

Mama would have wanted. Taking Nancy in would make up for lost time.

Floyd returned. "So I hope that doesn't mean you're gonna make yourself scarce around here," he said, "get all tied up with PTA meetings and peanut butter sandwiches."

"Me?" Cora laughed her husky laugh. "Nah, I'll bring Nancy along. She'll get a kick out of it here. She's debonair for a kid. She'll be thirteen next month. We'll have a lot of laughs. Just start polishing up your Shirley Temples."

Fortunately, the social welfare people hadn't thought to ask where Cora spent her evenings—never thought to question anyone who might say, "Oh, Cora, yeah. She's one of the regulars at Jolly Jack's. Lots of fun. A real looker, too. The GIs love her." The folks at the social welfare office had had trouble enough handling family turmoil in five counties—trouble enough finding homes for kids like Harold Kessler over in Snyder's Knob who had threatened to kill his parents with an axe after he had chopped holes in the walls and floors and demolished all the doors of their house. Nancy's case was small stuff. A disgruntled kid. An uppity schoolmarm saying the girl should be moved out of an unfit home. Small stuff. The hearing officers—a big blond who smelled like cats and a red-nosed man with a pock-marked face—had been thrilled to learn there was a married aunt with a spare room and upstanding habits. The rosy-nosed man had particularly noticed Cora working a *Reader's Digest* Word Power column as she waited for their interview. "Oh, I do it every month," Cora had said cheerily. "I think it improves the mind, don't you?" After that, everything was just paperwork.

Cora sank into bed a tiny bit tipsy. She'd been trying to go easy on the booze now that Walt was gone. She'd probably do better when Nancy moved into the spare room.

"A spare room," she whispered into the night. Stripes of light from automobiles driving by on Fairlawn Lane crept across the bedroom wall like ghosts.

The house creaked. That's what the nursery had been reduced to. A spare room. A pain zigzagged through Cora's chest as she thought of her two lost babies, little Lily and little Beth. She'd given them names even though she'd never known if they were girls or boys.

A car stopped, its headlights flooding a wall of Cora's bedroom like a movie screen. A car door slammed shut with a thud. Cora winced. Feet crunched on the cinders as someone walked across the street. Cora closed her eyes and thought of lying in the cinders, thought about the awful night as though maybe this time she might make more sense of it.

Cora carries little Beth with sunny confidence, already five months along and plump as a peach—well beyond the dangerous three months when she'd lost poor Lily two years earlier. Walt jokes about her cravings. "Pickles and ice cream," he kids. "The little woman likes to wake me up at 2 a.m. to get her pickles and ice cream." He smiles, shakes his head, and everyone grins in commiseration.

They find a flat closer to Walt's postal route—a bright white-walled place with four rooms, a washing machine, and a yard with a tire swing tied to a tree. Perfect for a kid. The only problem is the price—$10 a month more than the old apartment. Cora convinces Walt they can swing it with her savings from the Tune Time Record Store. She'll have to quit for a while, of course, but she'll go back. She'd get bored sitting home.

Walt resists at first, but Cora understands. He likes being the breadwinner. His own mother always worked and she browbeat his dad like a woodpecker going at a post. Walt always swore he wouldn't end up like his father.

Eventually, though, he agrees to the move. Cora suspects what swings him around in the end is Jolly Jack's being just down the road. Walt had been pulled over a couple of times for driving under the influence.

The trouble begins with a visit from Walt's mother, Estelle. Estelle makes snide remarks about Cora's housekeeping and carps at Walt over everything from his pompadour to his habit of folding the newspaper with the sports page in front. By the afternoon she leaves, Cora and Walt are limp. They go for a few at Jolly Jack's, then across the street to dinner at a small cafe they haven't been to before.

They order clam chowder, roast pork with gravy, apple sauce, and creamed corn. Everything goes well until the owner brings the check.

Walt looks it over and frowns. "Hey buddy," he booms, "you made a mistake. This bill says two packages of crackers. Two cents each. You gotta be kidding. Nobody charges for crackers. Crackers come with the soup."

"Well, no," the owner says. He is a large man with curly hair and a belly round as a beach ball underneath his stained white apron. "I asked if you wanted crackers. You said yes. If you hadn't a wanted them, I wouldn't a given them to you. I wouldn't a charged you."

"You gotta be kidding." Walt's voice rises, his face as red as a stop sign. "You're trying to rob us. This is robbery. That's what it is. Who eats soup without crackers?"

"Well, a lot of people. You'd be surprised," the man says, raising his voice to show Walt he isn't intimidated. "The places that give you crackers, they just charge more for the soup. You don't get any choice. Here you get a choice." The man has loose pouches of skin underneath his eyes that jiggle when he talks.

"You bastard, you're making that up." Walt pounds his fist on a rubber mat on the counter. A flurry of toothpicks flies up into his face and makes him madder. "If you think I'm gonna fall for a cock and bull story like that, you're dumber than you look." He reaches across the counter and pushes the man, makes a fist and waves it threateningly. "If you think I'm some goddamn sissy from the sticks that you can pull a trick like this on, think again." Several customers in the cafe turn to watch.

"Walt, please, let's just pay it and go," Cora pleads. She puts her hand on Walt's arm but he shoves it away with a jerk and gives her a dirty look.

"Whose side are you on, anyway?" he spits.

Cora looks scared. "Yours, Walt, you know that. I'm always on yours, but it's only four cents. Let's just pay it and go."

"Only four cents?" Walt's voice booms. "Look who's talking. Miss Big Time Spender. Had to have a fancy new apartment. Had to have a hotshot washing machine." He pushes Cora. She grabs the counter for balance.

"Christ, if you had your way, we'd end up in the poorhouse," he yells.

The cafe owner looks at Cora's swollen belly. "Look, buddy, let's forget it. It's been a busy night. Maybe I didn't make it clear about the crackers, that they were extra. Here, gimmee the bill. I'll take the four cents off. No hard feelings."

Walt steps back, rolls his body to establish equilibrium, burps, then opens the door and walks out without paying. Cora gives the owner a helpless, pleading look and follows.

She remembers only snatches of what happens after that. She remembers Walt's big voice imitating her, saying "Only four cents," in a loud falsetto as she runs up Fairlawn Lane behind him, awkward with her weight. She remembers that he stops all of a sudden, swings around, and then she feels a pain in her chest and hears a thud like a sack of potatoes being dropped and tastes the bitter, dusty cinders.

Two days later she hemorrhages. It might have happened anyway, the doctor insists. God works in mysterious ways. It was unfortunate that she'd tripped and fallen, but she shouldn't blame herself. "Give her some extra TLC," he tells Walt. "It's a touchy time. She needs some extra TLC."

Walt tries. He never actually apologizes—that's not in him—but he dries the dishes and stops teasing Cora about her cooking, and for a couple of weeks he rubs her back at night.

But things change. Without the jokes and the wisecracks, there's a distance between them. Cora starts drinking more, partly to forget the lost babies, partly because something else begins nagging at her. Sometimes when Walt roughhouses (that's what she calls it) she feels an enormous thrill, an excitement that she *likes.* He's never all that brutish. He might push a little, maybe squeeze her breasts too hard or twist her arm to pin her down. But he stops before he does any serious damage, then he treats her like a queen. He tells her how beautiful she is, how lucky he is to have her. Sometimes when the days and weeks become too humdrum and Cora begins to wonder if their dreams are just pie in the sky, the tussling and the making up break the monotony, remind Cora she and Walt aren't ordinary, they're special. At least, that's what she's always thought, but ever since she lost little Beth, she's started to wonder.

The Capricorn Charm School was located on the second floor of a dingy downtown building above a photo studio with pictures of GIs in the window and a sign that said "Give Her Something to Remember You By." Cora had stopped by at noon after her shift at the Tune Time Record Shop, telling herself it couldn't hurt to take a look around. The school had a reception area with gray carpeting, a gray settee, and a table piled with stacks of *Vogue* and *Mademoiselle.* Behind the settee, a large plate-glass mirror was well lighted so that it brought out pimples and black-heads and enlarged pores that a girl might otherwise miss.

"This could be fun," Cora thought, clutching yester-day's newspaper, blood pulsing in her fingertips. She straightened her pleated skirt and rearranged her powder blue sweater and pearls. "I can probably pass on a few pointers to Nancy. She's been having a rough time of it. She could do with a little glamour in her life. Mama would like that. And who knows? I might even make it big."

A counselor named Bonita invited Cora into a small office. Cora thought Bonita resembled Joan Crawford. She had velvety white skin, coral cheeks and spidery eyelashes, her hair pulled back in a chignon.

The school offered a 16-week self-improvement course or an eight-month professional modeling course, Bonita explained. Reading from a sheet of paper, she described the classes: skin care, makeup, wardrobe analysis, leg posi-tions, hand positions, personality, table manners, introduc-tions. "Did you know," she asked Cora, "that there are 45 different kinds of introductions?" Cora didn't.

Bonita put down the paper. "Now then, which course are you interested in?"

"Well, I'm not sure yet. What do they cost?"

"Let me see. Where is that price list? I don't see it here. I must have left it in the modeling room. Would you like to step into the modeling room? You're welcome to take a walk down the runway and see how it feels."

Cora felt her face flush. "Oh, that would be grand," she said. She couldn't remember ever before using the word "grand." She walked down the runway, watching herself in the mirror and felt a new kind of thrill. A man rushed into the room but stopped short.

"My dear," he said to Cora, "I think you might be a natural model. Such a lovely face. Such grace."

"Why, thank you," Cora smiled.

"Oh! And look at that smile, Bonita," he said to the counselor. "I think this one might just be a natural model."

Cora's smile tilted, her lips twitched at one corner. He's buttering me up, she warned herself. She'd anticipated this; she wasn't born yesterday. But she'd also thought about the alternatives. More years at the music store or go into a war plant. But she wasn't a Rosie the Riveter type, and even if she was, she had a feeling all the Rosies riding high now would get dumped pretty quick when the GIs started coming home. She let her smile stretch broader. Besides, maybe she was a natural model.

"She is quite attractive," Bonita agreed. "But her walk needs work. Her hand positions. Her head positions. They need work."

Cora looked in the mirror, frowned at her hands, and repositioned her head.

"But that's what we're here for, isn't it?" the man cut in. Then, addressing Cora, he said, "My dear, we can never promise anything, of course, the modeling business being unpredictable, but blonds like you . . . the June Allyson look . . . well, confidentially, it's very much in vogue right now. Isn't that right, Bonita?"

Bonita agreed that it was, and within minutes, Cora was the owner of an iron-clad contract for the eight-month modeling course at the Capricorn Charm School at an astronomical cost of $268.

The Clinton school was a dirty brick building with a tar playground. A row of bare-limbed trees on one side stretched like gray scribbles against the morning sky. I got there early the first day, nervous and shy. The girls wore sloppy joe sweaters and stood in tight groups, tossing their heads and giggling. The boys shifted on their feet and hunched over, as though they weren't used to being so tall. One of them farted and whirled quick toward some girls nearby and yelled, "Who did that?"

I laughed but nobody noticed. The air was thin, and I could feel my breathing as I nudged closer to the schoolhouse wall. I tucked my hands deep into my jacket pockets and stared at my bobby socks and loafers. Fingering a poem I had written the night before, I pulled it out and read, "The sad girl gave a soft moan, Like the cry of a lost soul, Carried by the ocean waves, To a land of pale cold blue skies." The paper was warm from my jacket pocket, and it felt good to hold it, as if it were a friend I could count on. I clutched it in my hand and stared up at the hazy Clinton sky until the bell rang to go in.

The rest of the day was a blur of sweater sets, crew cuts, the smell of chewing gum and sweat and the sound of short, quick laughs as sharp as broken glass. Nobody paid any attention to me except once I went to the bathroom and found a note taped to the back of my white blouse that said, "Oink Oink."

I started collecting insults. In two months I had a list of thirty-three, copied from a book Aunt Cora had called a thesaurus. All day at school I muttered them under my breath—saphead, doodle, dimwit—to get back at the snooty Clinton kids, but I never talked to anyone out loud until I met Molly Bobst.

Molly was in literary club with me. She had a birthmark on her cheek the color of eggplant and shaped like Texas. One day Miss Eberlee sat us together. "Both you girls write such nice poetry," she whispered, her glasses dangling on a string over the table as she leaned down, "I thought you should meet each other." But that wasn't the real reason Miss Eberlee put us together, and Molly and I both knew it. We were outsiders. We eyed one another with hate and distrust, but then I spotted a rage in the back of Molly's eyes that I understood, and she must have seen the same thing in mine. We smiled.

Soon we were roaming the halls together muttering insults at the world—blockhead, whale brain, goosy, foggy in the crumpet—exchanging looks and laughing so hard we'd hold our sides and bump into walls. Once we walked home together after school shouting insults into the wind in voices as loud as an Army band.

I entertained Molly with my Carmen Miranda imitation and I showed her how double-jointed I was. I bent down in front and put my hands flat on the floor, then lowered my head until my nose touched the top of my sneaker. I knew by now to do it slow and quiver every once in a while as if I wouldn't make it but I always did. Then I stood up and folded my hand in from the wrist until it curved back and touched the inside of my arm, making a loop like a letter "p."

"Oooh, that's awful," Molly hooted, her birthmark scrunching up on her cheek as she smiled. "Do it again." We pretended we were best friends: two girls who were poets, two girls who were smarter than the others, but we both knew if any other kids at school had given either of us a tumble, we would have dropped the other one flat.

I loved living with Aunt Cora, though. She treated me better than my mother and she was prettier and had more flair. You could see the difference just in the way she smoked. She'd inhale, then open her mouth slow and let the smoke sort of roll out. Not my mom. When my mom smoked, she'd take a puff and blow the smoke straight out in a stream like a train.

I'd meet Aunt Cora after school at Jolly Jack's and have a Shirley Temple while she sipped coffee and we played the latest Billboard Chart hits. "Taking a Chance on Love."

"That Old Black Magic." "You'd Be So Nice to Come Home To."

Later we'd go back to the apartment and she'd give me modeling tips. She'd enrolled in modeling school just before I moved in so I learned to walk with a book on my head and cross my legs at the ankles instead of the knees. One day she decided, "Lets get rid of those braids." Two days later, on a bright April afternoon, I sat on a swivel chair at the Hollywood East Salon of Beauty with a new hairdo—a straight shiny cap down to my ears, then puffed out into cute little clouds of curls.

"It makes you look a little bit like Jennifer Jones," Aunt Cora said, her head tilted to one side. "Especially from a three-quarters view."

I felt like a million dollars.

The kids at school started looking at me in a new way, and one day walking home from Library Club, I passed some boys wearing baseball hats who elbowed one another as I passed and one of them gave me a wink and a smile.

I even started getting along better with my mom and Eddie. Eddie had loaned Aunt Cora the money for the modeling course after I told her he had a stash from working the carnies once in a while, whatever that meant. And later, my mother and Eddie would come to visit on Sundays, and I'd pretend my aunt was really my mom and my mom was just a distant screwball relative. You could laugh at her witless ways because she'd soon say goodbye and go home and be somebody else's problem.

Eddie brought me presents—fruit scented erasers, a whistle shaped like a guitar—and he told circus stories. At first I tried to act uninterested, but one day, I couldn't help it, I started warming up to him. What happened, I'd had an English assignment to write about an unforgettable character, and then Eddie told us about Rosie, the headless woman.

Rosie was just an ordinary girl but they billed her in the freak show as someone who'd lost her head in an accident. They hid her underneath a huge dress with a ruffled collar like queens wore in the old days. Eddie showed us a picture. On top of the ruffled collar, there was a bunch of lit up glass tubes with red and yellow liquids running in and out like they were a part of Rosie.

"People'd pay a dime for a look at her," Eddie said. "But what was really a riot, sometimes the circus hired a guy who'd put on a doctor outfit and pretend he was keepin' her alive. Rosie would slow down the liquids into the tubes every so often and tug at the doc's sleeve when he was looking the other way. He'd ignore her—that was part of the act—and she'd slow the liquids down even more." Eddie snickered just thinking about it.

"Finally some mark in the audience would yell, 'For God's sake, doc, turn around. Rosie's dyin.'"

We all hooted and after Eddie left, I kept thinking about Rosie. I daydreamed that it was me instead of her in the curlicued stand-up collar, thrilled that people were paying to see me, all blinking lights and flashing colors, rooting for me to stay alive. Nobody had the slightest idea that the real me underneath the glitter was small and mean and bitter. I got out my Indian Chief tablet. "The most unforgettable character I ever met," I wrote, "Rosie, the Headless Woman."

One balmy Saturday in October, when I'd been in Clinton eight months, Aunt Cora and I went downtown. We stopped at an ice cream parlor called The Daily Scoop, where I ordered a paratrooper sundae that came with a marshmallow topping, and Aunt Cora got a commando sundae with crushed peanuts. I felt sophisticated, as though eating the sundaes somehow helped the war effort.

Afterward, we walked over to the Tune Time Record Store. I loved it at the Tune Time. I'd been there twice before. It was long and narrow with huge pictures high up on the walls: Cab Calloway, Dick Haymes, Dinah Shore, Tommy Dorsey, Hildegarde. You name it. There were racks and racks of records with yellow flags sticking up announcing "Super Selection."

Aunt Cora's boss, Mr. Kollwitz, was behind the counter, a short bald guy who wore a button on his jacket lapel that said, "We got the blues."

Mr. Kollwitz smiled and handed us a record called "I've Heard That Song Before."

"Just came in," he said. "Harry James. Give it a listen." He jutted his head toward a row of glass-enclosed listening booths on one side of the store. "Go ahead, be my guest. Enjoy."

"We always do," Aunt Cora sang with a smile, and we headed for a booth. She set the record on the turntable and we sat bobbing our heads and grinning out the glass windows at customers strolling by. I felt special, like we were movie stars.

Aunt Cora turned the record over carefully with the tips of her fingers, and I stood up and twirled as the music started, and that's when I spotted the familiar-looking shoulders bouncing two booths down from ours. I had seen those shoulders hunch and dip in Mr. Music's class.

"That's Bobby Felker," I said to my aunt, excitedly. "A guy from Marysville."

Aunt Cora turned to look. "No kidding. Well, go say hello."

She didn't have to tell me twice. I quick peeked at my reflection in the glass. Not bad. I had on a pink blouse that brought out the rosiness in my cheeks, and my curls were shiny and thick. I ran down to where Bobby was bouncing and knocked on the glass.

He turned and looked surprised, then grinned. He opened the door. "Hey, I heard you were living in Clinton."

"Yeah. I've been here eight months." I was so breathless I forgot to worry what else he'd heard. "So what are you doing here?" I asked. Bobby looked grown-up. He had a crew cut so his cowlick was gone, and his pants were pegged at the ankles.

"Well, I'm a real jazz nut, and you can't get any decent records in Marysville."

"Oh, no." I made a face to show I understood it was useless trying to buy decent records in Marysville.

"So I come to Clinton." Bobby's sandy eyebrows had little flicks of red under the store lights. "It's only twenty-five minutes on the bus, and I know I can count on Mr. Kollwitz for . . ." Bobby lowered his voice and pounded his chest . . . "a Super Selection."

I giggled as Aunt Cora came up and introduced herself.

She told Bobby she worked at Tune Time and said, "Hey, come and visit me and Nance sometime. Call ahead. Any record you want to hear, I'll bring it."

Bobby pulled his head back, as though he needed to get a better look, as though he couldn't believe his luck. Neither could I.

He called the next week and came on Wednesday night. We played Artie Shaw records. "Traffic Jam." "Dancing in the Dark." "Frenesí." Aunt Cora made us cocoa and suggested, "Hey, how about you two showing me some new dance steps." She knew I could do them because she'd been teaching me.

"Oh, that'd be great," I said. "Artie Shaw is my favorite to dance to." Aunt Cora had already told me to be sure to act interested in anything Bobby was interested in.

We slow danced one number and Bobby did a special little swoop with his shoulders, but I followed him fine. Then we jitterbugged. My aunt sipped beer and clapped and yelled, "Now you're cooking with gas," as we twirled.

Suddenly the Victrola went on the blink and stopped dead in the middle of Glenn Miller playing "Kalamazoo."

"Oh, no," Aunt Cora cried, but Bobby said wait a minute, and he fiddled around and fixed it.

"Hey, you're a real handyman," Aunt Cora said.

"Well, my dad used to repair things," Bobby said, looking at the floor for a minute. "I guess I got the know-how from him."

Bobby rubbed his fingers across the wooden base of the record player. "He hasn't been around for a long time though. My mom is married again. Barney Felker is my stepdad."

My aunt nodded, thoughtfully.

"Well, gee, thanks for fixing the Victrola," I piped up. "One good turn deserves another, right? I'll get some toll-house cookies. We made them this afternoon."

Aunt Cora told Bobby she went to modeling school and was teaching me some of her tricks. Bobby smiled at me and I smiled back, trying to keep my face at a three-quarters view, so I looked like Jennifer Jones.

After Aunt Cora said she had to hit the sack, Bobby and

I sat and talked. He told me how much he loved jazz. I told him I wrote poems and I'd probably work at a record store when I grew up. It was the best night of my life.

Sometimes Aunt Cora read me jokes from Uncle Walt's letters. "The rations here are so tough, they have to marinate corn flakes." But one day she got teary and said, "Listen to this." She started reading. "I just spent thirteen hours digging ditches. But I'm not complaining; a ditch could save my life. Anytime I get too far from one ditch I start digging another one. And I hope it's all wasted effort. I never wanted to do useless work so much in my life."

I looked at the tears on Aunt Cora's lower lashes and I saw a desperation in her eyes that I recognized from some of the soldiers and sailors we joked with at Jolly Jack's. All the corny jokes they hooted over and the second-hand store smiles they flashed couldn't hide the rawness you could tell they felt, frightened to death that they might not come back. I got up and gave my aunt a hug.

That night in bed I worried about what would happen to me when Uncle Walt came home from the war. I tried to picture him walking in and seeing my new curls and saying, "Well, get a load of you, turning into a real looker. Hey, Cora, let's just keep Nancy here with us." My aunt would cry and throw her arms around me and say, "Oh, Walt, I was hoping you'd say that. I love Nancy so much. She'll be just like our own daughter."

Still, I couldn't help but want things to stay the way they were, just me and Aunt Cora making tollhouse cookies and having a few laughs at Jolly Jack's and practicing modeling tricks. One thing I'd learned, you couldn't trust women around men.

8
CORA, 1944

The telegram came on a blustery March afternoon.

Cora was practicing leg positions in front of the giant round mirror above her Hollywood blond dresser while Nancy watched, sitting cross-legged on the matching blond wood bed.

"I'll get it," Cora sang when the doorbell rang. "Watch my going-down-the-stairs posture. See how I do." She swished past a tinted wedding photograph that showed her dazzling in a blue velvet draped dress, Walt flashing a mile-wide movie star smile. Sliding her hand elegantly along the bannister, she glided smoothly down the steps in new ankle-strap shoes. Nancy stood at the top, smiling.

When Cora saw the Western Union messenger through the glass of the door, her heart heaved in her chest like a water wheel.

"Oh, no," she cried.

Nancy sucked in her breath and clenched her fists.

"Dear God," Cora prayed, "don't let him be dead. I'll do anything you want but please don't let him be dead." She opened the door, her face a peaked mask. Nancy stood frozen at the top of the stairs.

The messenger gave a weak smile. "Cora Dowling?"

"Yes." Her lips barely moved, but still, the wind blew her hair into her mouth. She tried to spit it out, but it flew back, bringing with it the bittersweet taste of Colorinse.

"Telegram for you."

The envelope burned her hand, and she closed the door and stared at it for a long time. If he was dead, wouldn't someone come in person? Wasn't that the way they did it when Robert Walker got killed in "Since You Went Away"? Hadn't somebody come in person?

She raised the envelope to the tip of her nose, as if it might have the smell of Walt to it. Suddenly the smell of him after sex, the strong boozy, smoky, chemical smell seemed like the most important thing in her life. She lowered her eyes and tore open the envelope with a finger, a quick jagged slash. She squinted as she read, as though not sure she really wanted to see. Then her heart leapt. "He's alive," she shouted. "It's from Walt. He's alive."

Nancy clattered down the steps yelling, "I knew it. I knew he'd be alive," and the two hugged and twirled.

Cora read aloud. "Got a bullet in the thigh stop I'm okay stop Will be home for two weeks stop Arrive Thursday March 26 stop Letter follows stop Love Walt."

The railway station crackled with the soft electric static of bunny sweaters. Cora wore robin's egg blue to match her eyes. Her hair, freshly rinsed with lemons, shone like the sun. As the train pulled in, tears began streaking the women's make-up. Soldiers huddled at cloudy train windows like kids packed into three-for-a-nickel photo booths.

Cheers went up as the first GI appeared at the steps, then there was a momentary hush as everyone realized he was missing an arm. But he smiled and hurried toward a plump brunette who had pushed her way to the front of the crowd yelling, "Roger, it's me." They kissed in a lopsided embrace that twisted the pinned-up empty arm of his uniform.

Walt was twelfth off, looking so handsome Cora's pulse raced.

"Hey, gor-juss," he hollered, elbowing his way through the crowd, moving with the help of a cane.

"The same to you," she sang out and rushed forward. They kissed, and he gave her a bear hug. Suddenly she felt a tremendous surge of peace. Walt had gone close to the edge and he'd made it. She took that as a sign. After this they could come through anything together. They might get close to danger but they'd pull through.

Cora drove Walt home, gushing about how great he looked, who all had said to tell him hello, pointing out little changes around town.

"Boy," Walt wisecracked, "I'm home five minutes and already I can't get a word in edgewise." Cora laughed hysterically.

Then Walt got solemn. "You don't know what it's like to be back," he said. "On the train a guy was just reading the brand names from the paper, and they sounded so good, we all clapped."

He sat with a crooked grin, shaking his head and reached over to touch Cora's thigh. She noticed his face was thinner, showing more of his cheekbones.

Cora pulled into the driveway. She'd sent Nancy back to Marysville for two weeks. What the social welfare people didn't know wouldn't hurt them.

"But I can come back, can't I?" Nancy had asked with a panicky look.

"Of course," Cora had assured her.

"I bought a bottle of Canadian Club to celebrate," Cora told Walt as they stumbled into the apartment, half walking, half embracing, hands all over one another.

He sank into the sofa. "Jesus, if you knew how good it felt to sit on a sofa. Here, sit here. Christ, I missed you."

He nuzzled her neck and unbuttoned her sweater. "Oh, God, this is so good," he whispered. "Where's that Canadian Club? I could do with a little one. How about you?"

"Sure thing. I wouldn't want you drinking alone." Cora jumped up, taking special care with her leg movements, toes just slightly pointed out, as she crossed to the kitchen and returned.

Walt fingered his glass. "God, I feel filthy," he said. "I can't remember the last time I had a bath. Let me take this and sip it while I soak and think about you and what we'll do afterward." He winked.

"Sure, go ahead. I'll put some records on."

Cora picked up "I'll Never Smile Again," studied her reflection in the shiny black wax for a minute, then set the record on the Victrola. She sat listening and cried with joy as it played.

She heard Walt splash out of the tub and walk into the bedroom, his cane stabbing the floor with every other step. For a minute he sounded like Eddie. Cora wondered if he'd tell her about the bullet. In his letter he'd said he killed himself some Krauts. He said it had been worth being wounded to kill some Krauts.

She put "Sentimental Journey" on and sat down again,

closing her eyes until it ended. She picked up "Don't Sit Under the Apple Tree." Where was Walt? He was so quiet.

She tore up the stairs and into the bedroom. Her face froze in horror. Walt was sitting dressed on the bed holding the Capricorn Charm School contract. She'd stuffed it into her underwear drawer during a last-minute fit of tidying up. She'd forgotten Walt liked to run his hands through the silk and lace in her drawer before they made love.

"Isn't this a nice surprise?" he asked with a sneer. "Where the hell did you get $268?"

Goose bumps crept up Cora's arms like bugs. "I was going to tell you, Walt. I wanted to surprise you."

"Well, you already did that, didn't you? Answer me, dammit. Where did you get this kind of money?"

"I borrowed it. But Walt, I can make enough to pay it back. I can make money modeling. They said I was a natural model."

"Jesus Christ, Cora, you sound like a star-struck sixteen-year-old, falling for a line like that. Dammit, where did you borrow the money?"

"From Georgia and Eddie."

"Georgia and Eddie?" Walt's face tightened like a fist. "Jesus Christ, that's all I need. I come home after getting half killed, and my wife is in debt up to her tits and who does she owe it to? Her slut of a sister and a cripple." He pounded his fist on the bed, rattling springs against the wall.

"Walt, that's not fair. Georgia's no slut. Carl was a long time ago. Eddie's the only guy since then."

"Huh, the only one who's hung around, you mean. A cripple creep who's savvy enough to know a good thing when he sees it. Plenty of pussy and three square meals. No strings attached. Christ." He got up but lost his balance and fell back on the bed, his cane clattering to the floor. He glared at it as Cora picked it up, then grabbed it, got up and hit the door with his fist.

"Walt, I'm sorry. I'll pay the money back. I thought by the time you got home I'd have a job modeling. I thought you'd be proud of me."

"Well, you thought wrong, didn't you?" He grabbed his cane and hobbled down the stairs.

"Where are you going?" Cora ran after him.

"I'm gonna visit that slut of a sister and her cripple boyfriend. Tell them to keep their stinking noses out of our business. I can just picture them looking so smug. Poor Walt can't afford to send his wife to modeling school. Christ, Cora. Jesus P. Christ."

"No, Walt, please. You just got home. Let's have another drink. Let's sit and talk. Please."

"Shut up. Brother, what a homecoming." Walt stomped out the door toward the Packard.

Cora raced out after him. "Take me with you," she cried, hoping she could talk some sense into him on the way. He revved the engine and started backing out of the driveway, then screeched to a stop.

"You want to see the damage? Why not?"

Cora got in, trembling. Walt had a look in his eyes that scared her. She tried to reason with him, but he yelled, "Shut the fuck up," and started muttering to himself, "Christ, I'm off being blown half to smithereens and my loving wife is back here taking handouts from a slut and a cripple."

Cora remembered a conversation she'd heard in the record store, two women talking about boys who came home with shell shock. "They can't put the war behind them," one woman had said. "They want to keep fighting every minute. It must be terrible for them and their poor families." She prayed that Georgia and Eddie wouldn't be there. "Please, God," she said, "please don't let them be there."

But before she knew it, Walt was pulling up in front of Doc's, and she winced as she saw the light upstairs in the apartment window.

Eddie answered the door wearing an undershirt; red suspenders held up his pants and his mustache was askew as though he'd been scratching it.

"I'm gonna knock your block off, you twerp," Walt yelled.

"Hey, whoa there," Eddie said and put his arm out, but Walt shoved it aside like a dead animal and he hobbled into the apartment. Eddie hobbled after him, repeating, "Hey, whoa there."

"Who is it?" Georgia called in her little girl voice from the bedroom.

"Guess who," Walt bellowed.

Georgia peeked out and smiled. "Walt, you're back," she said.

But then she saw the scowl and her chin dropped as he mimicked her in a falsetto voice. "Walt, you're back."

Eddie ran to Georgia. "Look, fella, calm down," he cried.

Walt lifted his arm.

Cora raced up. "No, Walt, don't."

But by now Walt was too far gone to stop. "Stay out of this," he yelled and swung at Cora instead. She jerked and folded, her hair a silky yellow veil across her face as she dropped to the floor slowly and gracefully, like a movie star.

9
NANCY, 1944

When I found out what happened, my first thought was, Suppose the social welfare people found out? I didn't want to get sent away from another unfit home. But it didn't come to that. Aunt Cora called to say I should stay in Marysville.

"Nancy, I'm real sorry," she said, "but Walt has shell shock. He got it from the war." Her voice sounded like it had sand in it. "He gets episodes. It wouldn't be good for you here."

My chest was tight. "Well, maybe it won't last," I said in a tiny voice, my eyes fixed on the back window of our apartment. The glass had streaks of imperfections in it, like teardrops had got stuck there.

"Maybe not." I heard her take a drag on a cigarette.

"Just promise me you won't run to the teacher again. Give Eddie a chance. Promise me, okay?"

I promised because I was too scared not to. I didn't want to think of my aunt all bruisy blue. In a way I was glad I couldn't see her.

"Well, listen, we had some good times, me and you, didn't we?"

"Oh, yeah." My voice cracked.

"Yeah. So I'll talk to you soon . . . "

"Aunt Cora . . . " I held the phone tight with both hands.

"Uh huh . . . "

"I love you."

"Oh, Nancy, I love you, too."

At least I was a hot shot around school for awhile, bragging that my aunt was a model who'd showed me some of her tricks. I said she'd probably get me a modeling job any day; I wouldn't be hanging around Marysville very long.

Miss Sandercock wasn't my homeroom teacher anymore but she stopped me once in the hall after an assembly where some seniors had demonstrated table manners.

"Nancy, I'm glad to see you," she said, her eyes traveling around my face like I was sprouting weeds. She was probably trying to figure out what was up. I thought back to the day I'd sat in her quiet classroom and written the note asking for help. She'd been as sweet as could be and had written me asking if I wanted to go home with her for a while. I'd looked at her perfect handwriting, thrilled that it was intended just for me. I'd only ever seen a few words of her lettering before—"Good work, Nancy," or "Watch your mechanics, please" at the top of a paper. I'd nodded and she walked me to her house, sat me down in her sunny kitchen and poured me tea from a copper kettle, her nylon stockings rustling as she moved.

"Are you still writing?" she asked now in a soft voice.

"Oh, sure." I blinked and went tongue-tied. My poems were getting blacker and more bitter every day, full of insults, ghosts with huge square holes for mouths that bubbled out loud mocking laughs, babies falling headlong on the steel-sharp edges of low tables, shadowy mothers smiling from dark corners.

Miss Sandercock put the tips of her fingers on my arm. "If there's anything you want to talk about, let me know." Her eyes were so kind, I went weak, but I was too embarrassed to explain all that had happened.

"Oh, yeah, if there ever is, I sure will," I muttered. I remembered even when I'd been beside myself to get away, I'd begged her to make sure the social welfare people weren't mean to my mom, and later I heard her tell them on the phone, "I'm sure Mrs. Sayers means no harm, but the child is visibly shaken." She'd been thoughtful enough to call my mom Mrs. Sayers although everyone knew better. And later she'd come up with the idea we could tell my mom Aunt Cora needed company while Uncle Walt was overseas, and that would help her save face.

The bell for next period rang. "Oh, well, I gotta go," I muttered and hurried off, tripping over my feet. After that, whenever I saw Miss Sandercock in the hallway I turned around and went back where I'd come from, as though I'd forgotten something.

I ran into Bobby Felker a couple of times but he always seemed to be rushing off somewhere with older kids. He'd wave and give me a smile, but that would be it. I'd turn and watch him move and think of the cute little hunches and dips he made with his shoulders when he jitterbugged. I'd feel the way his jaw moved against the side of my head when we danced a slow number. But in the end, I figured the only reason he came to see me in Clinton was because Aunt Cora was able to bring Artie Shaw records home from Tune Time.

I started using my insults around school, muttering just loud enough so whoever was near me could hear. Kids would laugh. Sometimes when a teacher got uppity, I'd write "physicface" or "blubberbrain" on a piece of paper and slip it to Joanie Bonnadonna, who sat alongside me in math. Joanie would roll her eyes and slap her hands on her desk.

By the middle of April, the insults weren't enough, though. I wanted more attention. I started talking fancy, reciting lines from books and poems. I got the idea from a new teacher, Mrs. Gilbert, who used flowery sayings to make a point.

If a kid complained the work was too hard, Mrs. Gilbert would put a bony hand on her chest and scold, "Mark, you are the master of your fate, you are the captain of your soul." When she listed new vocabulary words on the blackboard, she always wrote underneath them in pink chalk, "Remember, language is the light of the mind." Then she'd stand back and smile as though she'd just unveiled the secret of life.

I didn't see any reason why I couldn't sound as poetic. It seemed like fancy language was just the thing to go with my new curly hairdo and my made-up stories about being a child model. On Saturdays I went to the public library and sat at a wooden table and read a book called *The Great Quotations: Ideas for Our Time,* memorizing quotes the way I'd collected insults. Whenever I had to leave a place, I'd say, "The time has come, the walrus said," and I'd get up and go. Whenever I walked into Mr. LaCrosse's algebra class, I'd spout, "Abandon hope, all ye who enter here."

I got friendlier with Eddie, too. He seemed to like me, asked about school, read my papers—stuff my mom never bothered with. I pictured Eddie as a dad. He wasn't the kind of dad I had fantasies about, like Judge Hardy in the movies, but at least if they married, my mom wouldn't be living in sin anymore, and having Eddie around put her in a good mood. She'd been nicer to me since I came back from Clinton.

I remember one day in June, I was in the bathroom trying on some of my mother's Ivory Invitation face powder and thinking I looked pretty cute in a coral colored blouse Aunt Cora had given me that fit just right. I was smiling at myself from a three-quarters view when my mother walked in. I held my breath as she looked at me and then at the open powder box, afraid she'd have a conniption fit, but she didn't.

"Oh, isn't that cute." She laughed her big laugh, but I wasn't sure what was funny.

"You're really growing up, huh?" she said, talking to my reflection. "You look cute."

"You think so?" I talked back to her in the mirror, feeling an unexpected thrill.

"Yeah, a little powder now and then won't hurt."

"Beauty is as beauty does, huh?"

She looked blank, then smiled. "Yeah. So what are you now, fifteen?"

"Fourteen."

"Same difference. It makes your skin a little fairer, more like mine." When she put her face closer, she smelled like pineapple puff. I liked it.

"The only thing . . . " She burst out laughing.

"What?" I laughed too though, I didn't know what was so funny.

"The only thing," she giggled again, "you're not supposed to put it on your eyebrows. You look like the union guy, what's his name?"

I peered in the mirror. My eyebrows were steely gray and bushy from brushing on the powder. "John L. Lewis," I answered.

"Yeah." My mom wet her finger in the sink and wiped the powder off. I could hardly believe it; she practically never touched me.

"There," she said. "That's better." We stood for a few seconds grinning at each other in the mirror.

That night I dreamed my mom and I were riding on a bicycle built for two. Then the bicycle turned into a Ferris wheel that broke down when we were at the top. All I could see down below was black churning water and I went shivery with terror. My mom and I hugged one another in fear, and suddenly she turned to me and said, "Nancy, I'm sorry I'm a loose woman. I'm sorry I'm an adulteress." She squeezed my shoulder. "But look what I got for it. I got you." I sagged against her and the Ferris wheel began to move.

The problems started up again in July when Eddie began going on the road more. When he'd first moved in, he'd just go for a couple of days at a time but things changed after Uncle Walt came home from the war, drove up to Marysville and threatened to beat Eddie and my mom up for being a cripple and a slut. Eddie started going away for a week at a time, and once he went to western P.A. for a whole month.

My mother called him at the boarding houses where he stayed in the different towns to say she missed him. She'd ask when was it, exactly, he was coming back, it slipped her mind. One night she called a place four times until the guy who kept answering the phone finally said, "Look, lady, why don't you just give me the message." My mom got so discombobulated she blurted out the truth. "Well . . . ah . . . all right . . . ah . . . please tell him Georgia called to say she . . . ah . . . misses him."

She hung up, banged on the wall by the phone, and ran her finger over a little ceramic statue of the See No Evil monkeys she kept on a rickety wood table by the phone. Suddenly she slapped at the monkeys and burst out crying.

"What happened?" I asked.

"All he said was, 'Oh, brother.'" She sobbed. 'You'd think he could have been a little nicer. You'd think he would have known I was just trying to be . . . uh . . . be, uh . . . oh, I don't know."

"Romantic?"

"Yeah. Romantic." Her nose was red and her jowls sagged like old pants. "You'd think getting all those long distance calls, and as poor as we are, he would have known I was just trying to be romantic."

I tried to think of a quote that would help but all I could come up with was, "'Tis better to have loved and lost than never to have loved at all," and I knew that wouldn't be right. I just sat and watched my mom stare at the phone with such desperation the air in the apartment seemed to smell of it. I hated her for being so helpless. I hated Eddie for not being there when she called. I hated Uncle Walt for driving Eddie away. I had plenty of hate to go around.

But that wasn't the worst of it. The worst happened five minutes later when I had to call a kid about a homework assignment. I picked up the phone and heard two women on the party line.

"It's shameful," one was saying. I recognized the voice. Mrs. Resh. I pictured Mrs. Resh at church with her henna red hair that was thin near the skin so the pink of her scalp showed through. She had pouchy cheeks and a hundred chins. She reminded me of Winston Churchill.

"Tying up the phone, making a fool of herself over a man," the voice went on. "She's a hussy. That's what she is. It makes you ashamed to be a woman."

I wanted to yell, "It's none of your business, you gossipy old bats," but I knew they'd turn that into gossip, too. I set the phone back onto the hook as though it was a baby bird.

Whenever Eddie went away, Reverend Mackey came around. Usually he came on Tuesdays at seven o'clock after we'd had our dinner, but every once in a while he came at 5:30 just about the time my mom got home from work. I usually hotfooted it out to the library when he showed up. I didn't like Reverend Mackey but I was polite to him on account of my mother. He seemed to cheer her up and calm her nerves. I worried about my mom's nerves. From the time I was a little kid I worried she'd someday start to bounce and not be able to stop. She'd be like one of those people you read about who get hiccups that last for years except she'd bounce. Year in and year out. The thought of it scared me to death.

She wasn't the only one I worried about. I was getting pretty odd myself. Before I went to school, before I went out anywhere, I had to read over my lists of insults and quotations. I'd get panicky if I couldn't remember all the words to a quotation. I kept the lists stashed in my bookbag as though they were stolen treasure. Another thing, I'd lie in bed at night and worry about Uncle Walt and his shell shock. How you could go along acting like a normal person, and then all of a sudden you're having episodes, trying to punch everybody out. I wondered if there were other kinds of episodes, if all of a sudden you went hysterical thinking you had bugs in your hair or you thought you could fly and jumped off a viaduct into cold black churning water. I wondered if you could get shell shock from someone else. If you could, I figured with our luck, my mom and I would get it from my uncle.

One Tuesday in August, Reverend Mackey came around at 5:15 when I was home alone.

"So, tell me, how are you doing, Nancy?" he asked. "I don't believe I've seen you in church lately."

"Oh? Well, I've been there."

"You have?" He raised his dark eyebrows and stared at me through his splotchy glasses. I knew he knew I was lying but I didn't care. Then I got nervous, wondering if it was more of a sin to lie to a preacher.

"Well, one week I had a cold," I mumbled.

"I see. Well, I'm sorry to hear that. Did you soak your feet in hot water?"

I shook my head. There seemed to be soot in the air, as though it had blown in with him.

"Too bad. Best thing for a cold, pulls it right out." He headed for the sofa.

"May I sit down? I'll just wait for Georgia. And while we're waiting, here, let me show you a new device I invented."

I perked up, remembering the gizmo he'd brought around before that sucked the poisons out of you. We'd all got a good laugh out of that one.

He opened a paper bag. "This is a muscle massager," he said. "Relieves your tension." He pulled out something that looked like the claw the guy wore in *The Best Years of Our Lives,* the guy whose arms were shot off, except this one was wood and had five curled-up fingers.

"Here." The Reverend patted the worn blue velour sofa. "Sit down and I'll demonstrate for you."

I wasn't sure I should but my curiosity won out.

He turned toward me. I could see the pores of his face. "Do you ever get tense in the shoulders, Nancy?"

Did I? I nodded.

"Well, just see how good this feels." He put the mechanical hand on my shoulder and squeezed the wooden fingers. They dug into my shoulder muscles. A dull pain stretched across my upper back. He jiggled the wooden fingers around on one achy muscle and it really did feel good. Then he opened the hands again.

"Pretty clever, huh?"

I laughed. "Yeah. It felt funny."

"Is that a new hairdo?" he asked, leaning closer. "You're looking more grown up these days."

"Uh . . . yeah." I started moving away. He looked me up and down. "I can see you're starting to fill out," he said. "Starting to flower."

Fill out? Flower? What kind of talk was that? I peeked down at my yellow cotton skirt and white eyelet blouse.

"Before you know it, the boys will be after you." The reverend's voice was low and full of breath. He picked up the mechanical hand and squeezed my left breast with it. "They'll be after you like that."

I jumped up and screamed. "What do you think you're doing?"

"They'll sweet-talk you and say, my, isn't that a nice new hairdo, and before you know it they'll have a hand on your breast. Then they'll tug at your panties." He waved the mechanical hand toward my crotch. It caught on my skirt and swooped up the hem of it.

I smacked the wooden hand away and stood. "Get out," I screamed.

"Wait, wait." The reverend was panting like when you run fast. "Calm down now. I'm just trying to warn you about the ways of the world."

"You are not. You're doing dirty, disgusting things." I was shaking so much I felt like one of those blizzards in a paperweight.

His head snapped and he looked up to me. "Now, now," he said, "sit down and we'll pray together. We'll ask the Lord to keep you pure. We'll ask the Lord to help me. You. I mean you." There was sweat above his upper lip. The mechanical hand hung down, limp in his fingers.

"No, I won't sit down. How could you do such a filthy thing?" My voice sounded shrill.

He didn't move, so I ran out.

10
NANCY

I raced down the stairs, my legs spinning like bicycle wheels, circled the pavement in nervous, jagged steps, and dashed toward Third Street. When my mom came around the corner, we crashed into one another.

I jerked back. "Do you know what that filthy Reverend Mackey did?" I screamed. "He grabbed me. Here." I pointed to my chest, then quick crossed my arms as though my mother might grab for me herself. "And he reached for my crotch."

My mom's jaw dropped. "Grabbed you?" She looked at my arms clutched together in front of my eyelet blouse and then at my face. "Are you sure?"

"What do you mean am I sure? Of course I'm sure. With a mechanical hand."

"A what?" My mom started to smile, then she realized I wasn't joking and her face went white.

"We should call the police," I yelled in a rusty voice. I threw my hands out in front of me in frantic spurts as though trying to fling dirt off them. "We should have him arrested."

"Nancy, shhhh." My mother pulled me into the doorway of Sunny's Just-Rite Appliances murmuring, "Shhh."

"No, I won't shhhhh," I screamed.

"Nancy, don't . . . don't make a scene." She put her hand over my mouth. It smelled like powdered doughnuts. "People are looking at you."

I shoved her hand away. "I don't care." I turned toward the street and raised my voice. "We should yell it at them. Reverend Mackey is an evil old man."

"No, no, no." My mom looked panicky and clamped her hand over my mouth again, her fingers trembling. Or maybe it was my lips trembling. I closed my eyes, feeling like a prisoner in the doorway of Sunny's Just-Rite Appliances. I thought I might suffocate, and for a minute I gave in to it, as though it would be the answer to all my problems. My mom took her hand away, and when I opened my eyes, her face was a watery blur, then it became two faces, then three all swimming in the late afternoon sun. I wanted to slap them, all three of them, wanted to knock them off and watch them roll like cantaloupes across South Market Street. For a minute I hated my mother so much it scared me.

She leaned forward and whispered, "You're all upset. Let's go back to the apartment. You have to calm down." Her lipstick was just a ridge around the rim of her lips.

I pulled away, yelling, "I don't have to calm down." I put an extra screech into the word "don't" to show I meant business. I'd never yelled at my mother before. A part of me liked it.

Her face crumbled. "Please . . . you're embarrassing me." Tears started up in her eyes.

That did it. I felt something blur and fade inside me, like the ink on a letter that's been left out in the rain. "Of course," I said to myself. "I've always embarrassed her. Just being alive I embarrass her." I went limp and stared at a red and white sign in Sunny's window that said, "You'll be proud to have the neighbors talk when you wash with Maytag."

We walked back, wiping our eyes, not talking except once when we passed Mrs. Stiles getting out of her Packard. There was a big black A on the window that told how many gallons of gas she could get in a week.

My mother flashed a bright smile and shook her head. "These summer colds. Sometimes they're the worst, aren't they?"

"Isn't that the truth?" Mrs Stiles said back, looking at us as though she knew something was up.

At the apartment door, my mom fiddled in her purse for a long time searching for the key, then started up the stairs with draggy steps. I noticed her slip stuck out. She didn't keep herself up as much when Eddie went away. At the top, she turned and looked down at me, her face blank as a paper doll's.

"He's gone," she called out in a flat voice.

When I got upstairs, she lit a cigarette and put it down in the ashtray on the end table by the sofa. The smoke curled around the See No Evil monkeys. She brought two cold Cokes.

"Now, what's this about a mechanical hand?" she asked, with a hint of a smile again. I realized myself how ridiculous it sounded and that made me feel even more furious.

"He said it was a muscle massager. But he grabbed my chest with it and then he reached toward my crotch."

My mom frowned and put the Cokes on the scarred wood coffee table. She took a drag on her cigarette. "Nancy, I think your imagination is . . . uh . . . getting the best of you." She gave me a look like you do at a pet that's misbehaved.

My insides churned with a mix of rage and pity. My mom hardly ever got a chance to look superior. Everyone else knew more than she did, had more confidence, understood the world better, and everybody knew it. I was the only person my mother could look down on.

"It's true." I raised my voice to make up for the weakness I was starting to feel in my stomach and my toes. "I wouldn't make up something like that. Why would I make it up?" My voice came out in harsh bursts. "He said the boys are going to start grabbing at me and we should pray to the Lord to keep me pure."

"He said that?"

I nodded. My throat ached; my head throbbed.

My mom's eyes flickered for a minute as though she remembered something, then she looked around at the walls and the ceiling. She plunked onto the sofa and started crying, not just tears, but real sobs.

I barely breathed, "I'm sorry," without being sure what I was sorry about except that I knew it was going to be hopeless trying to talk to my mother.

The untouched Cokes sat fizzing and hissing as I slumped on a chair and stared at the shadow of a tree dancing on the wall. One leaf kept dipping toward my mom's cheek and then away again. Up, down, up, down. It got close but never quite touched her.

11
CORA, 1944

Reverend Mackey hooted. "A mechanical hand. That girl! What will she think of next?" He looked at Cora and laughed so hard, tears steamed his glasses. He took them off, pulled a crumpled handkerchief out of his pocket and rubbed it in a circle on the lenses with a large thumb. "A mechanical hand. Wait until I tell Enid that one. That's even better than the Foul Rift story. A mechanical hand."

The telephone rang. The reverend stuffed the handkerchief back into his jacket pocket with a quick, sharp jab and picked up the receiver. Cora closed her eyes, listened to the rectory clock tick, and thought back.

It's two days earlier. The phone call comes from Nancy, sobbing, "Oh, Aunt Cora, something terrible has happened." "What?" Cora asks, and Nancy explains, talking in short, raggy bursts, saying that Georgia won't believe her. Cora drives to Marysville right away, telling Walt Georgia is feeling under the weather, knowing she can't tell Walt the truth. Walt would be too cruel about news like this, would taunt, "Well, what do you expect? Like mother, like daughter, right?"

Nancy is waiting, pacing on the sidewalk outside the apartment, running her fingers through disheveled hair.

Cora parks the Packard, says, "Let's walk," and they start up Broadway. The air is chilly and dusty. "I've heard stories about the reverend," Cora tells Nancy as they pass a dry cleaner's with a dying rubber plant and a "Remember Pearl Harbor" sign in the window. "But more that he's a voyeur."

"A what?" Nancy's lips tremble and droop at the corners, as if little invisible weights were pulling on them.

"A voyeur. He likes to peek into people's lives, listen to them confess their sins." Cora laughs bitterly. "Especially their sins of the flesh."

Hank Bailey waves from his stool behind the ancient counter of his News and Cigar Shop. Balding now, Hank has sat in the same dusty window for as long as Cora can remember, watching the world go by. Cora wonders what Hank knows about the reverend.

She nods to him as she continues talking to Nancy. "I always figured if Georgia felt better for confessing, what was the harm? Georgia is so . . . " Cora stops walking, looks at Nancy and her expression softens " . . . so Georgia." She laughs a forced husky laugh, then grabs Nancy's hand. "But taking advantage of a child. We can't allow this." She promises Nancy she'll go to talk to the reverend.

Now, as she sat in the rectory, however, Cora was non-plussed. She'd expected a denial, had even planned a response: "Well, of course, we expected you to say it wasn't true, but you should know there've been rumors, Reverend Mackey. We all know about your so-called private confessions. But this. An improper advance to a child. This is serious business."

The reverend hung up the phone, looked at Cora and said, "Now where were we? Oh, yes, a mechanical hand." He roared again, a loud, forceful laugh that filled the room. Suddenly Cora felt weak and confused. Walt could do the same thing to her, use his deep, strong voice as a weapon, loud and cruel, knowing the words didn't matter, it was the hugeness of the sound that intimidated her. Beads of sweat dampened her forehead. She felt a little ridiculous, but pulled herself erect.

"It's no laughing matter, Reverend," she said quietly. She kept her eyes on him. She'd be damned if she was going to let him get the better of her.

The reverend dropped his head for a second, then looked up with a pious expression. "You're right. I shouldn't laugh at one of my flock." His voice quieted and took on an apologetic tone. "Tell Georgia she shouldn't punish the girl, just pray for her soul. Tell her I'll come to the apartment and we'll pray together."

"I don't think you should do that, Reverend Mackey." Cora realized the reverend would overwhelm Georgia with his phony piousness. "You can deny whatever you want, but there's a child at that apartment who is shocked and suffering." She noticed a quick frown come and go on the reverend's face as she spoke. Mama would be proud of her. "And I don't want you frightening her more."

She got up resolutely. "And another thing," she said, picking up confidence as she rose, knowing she had a model's poise. "You haven't heard the last of this." She grasped the polished brass doorknob of the rectory with sweaty palms but a sure steady pressure, opened the door, and marched out.

But later at the apartment when Cora told Georgia what she'd done, Georgia lit up a Raleigh, waved the match back and forth. "Look," she said, "I don't want to . . . uh . . . stir up trouble. You know, Nancy has told a lot of tall tales." The match flame quivered in the late afternoon light, like a tiny warning signal. Georgia looked haggard and her short blond lashes looked wet. "After all, we don't know what . . . happened. We weren't there."

12
NANCY, 1944

I wouldn't drop it. The hate in me was too big. On the Monday after Aunt Cora's visit, I told bigmouth Florence Butz about it just before gym class, knowing Florence would tell everybody else. I sat down next to her on a bench in the locker room and almost gagged on the words. "Reverend Mackey squeezed my bosom . . . with a mechanical hand," I said. "Last week." Blood pounded at my ears. "And he grabbed at me down there." Describing it was almost as bad as when it happened, in some ways worse, as though admitting it was like saying I'd agreed to it. I forced myself anyway. I was determined not to let the reverend get away with it.

Florence dropped her gym shoes on the floor with a thud and looked at me. "Oh, my God," she said. "That's the most terrible thing I ever heard." It was so terrible she wanted to know every detail, where he sat, what he said,

what the mechanical hand looked like. I told her everything, trying to pretend I was repeating something I'd memorized from a book. "Yes, the hand was wood. Light colored. Maple maybe. Or Hollywood blond. His breathing
went funny, like he was breathing through his mouth instead
of his nose." The more I talked, the more I felt like just a
voice in the air rather than a real person, a shadow that the
wind could blow through.

By Wednesday morning, everyone in school knew, but
things didn't turn out the way I expected. A girl in my
homeroom hissed in my ear, "My mom says you must have
asked for it." At noon in the lunchroom, a boy stared at my
chest and asked, "Hey, when do I get a turn?" and later
another one said, "Hey, how about I give you five cents for
a real feel?"

The principal, Mr. Ecoles, called me in after school on
Thursday and scolded, "We have a serious problem here,
Nancy." Mr. Ecoles had a pale thick face, and the collar of
his white shirt stuck out from his neck like one of the rings
around Saturn. "If you don't stop spreading rumors about
Reverend Mackey, I'll have no alternative but to suspend
you. I'll have to call in your mother."

I knew I couldn't allow that. My mom had been avoiding me more than ever. The day after the reverend groped
me she decided to clean the kitchen cabinets while Eddie
was on the road. The next day she started on the closets,
hauling out boxes of summer clothes, examining each halter top and sundress under the kitchen light, shaking her
head. She washed and ironed every piece and then stashed
the boxes away again, kicking at them until she got them in
just the right tight spot in the backs of the closets.

In the end, even Aunt Cora let me down. The next
Saturday afternoon when she came to Marysville, I told her
what the principal had warned. We were sitting on a bench
at Marysville Park. It was a gray, overcast day. The air in
the park had a sickly sweet smell, like rotting flowers.

My aunt sighed. "Well, maybe it's better if you just . . ."
She put a hand over her forehead " . . . just join another
church."

"But why can't we report him? Why can't we get him arrested?"

"Because he'll tell them you're lying." Aunt Cora pressed her lips together. "Because he's a minister. It'll be his word against yours, and people don't like to believe anything bad about a reverend."

I didn't say anything. I just sat alongside Aunt Cora in the gray afternoon and inched closer to her warmth, wishing I could go back and live with her in Clinton.

"I'm sorry, Nancy." My aunt studied her red fingernails. "But another thing, Walt says I'm spending too much time coming up here, he needs me himself these days."

I looked at my aunt, saw her jawbone move underneath her skin, and felt guilty. My breathing became shallow, as though I shouldn't take so much air.

"How is Uncle Walt?" I asked in a tiny voice.

"I don't know. One day fine, next day terrible. He goes along okay, and then suddenly something happens like no cold beer, and that'll set him off. Plus he won't put on civilian clothes. He'll only wear his khakis. He and some other vets sit around and drink and talk about the war."

I glanced at my aunt. She was so smart and gorgeous, it didn't seem fair. Uncle Walt had made her quit modeling school, but she'd got a job modeling anyway for the Finkel's Department Store Mail Order Catalog. "Only corsets, but it's a start," she'd giggled and told us, "You know what they say, if you want to be a success in a career, you need a good foundation."

Aunt Cora looked at me and sighed. "Sometimes I think he resents my modeling, resents that I've got a good job, but I need it. For the money, God knows. We both need it for the money, but I need it for me, too."

She squinted her eyes and looked up toward the sky. The sun came out for a minute and turned the tiny hairs on her cheeks golden. "I know women are supposed to stand by their men," she went on, staring at the white clouds, "but we need to take something for ourselves, too. We only go around once, you know."

"Oh, Aunt Cora, I bet Uncle Walt is real proud of you, being a model. Everybody is."

She turned and smiled sadly at me and I noticed how haggard she looked. I couldn't ask her to do anything else for me.

I was ready to give up on the human race when Bobby Felker stopped me the next Monday after school at the edge of the playground. He had a serious look on his face, like Buster Keaton.

"Listen, Nancy," he said, "I've been meaning to call you. I—uh—had a real good time that night in Clinton."

"Oh, sure, thanks." I held my breath. If he made some kind of cheap remark, that would be it. God might as well whoosh me off the face of the earth, because if He didn't, I'd find a way to do it myself.

Bobby studied his hands. "Look, I'm real sorry about what happened with the reverend."

I felt like a dam was bursting in my brain. I couldn't talk.

He looked up at me with a pained expression. "I—uh—think you did the right thing, speaking up."

My breath caught. "You do?" My voice was a whimper.

"Yeah, I do." Bobby looked around. A breeze ruffled his hair. "It's a small town. People are narrow-minded. I know they're saying unkind things, but what you did was so brave, I wanted you to know I think it was the right thing. Speaking up, it might keep the reverend away from another kid."

I looked at Bobby, grateful, but suspicious, too. How come he'd practically looked right through me ever since I got back to Clinton until now? My skin seemed too tight, and my eyes felt like deep tunnels in my skull.

He started to reach his hand out to me but I jerked away. He pulled his arm back. "I'm sorry. I didn't mean to do . . . anything out of line." He blushed.

"Sure." Tears started up in my eyes. I stared at Bobby. Maybe being a musician, maybe he understood things better than the others. He backed away. "Well, I better go," he muttered.

I wanted to cry out, "No, don't go." There was something about Bobby that always made me think things would turn out all right. But I hesitated, afraid I'd sound too pathetic. I just lowered my head and nodded.

"So—I'll—see you around," he said and hurried away looking like one of the cross-country racers you sometimes saw in newsreels, all arms and legs, while I stood in the afternoon sun with tears streaking down my cheeks, my legs turning to jello.

I watched Miss Sandercock's homeroom kids file out, then I stumbled in. She was erasing the blackboard. When she turned and saw me in the doorway, she rushed over.

"Nancy, I'm so glad to see you," she said. We sat at two empty desks. "I've wanted to talk to you, but I . . . ah . . . I didn't want to interfere." She reached out and took my hand.

Hers was warm. She looked cute sitting at a kid's desk wearing a brown knit dress with a pocket over the heart. A bright red hanky peeked out, like a flower.

I knew I didn't have to explain why I was there. "What would it be like if I wanted to take the reverend to court?" I blurted out. A thin slab of sun fell on the old waxed oak floor. "My aunt said Reverend Mackey would claim I lied, and people would probably believe him."

Miss Sandercock bit her lips. "She's probably right."

"My mom already doesn't believe me. She doesn't like to talk about it at all." I didn't mention all the lies I'd told in my life. I didn't mention how I went to bed at night torn between hating my mom for siding with the Reverend and hating myself for being the wages of her sin.

Miss Sandercock took my other hand. "Sometimes in life," she said, "you have to take a stand even if you can't win. You have to stick up for your principles." She had a warm, powdery smell. "If you want to go to court, I'll help you. If I can."

"Oh, Miss Sandercock, I don't know." I looked up at the ceiling. There was a string of stains, like little amoebae chasing one another. "What would I have to do?"

"Umm . . . ." She ran a finger over one of the grooves in the old wood desk. "I'm not exactly sure, but I think your mother would have to press charges for you. At the very least, they'll want her to testify." Miss Sandercock cleared her throat. "They could ask her questions about her personal life. It could, I suppose, get . . . ah . . . nasty."

I closed my eyes and tried to picture my mom in court. I saw a stern-faced judge with beady eyes like Herbert Hoover ask her questions. I saw her look confused and watched her hands begin to flutter. I saw her start to bounce.

Miss Sandercock shifted in her seat. Her knee bumped the desk. "On the other hand," she said, as though she'd read my thoughts, "it might be harder on you and your mother than on anyone else. It might be you've already helped enough, speaking up. People may rally around the reverend in public but deep down they'll always wonder."

"Do you think so?" I asked. I looked at Miss Sandercock's face, her pale skin. "A friend told me the same thing yesterday."

"Mmmm hmmm. I do think so." She gave me a glimmer of a smile and squeezed my hand. "It sounds like you've got a good friend."

One day the next week Sylvia Staples came up to me on my way home from school. "You live over Doc's, don't you?" she asked. Sylvia came from a poor family with a ton of kids.

"Yeah. So?" I glared at her. She had a lopsided face. Everything on one side was a little bit higher than the other. She made you want to tilt your head. Her hair was only combed on the top and sides. A hunk in back looked like it hadn't been touched since Columbus discovered America.

"How about if I walk with you? I have to go buy some Pepto Bismol for my mom. She don't feel good."

That just showed how low I'd sunk. Ordinarily Sylvia wouldn't have the nerve to ask to walk to Doc's with anybody. Sylvia was even lower on the totem pole than I was.

"It's a free country," I muttered. A shadow flitted across Sylvia's eyes, but she smiled again. Her cheeks were chubby even though she was skinny as a stick everywhere else.

Walking alongside me, she smelled a little like sour milk. "I thought that was really funny, the joke you made at the spelling bee last month," she said.

"The spelling bee? Jeez. What did I say?"

"Oh, you should remember." Sylvia stopped for a minute and scratched her ear. "You spelled archaic and then said, 'Like in the saying, we can't have archaic and eat it, too.'"

"Ha ha ha." I laughed loud, like my mom. "I said that, huh? I'd forgotten about that." The truth was I hadn't forgotten at all. It was one of my best jokes. I looked at Sylvia in a new way. "Well, our team won, huh? You were on it, weren't you?"

"Yeah. I spelled hyacinth."

"You did?" Sylvia wasn't much of a student.

"Yeah, but only cause I have a cousin named it. Hyacinth. My aunt never made it to the hospital. Her baby got born in the hyacinth bed outside the house so that's what she named it."

"No kidding." By the time we got to Doc's I decided to take Sylvia under my wing, show her my list of insults, teach her a few quotations. I liked the idea of having a friend I could feel superior to. I invited her up to the apartment for cocoa.

"This is Sylvia," I told my mom with a bright smile when she arrived home from work and I saw her eye the cocoa stains that dribbled down the sides of Sylvia's cup.

"How do," Sylvia said. She scratched inside her ear, then inspected her finger.

My mom cringed, and after Sylvia left, she said, "I'm not sure I like that girl. She doesn't look . . . uh . . . clean."

"That's not a very Christian thing to say," I shot back, and then I knew I was going to make Sylvia a bosom buddy.

The next day I went home with her after school. She lived in a dump on Division Street with peeling paint and a rusted car without wheels in the yard. The grass was overgrown. We went in the back door, across a saggy porch with old egg cartons and empty potato chip bags strewn around.

Sylvia's mom was ironing in the kitchen. She was scrawny as a bean, with the longest arms I'd ever seen, as though too many kids had pulled on them. Two boys in torn shirts stood slurping Kool Aid through straws. One had a smudged bandage over his chin. But what really caught my eye was an older girl sitting at a tiny table in a corner, writing.

"That's my sister, Clarissa," Sylvia said. "Clarissa's seventeen."

Clarissa glanced up and smiled. "Nice to meet you." It was hard to believe she was part of the same family. She had creamy skin like the Noxema girls and eyes as green as a cat's and shiny black hair.

"Clarissa writes to soldiers," Sylvia said. "She cheers them up."

Clarissa laughed and pulled a magazine called *Homefront* out from under a box of airmail paper with red and blue borders. Sylvia and I moved closer. The magazine cover had a picture of a beautiful girl and a slogan that said, "There's Something about a Man in Uniform."

"Soldiers who want to get mail send their names in," Clarissa explained.

"Clarissa already got a marriage proposal just from one soldier looking at the pitcher she sent 'im," Sylvia piped up. Clarissa blushed.

"Are you going to marry him?" I asked.

"Oh, I don't know," Clarissa laughed. "I'm saving up my money to go to commercial school. I thought I might move to a bigger city someday. Maybe get a job in a nice office. There are lots more opportunities for women these days, you know." She drew circles on a scratch pad.

I stared at the pad as though it might tell me secrets about life, then peeked back up at Clarissa. She had a look about her as if she knew where she was going. I'd seen that look sometimes in Aunt Cora. I wouldn't in a million years have thought Sylvia had a sister who talked about moving out of Marysville, as though she could do anything in the world she wanted.

Sylvia and I started hanging out together. I didn't have much to lose. Most of the other kids looked down their noses at me anyway except Bobby Felker, and all he ever did was stop me once in the hall after an all-school assembly. "How are you doing?" he'd asked, books cradled under one arm. "Oh, great," I'd lied. "A lot better." He'd opened his mouth and then closed it again. He put his free hand on my elbow. "Well, that's good," he said and took off, and that was it, as though he'd done his good deed for the week.

I didn't care. I liked Sylvia. She wasn't as dumb as she looked; she laughed at my jokes, and treated me like a queen. I liked the attention and I liked that Sylvia had a sister who had turned out as well as Clarissa, as though some of what she had might rub off on me.

It was an added attraction that Sylvia got my mom's goat. I felt smug bringing Sylvia around, watching my mother's eyes darken, knowing she wouldn't complain again. I knew she still didn't know what to make of me since the day I yelled at her on the street and spilled the beans on Reverend Mackey.

I looked for more ways to irritate her. I brought home dust from the cloakroom at school and scattered it under the kitchen table and bed. I placed a little hairy ball in one of her blue satin bedroom slippers. I put on some of her Tantalizing Red lipstick and smudged two coffee cups so she'd think she hadn't washed them well enough.

One night I put a poem on the kitchen table that said, "I am pain and anger, I am a wild scream in the night. I am manicured red claws yearning to rip into creamy flesh. I am a heart that beats unnoticed."

The next morning the poem was gone and when I asked about it, my mother swiped away with a dishrag at the tile behind the sink and said I shouldn't leave scraps of paper around, it probably got thrown out with the trash, but I noticed that she swallowed hard as she spoke and I got an evil satisfaction from it. Being spiteful was the only way I could help quiet something that was building inside me, as though I'd swallowed one of those firework capsules that you light and it burns into a snake of ashes that grows and grows.

13
NANCY, 1944-45

In December, after two months of hanging out with Sylvia, I got antsy. Sylvia looked up to me too much. I wasn't used to it. I'd wake up at night from vague dreams with icy shivers on my arms. I'd scramble in a panic for my lists of insults and quotations and sit hugging them against my chest for dear life. That was the other thing. I couldn't use the insults and quotations with Sylvia. I'd tried a couple of times but Sylvia had looked at me with an odd expression as though she knew all the recitation was just a cover. I'd felt my face flush and my stomach tighten and eventually I gave up.

I started eyeing Joanie Bonnadona, who sat across from me in math. Joanie wore huaraches even in the winter, sassed teachers, and snuck off at lunchtime with Itchy Kessler to smoke on Beale Street behind the school.

One day in January when the lunchtime bell rang, I leaned across the aisle and asked her, "Hey, how about if I come along with you and Itchy for a cig?" Joanie lifted her fuzzy eyebrows at me. "You smoke?"

"Hey, where there's smoke, there's Nancy." I had a couple of squished Raleighs tucked into my pea coat pocket and a cooked throat from practicing the night before in the lot behind our apartment.

The next day Joanie and Itchy, who had teeth like stalactites, and another guy, Darryl, came to my apartment after school. Itchy pulled a flask from the hip pocket of his dungarees and passed it around. We all took swigs, smiled goofy smiles to hide how bad it tasted, and announced, "Hey, great!"

Itchy was a card. He grabbed the phone, dialed a telephone number at random, put on a fake voice and said, "This is yoah president speaking. Remember, I hate wah. Eleanor hates wah." He slammed the receiver down, and we howled. We decided to call the Golden Nursery and ordered six fruit trees to be delivered to Mr. Fenstermeyer, the math teacher. Itchy got on the phone.

"What kind of fruit trees?" the nursery woman asked as we all clustered around the receiver, listening.

"I don't care," Itchy said in a deadpan voice. "I just want some nice fruits." The rest of us shrieked, and ran into the kitchen.

We started hanging out at my place every day after school. We'd sit in the same seats, I'd get Cokes and we'd light up cigs and swig whiskey, planning what to pull. The way we did the same thing every day reminded me of the rituals in church. Prayers. Songs. Standing up, sitting down. Like if you didn't have the rituals, everything else would somehow fall apart.

The stuff we pulled wasn't very churchlike, though. We snuck into movies and palmed candy from the Five and Dime. One afternoon in March we went out to Stern's Dairy on the edge of town and dressed a cow in some of my mom's old clothes. We tied a ruffled dickey around its neck, threw a fringed shawl over its back, put two pink garters on one of its legs and fastened a beige straw hat with plastic cherries to its head. We led it into town through some back alleys and tied it to a telephone pole in front of City Hall.

Another time on a dare I roller-skated through the lobby of the Colonial Hotel wearing a Lone Ranger mask, the wheels of my skates clacking like a racing train on the old marble floor. When I rolled out the front door again, the four of us fell against one another, roaring like wild animals just as Sylvia Staples came around the corner.

Sylvia smiled at me but I could see the hurt in her eyes. I'd told Sylvia my mother said I had to stay home alone after school and study. I said, "Oh, hi, Sylvia," and busied myself taking my skates off, but a couple of minutes later I told Joanie I had to go home. At the apartment I pulled dust balls out of my bookbag and watched them float to the floor. If my mother ever noticed the extra dirt, she never said peep, as if she didn't want to give me the satisfaction of knowing I got her goat. She was back to being her phony cheerful self and avoiding me as much as she could.

She'd started working overtime, too. Sometimes I wondered what my mother's life was like at work, what she thought about and said. As pathetic as she was, her work was a part of her she had all to herself.

I opened the kitchen window that looked out on the empty lot out back and propped a stick in it. I stared at the budding limbs of a tree jiggling in the warm breeze like a girl who's itching to dance, a girl swaying with the music, dying to be asked. A train whistled somewhere. I stared at some dandelions wilting in the too early March heat, and their bent little stems seemed like the saddest thing I'd ever seen. The air was so still I was afraid everything might stop just the way it was. For a minute I wondered what would happen if I went up the fire escape to the roof and jumped.

One warm day in April, Bobby Felker was standing outside my homeroom after school. "Hi," he said, with a small smile. He wore a blue shirt and dark pants pegged at the ankles. His face was lean and he looked so debonair, my knees went rubbery.

"Hi." My voice sounded like it came from under water. "Listen," Bobby said, "you know, they've started up the twilight dances on Friday nights at Marysville Park. I thought if you weren't doing anything Friday, maybe we could go together."

I looked at Bobby in disbelief. How could he just mutter something so momentous in a hallway full of kids with the smell of chalk and stale sweat? "Maybe we could go together." The words pounded in my brain. They should be written in the sky, draped in crepe paper letters over the front of the school.

"Well, yeah, sure." I studied his face like a map, wondering what the catch was.

"Good." He smiled. "I figured we cut a mean rug that time at your aunt's. So, hey . . . " He put his hand on my arm. " . . . Why not do it again?"

"Yeah. Great." I smiled idiotically, my arm burning underneath my pink blouse where he'd touched it. "That will be . . . " I put my hands out, palms up, and laughed, as though there were no words for what it would be.

Bobby laughed too. "So are you on your way home? I'll walk with you." He turned toward the front of the school and a shaft of sun winked in his hazel eyes.

I spotted Joanie and Itchy shifting from foot to foot at the schoolhouse door and knew I was trapped. "Oh, gee, some friends are coming to my place to do homework," I stuttered and smoothed the pleats in my navy blue skirt. "If I could get out of it, I would."

"Hey, I understand." Bobby turned back to me. His sandy hair was cut short and his eyes had slight dark rings around them, making him look sophisticated. "So the dance starts at seven. Shall I pick you up at your place?"

All the dread I'd felt the day Eddie moved in when I'd run into Bobby on the playground came flooding back. I had no idea how much Bobby knew about my mother or about Eddie.

"How about I just meet you at the park?" I studied my saddle shoes, then looked sort of at Bobby's ear. "I—uh— the weather is so nice these days, and I just love the outdoors. Nature. You know, what do they say? 'Nature never did betray the heart that loved her.'" I felt my face go red. "What I mean is, it'd be fun to meet at the park."

Bobby frowned for a second but shook it away. "Sure. Let's make it over by the barbecue pit. At seven, okay?"

I nodded and watched him walk away as though I'd never seen a human being move before.

All week I practiced looking glamorous. I swiped some Ravishing Red lipstick from Doc's and ran upstairs to the bathroom mirror and tried it on. It seemed to really do the trick. I kept eyeing myself from a three quarters view to be sure I still looked a little bit like Jennifer Jones. I brushed my hair one hundred strokes every night; the scent of the oil from my hair on the brush seemed grown-up and full of promises. I tried on all my clothes and tried them on again. I studied my list of fancy quotes, repeating them alphabetically as I went to sleep. " A man's reach should exceed his grasp or what's a heaven for." "By their deeds ye shall know them." " Come live with me and be my love."

On Friday at seven o'clock, I sat on a bench by the barbecue pit underneath a pale purple sky that was huge and cloudless, as though it knew the day was special. I had on a swirly black ballerina skirt and a lilac sweater Aunt Cora had said highlighted my complexion. I picked up a stretched-out wire coat hanger that had a piece of burnt marshmallow sticking to it and started carving vowels in the earth, trying to make each letter perfect. I wrote out nature words . . . "honeysuckle" . . . "pink tulips" . . . "pines" when suddenly Bobby peeked over my shoulder.

"Now that's what I call a dedicated poet. Writing in the dirt." He smiled and sat down by me.

I blushed that he remembered I wrote poems, and scratched over my words with the hanger. "Just warming up for it," I said. I looked at Bobby and smiled. He smelled like after-shave lotion. My nerves felt like shooting stars.

"I see. I do the same thing myself, drum my fingers on anything handy when I hear music in my head." He nodded his head and jiggled his shoulders in rhythm. "Which is most of the time." Across the way in the park, two older couples who were chaperons for the night walked onto the glassed-in pavilion dance floor and put money into the juke-box. The women wore their hair in swoopy waves in front, then pulled up behind their ears with barrettes. They had on flowered dresses with V-necks.

A record came on. Violins. "Ah, music . . . " I grinned at Bobby. "Charms to soothe the savage beast, huh?"

Bobby grinned back. "Well, yeah, I suppose so, but with savage beasts, myself, I'd try a revolver first."

I giggled.

Rudy Vallee started singing "Cheek to Cheek" and Bobby stood up. "Shall we?"

"Yeah. Sure."

Heaven, Rudy sang, *I'm in heaven . . .*

Rudy, you don't know, I thought to myself as we walked across to the dance floor. I noticed some kids from school inside the pavilion, and suddenly I worried I'd do something crazy. I'd throw an episode like my Uncle Walt. I'd fall and shake and not be able to stop or I'd jump and yell and drool.

But when Bobby put his arm around me and took my hand, I knew I didn't have to worry. *And I seem to find the happiness I seek*, Rudy sang, *when we're out together dancing cheek to cheek.* I leaned against Bobby, and we moved together like we'd been glued.

We danced to "You'll Never Know," "Till the End of Time" and "Oh, What It Seemed to Be." When Bobby dipped a knee, I dipped a knee. When he rotated a shoulder, I rotated. It was as though I had a force in me I'd never known was there, as though I had just been waiting for Bobby to bring it out.

We jitterbugged to "Jingle Jangle Jingle" and "In The Mood," swirling past other kids from school and older couples who were all elbows and pumping arms, whizzing by posters of Frank Sinatra, Duke Ellington, and The Andrews Sisters. Sometimes Bobby moved his mouth to the music but he wasn't singing words, just sounds.

Later, we stopped to get Cokes at the snack bar in the corner of the pavilion and stood watching the other dancers. I should say Bobby watched the other dancers. I watched Bobby, afraid he'd disappear if I didn't. I studied the pores of his skin, the patch of sand-colored stubble near his ear that he'd missed when he shaved, the little swoop at the end of his nose. I stood with one foot pointing slightly out like Aunt Cora'd taught me models did to look more poised.

Kids from school passed by and said "Hi," surprised to see us together. Once Bobby leaned toward me to say something above the music and put his hand on my shoulder. I thought I might explode from joy.

After the dance, we went to sit on a bench back near the barbecue pit.

"Our spot," Bobby said, grinning.

"Yeah. Our spot." I surprised myself, sounding so bold, but somehow it seemed natural, as though Bobby and I belonged together in a special spot.

"So how's your Aunt Cora?"

"Oh, she's good. She got a job modeling for Finkel's Catalog."

"No kidding? Good for her. She seemed like a woman who was going to go places."

I decided not to mention that she modeled girdles. I thought of saying my uncle came back from the war with shell shock but decided no, my family was weird enough already. Anyway, Aunt Cora said he was doing better except he'd still only wear his khakis.

Bobby looked toward the dance pavilion A woman was locking up the snack bar. A couple danced without music. "I guess you heard the reverend is doing all his counseling at the church these days," he said in a soft voice. He turned and looked me in the face. "And Mrs. Mackey is helping him."

I felt my fingers turn to fists. My eyelids fluttered. "Yeah, I heard." Aunt Cora had told me. If my mother was visiting Reverend Mackey at the rectory, she hadn't said anything to me.

"She told my mom she'd always wanted to do more for the needy people in his flock but never knew what. Then one night it came to her when she was canning pickles." Bobby looked at the ground for a second and a smile flitted across his face. "She told my mom the Lord said the reverend needed her to help him counsel the women in his flock. He needed the woman's point of view."

I nodded, staring at my fists.

"What I'm trying to say . . . " Bobby raised his hand toward my chin but he didn't quite touch it " . . . is that your speaking up made a difference."

"Yeah, I guess so." Suddenly I felt tired and teary.

"I admire you for it. A lot. I know it wasn't easy."

I raised a foot and looked at my ballet slipper. "Thank you," I whispered in a small voice, but I felt a surge of satisfaction, too. Maybe I had made a difference. Maybe I was going to be a woman who would go places, too.

We didn't talk for a minute, then Bobby said, "Tell you what. If you recite one of your poems for me, I'll sing scat to you."

"Scat?" I figured it must be a new song.

He grinned a mischievous grin. "You'll like it. Just wait. But you first. Poem first."

"Oh, I don't know. My poems are mostly silly," I lied, then looked at the ground and frowned, thinking of all the bitter verses I'd been writing lately.

"Try me."

I tilted my head and figured what the hell. The night was like a dream anyway.

"Okay, I'll recite a poem about poetry." It was an old one, harmless. It didn't give anything away about me,

"Perfect." Bobby stretched his legs and leaned back on the bench.

"Okay. 'A poem is a secret, a memory that lingers at the edge of your thoughts.'" My voice was whispery. "'Images gather like birds. Baby fists. A quick blonde smile. A cage.'" Bobby's eyes were closed and he nodded. "'Pinpricks of neon flicker between the leaves outside your bedroom window.'" Suddenly I realized the poem was giving away more of me than I realized, and my mind went blank.

"Uh, I'm sorry." I put a palm up to my mouth and laughed a fuzzy laugh. "I forget the rest." I felt foolish. Bobby opened his eyes and turned to me with his eyebrows arched.

"Okay." He smiled. "I'll give you a provisional A." He patted me on the back. "You can recite the rest next time." My heart leapt. Next time. He said next time.

"Now you," I whispered. "Now scat."

"Okay." He leaned close to my ear and sang, "Beeyoop de doop dooey beeyoop de doop." He drummed his fingers gently on my knuckles until my fists fell open.

"I figured a poet would enjoy scat," he said. "Scat is a kind of poetry for a jazz nut like me."

I smiled and wanted him to drum on my hands again. "I like it," I said. "It's cute."

"Good. Here's some more." He put his mouth even closer. "Doo wee beeyop doo ee yop," he sang. His lips touched my ear and sent a shiver through me. I turned toward him and he kissed me on the mouth, soft at first, then harder until I felt it in my fingertips and toes. The trees could have crashed down around us and I wouldn't have known.

14
NANCY, 1945

I didn't see Bobby again until next Wednesday except in my brain. The morning sun would splash a patch of light on the foot of my bed and I'd see Bobby's face in the blaze, bright as a movie. At night in my dreams we danced on streets of gold, a white rose in my hair, while kids from school craned their necks to gape as we whirled past.

When I found Bobby waiting for me outside homeroom on Wednesday after school, I wasn't surprised, and then I had to laugh to myself. A couple of weeks earlier if someone had said Bobby Felker would take me to a twilight dance, I'd have joked, "Oh, sure, and we'll take a trip to the moon on gossamer wings."

But suddenly looking into Bobby's hazel eyes in the dusty hall as he leaned against the wall with one sneaker on top of the other, I moved to him as though we were two pieces of a puzzle.

We went to another twilight dance, and then another. On May Day we watched the parade on Main Street together. We bought little American flags on toothpicks and I stuck one in Bobby's shirt pocket while he fastened one in a buttonhole on my sweater. We walked to our spot in Marysville Park holding hands for all the world to see. I took it as a sign that Bobby and I were meant to celebrate May Day together forever.

I still wouldn't let Bobby come around to the apartment, though. He was a part of my life I wanted to keep away from my mother, as though she might tarnish him. I just kept gushing to him about how much I loved the out of doors as an excuse to meet wherever we were going.

I rattled on about the smell of sweet corn and cut grass and the silky velvet feel of rosebud petals. I memorized the constellations. I looked up nature quotes. "I love not man the less but Nature more," I'd say with a smile. "Speak to the earth and it shall teach thee," I'd quote with a grin. I knew I was overdoing it but I couldn't stop, and I could tell Bobby wasn't ever sure if I was kidding or not, but in case

I was serious, he was too polite to laugh, so he'd just smile back.

One Sunday we took a walk on Kessler Junction Road that led out of Marysville to even tinier towns nearby: Bethel, Pumphrey, Pool Creek.

Sitting underneath a poplar tree in a grassy meadow near Kessler's Creek, Bobby told me his mother had been married before to a traveling machinery repairman who moved around the country a lot and that his father had walked out on his mother one spring night in 1932. "Just left her there with three boys." Bobby shook his head and looked as if he tasted something sour. "We never saw him again."

"Oh, that's so sad," I said, wanting to grab Bobby's hand, wanting to say I understood, I hadn't ever seen my own father at all, but I decided I shouldn't, it would sound as if I was saying I had an even sadder story than his. Not to mention I'd be too ashamed to admit to Bobby out loud I was a bastard, although I supposed he knew. I'd always supposed everybody in town knew.

He told me he wanted to be a jazz musician but that he'd probably go to college just in case.

"My stepdad wanted my older brothers to go, but they never did. Too much wanderlust. They're living all over in different places now." Bobby waved his hands in the air. "I guess I'm his last hope." He smiled a crooked smile.

I told him I might go to commercial school, I was already a whiz in typing class. He said that was great, he'd worked on yearbook write-ups and a lot of girls didn't seem to know what they wanted to do with themselves. I told him I was double-jointed and he said let's see so I jumped up and demonstrated a couple of my backbends and twists. The ground smelled fresh and minty as I performed and the tiny points of grass pricked at my legs and wrists, making me tingly all over.

Bobby howled when I finished. "That's great," he said. "No wonder you're a natural dancer. Same principle: a bend here, a twist there." He got up and started jitterbugging underneath the poplar tree. "Here a bend, there a bend, everywhere a bend, bend."

I laughed and began jitterbugging, too, chanting, "Here a twist, there a twist, everywhere a twist twist." We danced for a while facing one another, floppy armed, grinning, something strong and sweet pulling between us as though one was the moon and the other the tides as butterflies twirled around us and birds cooed their springtime songs. I started to understand how Aunt Cora must feel about Uncle Walt. I wondered if my mother had felt the same way about my dad.

The next Monday I dumped Joanie and Itchy. All of a sudden, they seemed too crude and vulgar. At lunchtime on Beale Street I squished out a cigarette with the toe of my saddle shoe and told them we couldn't hang out at my house anymore, my mom's shift at the factory had changed so she'd be home during the day. I thought they'd see right through my lie, but Joanie was real sympathetic.

"Jeez, that's tough, Nance," she'd said, shaking her head, cheeks flushed. "Gettin' stuck with your mom home during the day. Jeez."

I was surprised Joanie didn't made a wisecrack, but later I figured out pretending to believe me was her way of saving face.

In early June I started inviting Bobby around to the apartment after school. Eddie was on the road and I knew my mother wouldn't get home until 5:30. I showed Bobby my Rosie the Headless Woman essay. We played records, sat on the sofa and smooched. He sang scat in my ear.

One day he slipped his hands inside my blouse and I let him. He loosened my skirt and rubbed my stomach and I let him do that, too. It felt as though he was stroking all the nerve ends in me with his fingers. Then he gently took my hand and put it on his crotch and I felt his thing. It was stiff and warm and I sort of liked the feel of it, but I jerked my hand away, scared. I didn't want to end up like my mother.

Bobby just smiled, got up and put another record on, but I couldn't take my eyes off the lump in his blue jeans. "Bésame Mucho" began playing.

He sat down, kissed me again and started rubbing against me, moaning my name. All of a sudden something happened that was like a volcano inside me. There was a huge eruption of feeling in my crotch, then it was like somebody had poured honey into me and it was flowing through my bloodstream, into my arms and legs and toes, everywhere. It was the most wonderful thing I'd ever felt.

I looked at Bobby and cried. He asked what was wrong and I said I didn't know. He wiped my tears away with his fingers and kissed my ear. Finally I sniffed and swallowed and said I must be coming down with the flu, I felt funny in the stomach. Bobby looked down at his lap for a minute, then raised his eyes back to my face and said he better get going.

For days I couldn't think of anything but the honey in my blood. When Bobby and I were together, we kissed and petted and rubbed against one another more than ever, but the volcano never erupted again. I wanted to say, "Could you rub against me the way you did that Wednesday afternoon when 'Besame Mucho' was playing? I was sort of on this end of the couch and you had your arm over there against the cushion. You were wearing your blue jeans." But I never did. I was too embarrassed.

Two weeks later on a Saturday when his parents were away, he took me to see his house. The living room had a huge blue sofa, three big easy chairs, and a gigantic Persian carpet that was kind of threadbare but looked good that way. The air in the house had a cinnamony smell to it.

Bobby stopped by a brick fireplace with photographs above it. "Here I am with my brothers when I was six," he said. I stared at a black and white picture of three boys clowning for the camera. Bobby, wearing a little sailor suit, looked so cute I had to smile. It seemed like there was something familiar about the others, but I couldn't figure out what. Maybe they just looked a little like Bobby.

A tinted photograph showed Bobby's mother and Barney Felker on their wedding day. She wore a peach-colored suit and a huge corsage of orchids. Her sandy hair was swept up and her mouth stretched into a soft sweet smile. Barney looked like he barely fit into his dress-up suit, like a barrel stuffed for shipping, but he had a proud expression.

Bobby seemed to read my thoughts. "Barney has been

really good to my mom. He loves her. A lot of men wouldn't want to raise somebody else's kids."

I nodded but wondered if that's why nobody wanted to marry my mother, nobody wanted to raise somebody else's kid.

He brought Cokes and Cheez-Its from the kitchen as I studied a bookcase near the fireplace.

"My mom is a real bookworm," he said, setting the Cokes down on a table in front of the sofa. "She'd rather curl up with a novel than go into town and gossip like a lot of women."

I nodded and smiled. I couldn't imagine what it would be like having a mother who was a bookworm. I wondered if Bobby's mom stayed away from town because the women used to gossip about her and the husband who ran off. I could sympathize with that. Maybe Bobby's mother and I would get along just fine.

Bobby got out his clarinet, stood by a window, and played "In the Mood," arching his back and squinting his eyes as the sun framed him from behind like a spotlight. I sank into the sofa and thought of the days I'd gone out of my way to walk past Bobby's house and study the pavement, wondering when he'd walked on it last. I could hardly believe I was inside that house now listening to him play "In the Mood" just for me. When he finished, he set his clarinet on a chair, put "Paper Doll" on the Victrola, stretched his hand out, and pulled me up to him. We danced so closely I could feel his ribs against me.

The music stopped but we kept dancing, out into the hallway, then to the back of the house, and finally into Bobby's room where we stopped and sat on a window seat covered with a yellow striped cushion. Outside a huge birch tree swayed in the breeze. Bobby crossed the paneled room to where he had his own Victrola and a wooden cabinet full of jazz records. He put on Artie Shaw's "Begin the Beguine" and boogied back and we sat together on the window seat, holding hands and gazing out at the world.

He got up and put on "Who Wouldn't Love You?," then walked to the bed, sat on it and looked at me, serious as a preacher. He lifted his hands, palms up, and wiggled his curved fingers at me to come to him, and there wasn't a thing in the world I could do except go.

Later I opened my eyes to look at Bobby. He smiled and ran his fingertips across my hairline. I touched his earlobe. I caught my reflection in the pupils of his eyes and trembled. Suddenly my lashes filled with tears and shame welled up inside me as I realized I was Georgia Sayer's daughter after all. I rolled away.

Bobby ran his fingers over the back of my hair. "Nancy . . . " he whispered . . . "look at me."

I didn't move.

He picked up my hair and kissed the back of my neck. I shivered.

"Please," he said.

I turned to face him and his eyes were so kind I didn't care if I was destined to be a slut like my mother, after all. I loved Bobby too much to care.

For the next two weeks we couldn't keep our hands off one another. Afternoons at my apartment. Picnics in the grass near Echo Lake just outside of town. Walks to the meadow on Kessler Junction Road. Things were going so well I decided to let Bobby pick me up at home one night. We were going to a movie and I knew sooner or later I'd have to let him meet my mom so I gritted my teeth, crossed my fingers, and wished on a star that my mother would act decent and it worked. She just gave Bobby a big smile and hello and commented on how humid it was. "I always say it's not the heat that gets you, it's the humidity," she said, fanning her face with her hand. Bobby smiled back and agreed and my mother said now don't keep her out too late, we Sayers girls need our beauty sleep, and that was it. She wandered off into the kitchen and the next day at breakfast she chirped, "So he's what you've been doing all the primping for, huh?" and I grinned and said "Yeah," and we both laughed. My mother was in a good mood because Eddie was due back from a sales trip that day, but I still took it as another sign that maybe my luck was changing.

The trouble started when Bobby invited me to a backyard barbecue at his house on the Fourth of July. Two of his older brothers were going to be there, too, with some friends.

At first my heart soared, thinking he must be serious about me, taking me home to meet his family, but then I started to worry they might pry. One thing about Bobby, he never once asked an embarrassing question, but that didn't mean his folks wouldn't. I figured by now everybody in town knew who Georgia Sayers and her girl were but I couldn't be absolutely sure, especially since they used to live out in the R.D. and his mother was too much of a book-worm to come into town. Suppose somebody said out of the blue, "And what does your father do, Nancy?" At night in bed I went achy trying to rehearse how to act. Maybe I could just lower my eyelids and whisper, "Oh, he died." For all I knew, maybe my father did die so it wouldn't be an absolute lie. Or maybe I could just pretend I didn't hear the question and rattle on about how beautiful the lilies of the valley or the hollyhocks or whatever flowers they had in their yard were. I could even throw in a quote about flow-ers. That would be good, a quote. Or, wait, maybe it would be better to just let my lip quiver a little bit and say, "My father isn't with us anymore," as though something hap-pened that was so tragic I could hardly bear it. That should stop them, shouldn't it? Plus it would be pretty much true. But then what if somebody asked about Eddie? I'd just have to stick to my mother's story, that he was a boarder.

I could tell one of Eddie's funny carnival stories and make them think I was cute and witty. I went through so many maybe thises and maybe thats I woke up every morn-ing with sore jaws, pulsing teeth and knots in my neck. I almost backed out, but then I'd see Bobby, go weak with love, and hope for a miracle.

One thing, I knew I had to look right. I bought a copy of Silver Screen with a picture of Margaret O'Brien on the cover and studied how to look more like her. I figured sug-ary demure Margaret would go over better with the Felkers than saucy, sultry Jennifer Jones. I pictured myself sitting on a striped lawn chair across from Mrs. Felker, daintily holding a tea cup and gushing, "Oh, you're so lovely to invite me. Everyone in your family is so lovely." I practiced pulling my hair back behind my ears and fastening it with barrettes so the curls fluffed out behind me and made my face look baby sweet. I studied myself in the mirror, smiling with my upper lip firm across my teeth like Margaret did instead of loose and floppy like I usually smiled.

The morning of the picnic I washed my hair, rinsed it with the juice of a lemon to make it shine, and rolled it up with setting lotion. I wore a white cap-sleeved blouse with a Peter Pan collar and pearly buttons above a gathered print skirt with red roses that trailed around and around on a white background. Even my mother said, "Oh, you look so cute, so fresh and summery. And there's more bounce in your curls." Eddie even whistled and winked at me as he and my mom left at eleven o'clock to go to a Fourth of July picnic.

Bobby picked me up at noon in Barney's pea green Buick. It was a clear bright day and the sun felt so warm on my face through the Buick's windshield as we drove up Broadway, I took that as another sign things would work out just fine.

But by the time we reached his house I started getting stage fright and as Bobby pulled the Buick into his parents' driveway I felt my face freeze into a smile I could only hope was a Margaret O'Brien one. After that, all I remember are bits and pieces of the afternoon, all mixed up with the furious rat-a-tat of firecrackers neighborhood kids were setting off.

I remember Barney giving us a tour of his victory garden, bragging about the size of his carrots, radishes and dwarf lemons as I gushed, "Oh, they're lovely. They're so lovely." Bang bang. Bang. I remember Bobby's oldest brother, Cory, wearing a stretched out T-shirt and a scowl, eyeing Bobby's pegged pants and waving a beer can at him and saying, "Well, Bobbo, a li'l bird tole me you were a real Zoot Suiter these days, and damned if that li'l ol bird wasn't right," as Bobby grinned and pretended to tip a wide-brimmed fedora and twirl a key chain. Bang bang bang. Oh, and one real good thing. I remember I offered to help Mrs. Felker set the table and she said Well, how nice, let's see I think we're eight people and I looked around and counted and faced her and said, Yeah, eight, as though we'd just agreed on an important theory about life.

But the main reason my brain went blobby and everything else turned into a blur was what happened at the end when the boys went inside to turn a Phillies game on the radio and I stayed in the yard to help Mrs. Felker clean up.

"And how is your mother, Nancy?" she asked as she stood at the head of the wooden picnic table scraping the remains from one melamine plate onto another.

"Oh, she's fine." I felt my chest tighten. "Just fine." I dipped my head and started gathering up used napkins.

"Well, that's good. The last time I was in the gas company office, she told me she'd had a touch of neuralgia."

I bounced. Gas company? Neuralgia? I glanced toward the screen door as though somebody might be there to explain but there were just the silent rhododendron plants gleaming in the sun.

Mrs. Felker started collecting Dixie cups with her thumb and forefinger. "She said she was thinking of going on part-time. Has she done that? That may be why she's feeling better."

I realized Mrs. Felker had my mother mixed up with somebody else. "Uh, my mom works at the Rutt Ridge Silk Factory," I said in a small voice, "not the gas company."

Mrs. Felker looked puzzled for a minute, but she smiled and said, "Oh, forgive me, Nancy. I've been so excited getting ready for the boys coming home, my brain isn't working right." She put a hand on my arm. "Forgive me. What is your mother's name?"

I held my breath for a second. "Georgia Sayers." My voice was just a whisper.

"Oh." Mrs. Felker's face flushed and her hand dropped from my arm. She looked at Bobby with a kind of desperate expression, then swung her eyes back to me and studied my face for a minute as if she was reading a map.

I wanted to run.

Then she broke into a smile again. "Well, my heavens, of course. The woman at the gas company, her last name is

Saunders. How stupid of me! I believe I did meet your mother once at the drugstore in town."

"Yeah, probably. We . . . uh . . . live near there."

I smiled back but I could tell I had an expression like when you're waiting too long for somebody to take your picture and I was so relieved when Bobby walked back out and said, "Here, let me help you ladies bury these remains," I wanted to hug him right there but at least I had enough sense to wait until later in the car and then I hugged him like I never wanted to let go

The next afternoon Bobby showed up at my house looking like he hadn't slept. The rings around his eyes were dark and his shoulders slumped.

"Nancy," he said, "this is the hardest thing I ever had to say, but . . . " He heaved, as if he was having trouble getting air. "We can't see each other anymore."

"What?"

"I'm sorry. It's not your fault. Something has come up." His voice was raspy.

"Just like that? All of a sudden? Why?"

"I can't tell you. It's too . . . oh, God, I don't even know what the word is." His voice trailed off. "Just believe me, it's not your fault. It's not mine either."

But by now I felt my breath catch as I figured out the answer. Once Mrs. Felker learned my mom was Georgia Sayers, my name might as well have been mud. What was worse, I'd behaved with Bobby exactly the way everybody would expect Georgia Sayers' kid to behave. Like a scarlet woman. A slut.

"Nancy, look, I wish it could be different . . . "

"Sure. I understand." I hoped he didn't hear my thumping heart. "C'est la vie, huh? Fun while it lasted, right? Well, why not?" I turned away quick to hide the tears. "To tell you the truth, I was getting bored myself."

My head felt like it had just fallen on the floor with a thunk. At least I wasn't going to become pathetic like my mom, desperate to hold onto any man who paid her a little attention. If I was destined to be a loose woman, at least I could pretend I didn't give a damn.

"Nancy . . . " Bobby sounded more like his old self for

a minute. "If I could change things . . . if there was anything I could do."

"Hey, sounds like a song title," I quipped. Now the other parts of my body started to float away until I felt like I was just a huge beating heart.

15
NANCY

I stared at the apartment door as though I could somehow bring Bobby back to say it had all been a silly mistake, and pounded on it with my fists, and dropped my head against the hard wood.

Even though my mouth felt dry as old socks, I needed a cigarette. I staggered into my mother's bedroom. Eddie's black sample cases and the catalog that listed the novelties he sold were stacked along one wall near the radiator. An extra pair of his special shoes was tucked into a corner by the bed, one sole five inches higher than the other. I thought of the time I'd tried Eddie's shoes on and hobbled around the apartment in them. I'd been extra nice to Eddie that week. Tears pricked at my eyes now and I quick looked away.

I grabbed a crumpled pack of Raleighs from the drawer of the nicked maple night stand, stomped out and stumbled around the block, then started towards Marysville Park, thoughts of Bobby running through my brain like a speeding train. Bobby singing scat. Bobby's lips against my cheek. But when I got to the park, I took one look at the dance pavilion and tears started streaming down my face. I sat on a bench by the barbecue pit and thought of walking out to the R.D. to see his mother. She'd been through some misery herself, a husband running off. Maybe she'd be able to understand how I felt if I told her I hated having a mother who was a slut.

A breeze brushed my ankles and I looked down at my

scuffed sandals and faded gray skirt. I couldn't go to see Mrs. Felker. There wasn't anyplace I could go except back home, and that made me saddest of all.

I slumped on the bench and sobbed. The sky was darkening into the purple color of a giant bruise. In the distance I could see the dark shapes of pine trees like black slashes on the hills.

I stood up and dragged myself back toward town. The sharp air cut my lungs and the silhouettes of chimneys looked like men from Mars. I shivered.

Outside Doc's, I stopped and stared up at the lighted apartment window and shook with fury thinking if it hadn't been for my mother I could be in Bobby's arms right now. I shouted at the top of my lungs, "Stop it, you old witch. Stop ruining my life." I couldn't go in.

I edged into the alleyway alongside the building, my eyes half closed as white lights zigzagged through my brain, crashing into one another. I tiptoed into the empty lot behind the apartment, sat down on the dirt, and lit up a Raleigh.

The nicotine made me woozy. I hadn't smoked much since I'd been seeing Bobby. I closed my eyes and saw the two of us lying side by side in the grass at Kessler's Creek as Bobby ran his fingertips around the edges of my face. I shook my head, clenched my jaw, and looked up at the back window of our apartment.

My mother was ironing. You could see her shadow on the wall through the window, dipping her fingers into a bowlful of water and spritzing clothes with it like a preacher blessing babies.

I was still furious at her for siding with the reverend. Why couldn't she at least have said, "You know, Nancy, I've been thinking. Maybe you were right. Maybe it wasn't your imagination this time." Other kids' moms stood up for them. Why couldn't mine? It was bad enough Bobby dumped me on account of her. Couldn't she at least give a damn?

I squished the cigarette out and got up and started twisting. I needed to feel my muscles stretch and scrape and ache until I was exhausted. I bent down in front and spread my hands out flat on the ground. I lowered my nose until it touched my knuckles.

I threw myself into a backbend and tried to walk on all fours but lost my balance and caved in. Lying on the dirt, I started bawling and then I heard footsteps in the alley. A woman giggled.

A man's voice said, "So what do you get if you cross a cow with a kangaroo?"

"I don't know." It sounded like Shirley, Doc's waitress.

"I don't either, but you have to milk it with a pogo stick." It was definitely Eddie. I recognized his laugh, like sniffles. I stood up.

"So thanks for walkin' me through the short cut," Shirley said. I heard the back door of Doc's open and close. Eddie struck a match and went on down the alley when something furry rubbed against my leg.

I shrieked, then looked down. It was only a cat. Damn! It yowled and raced off.

Eddie ran back. "What the hell? Nancy, is that you? What the hell are you doing here?"

I felt trapped. "How about you?" I demanded. "What are you doing in an alley with some lady?" The minute I said it I got irritated that I had to stick up for my mom.

"Jesus. Women. I ran into Shirley over on Broadway. She was late for work. I walked her through the alley. It's a shortcut."

"Oh."

"So . . . " Eddie's cigarette glowed orange in the dark.

"I was just . . . doing some of my twists. Sometimes when I get nervous I come out here and do twists. They help me relax."

"Twists?"

"Yeah. I'm double jointed. I can twist myself into weird shapes."

"I never heard that."

"I don't do it in front of my mom. She says it's not lady-like."

"What kind of shapes?" Eddie took a drag on his cigarette, his face flickering in the light from the ashes.

"I can bend down and touch my nose to the ground. I can curl up in a bundle and roll."

"No kidding. So let's see."

I could tell he didn't believe me. Some of my spunk crept back. I eased forward and did my nose touch better than I'd ever done it before, Eddie's breathing adding a kind of quiet rhythm as I moved my head toward the ground, slow but sure. I stood up, then hurled myself quick into a backbend, hard and determined, drawing up every inch of energy I had in me, and this time I didn't cave in one bit. This time I walked in a perfect circle on all fours, stomach in a high arch, although my palms and feet grasped at the ground in rough jerky moves, like a confused animal.

"Jesus, you can bend backward, too?"

"Yeah."

"You realize only one contortionist in fifty, maybe a hundred, can do that? Bend forward and backward, too?"

"Contortionist?" I didn't have the slightest idea what Eddie was talking about.

Rhonda the Rubber Woman

Part Three

16
NANCY, JULY, 1945

The late afternoon sun winked on the spires of the Old Welsh Church as I opened the creaky iron gate to the maple grove in back. Eddie was already waiting for me on the bandstand, grinning. I wiped a smudge of dust off my blue jeans and waved. We were getting along great, me and Eddie. Every Tuesday and Thursday we met at the grove, where he was training me to be Rhonda the Rubber Woman.

I was throwing myself into being Rhonda, the world's youngest female contortionist, the way a dog went at a bone. I practiced for hours every day. Rhonda was going to be my real ticket out of Marysville. Rhonda was going to help me forget I'd ever met Bobby Felker.

"Good news," Eddie called from the stage. Eddie was a real good teacher. Already I could walk on all fours in a circle smooth as a daddy longlegs.

"What?" I yelled as I headed toward him. He'd also started training me to bend forward from the hips and put my head through my legs so it came out in back. He had a book that showed a rubber man who could stick his head all the way through and stare up in back at the sky. It looked pretty disgusting to me but I kept trying anyway. All the muscle stretches, all the pulls and strains and shooting pains in my body were nothing compared to the heartache over Bobby.

"One of the circus gals I know over at Belvedere is going to make you up a fancy costume. Spangles, beads, sequins. You name it."

"Oooh, that's great." I grinned as I reached the bandstand, picturing myself on a stage, arms outstretched, blowing kisses, mouthing the words, "Everyone is so lovely."

"And maybe I'll work up a musical accompaniment," he said, narrowing his eyes. "Yeah. Music would give the routine a lot of class. What say we give it a try right now? Give me the routine where you twist yourself into a ball and roll. I'll sing along."

"Sure." I stepped back onto the grass, sat and began to

pull my legs up toward my stomach, like the pictures you saw of babies in their mother's bellies. Eddie perched on the bandstand, legs dangling lopsided over the edge, and sang, "Would You Like to Swing on a Star?" He had a nice singing voice, sort of whispery, like Gene Kelly.

Slowly I gathered myself into a ball as Eddie finished "Swinging on a Star" and started on "I Got Spurs That Jingle Jangle Jingle," clapping a little bit in rhythm.

When I'd pulled myself together as tight as I could, I started to rock to get myself rolling but I didn't budge. I felt myself flush and sweat with the effort when suddenly Eddie broke into a loud chorus of "Ac-centuate the Positive." I rocked faster to keep up with the beat and that was all it took. I rolled a few feet in one direction, then a few feet in another, then I let myself go loose all at once, as though I'd been sprung from a rubber band.

Eddie and I exchanged sly looks and laughed. The music was going to make a big difference.

"Take a breather," he said so I sprawled out on the ground, grabbed a blade of grass and stroked it between my thumb and forefinger. Eddie told me his mom had been a piano teacher and she'd given him lessons when he was a kid, but he goofed off, so eventually she gave up on him.

"I'm sorry now," he said. "I wish I could play now, but my mom . . . " He shook his head and slapped his hands on the jiggly wood planks of the stage.

"I'd be playing a tune, thinkin', hey, not bad, but all she saw was mushy knuckles." He imitated his mom. "'Knuckles up, Edward. Knuckles up,' she'd say. She was always findin' something wrong, somethin' wouldn't have occurred to me in a million years."

I thought about Eddie as a kid. It must have been tough with his clubfoot. For a minute I wanted to give him a hug, but he'd think I was crazy so I jumped up and did a quick backbend and walked around in a circle on all fours. The maple trees looked weird upside down, as though they were about to hurtle off the earth.

"One good thing about your mom," Eddie went on as I squatted again, "she doesn't bellyache. Georgia's always got a smile for ya. I only know one other woman always

has a smile. A gal in western P.A. She's a looker, too."
Eddie stared up at the sky for a minute, then out toward
western P.A. The sun was going down. It looked like a
huge orange ice melting, spreading out along the edge of the
earth.

"Too many women, all they do is bellyache," Eddie
frowned, "Seems a cryin' shame, a waste. You only go
'round once in life." He looked at my face as I sat on the
grass now, hugging my knees.

I turned away as I thought about what Eddie said, but I
didn't go for it. You couldn't stop a bellyache, only what
you did about it. I bellyached all the time inside, telling
people off in my head, dreaming up ways to make them
sorry they'd been mean to me. I grabbed another blade of
grass and pictured my mom sitting in the kitchen when
Eddie was off on the road, smoking Raleighs and staring at
the linoleum. I pictured how she looked at me sometimes
as though I hurt her eyes.

You couldn't tell me she wasn't bellyaching inside. I
looked at the blade of grass, shiny on one side, rough on the
other. The difference between me and my mom, she didn't
know what to do about it, and I did. I gazed out at the huge
orange rim on the horizon.

"Enough of a breather. Let's practice the ball and roll
again," I said to Eddie in a voice so loud it surprised us
both.

17
GEORGIA, JULY, 1945

Eddie came into the kitchen one Saturday afternoon and
said he had to go to Pittsburg for a week. Nancy was out.
I'd been shining the chrome on the stove.

"The firehouses and churches, they're holdin' their
summer carnies," he said. "I got some new novelties that
are supposed to go over big with the kids playing pitch

penny. Hand buzzers. Fake dog-do. Candy that makes your mouth turn green."

"Oh, Eddie, that sounds awful," I said but I couldn't help laughing. "So I'll leave in the morning." He came up behind me and folded his hands in front of my waist.

"Okay. Sure." I felt tired and tiny, like a floppy doll. For a while it had been fun, Eddie going off, like the good-bye scenes in war movies. He'd give me hugs and kisses and tell me what a looker I was. I'd feel special. But he didn't make as much of a fuss anymore.

He kissed me on the back of the neck and I peeked at myself in the chrome and thought about turning thirty-five in August. Ugh! Except I knew I didn't look it. People were always saying I still looked like a kid. I worked at it, though. I'd been massaging my neck, bottom to top, throat to chin, the way it had said to do in the *Marysville Gazette* that we read down at Doc's. For a while I'd tried to tilt my face up a little bit all the time, like the paper had said to, to keep the skin on my chin tight, but then people'd started asking me if I had a stiff neck so I stopped. Later I sent away for a chin strap that was advertised in a magazine but when Eddie saw it, he practically died laughing so I didn't use it. I thought about it now, though, and decided to put it on while he was gone.

He started edging me toward the bedroom, in little steps, the washrag hanging from my hand. We'd stopped pretending he was a boarder when Nancy went off to Clinton. Sometimes I wanted to tell him if we were married I wouldn't mind his going off on business trips so much. I could talk to the other girls about how my husband was off on a business trip, same as them. Eddie had hinted a couple of times about getting hitched, but he hadn't said anything since the time Walt came up to Marysville and tried to slug everybody in sight.

"Walt certainly would be a whangdilly of a relative," Eddie'd said the next day. "Walt as a relative, whoooo, that's one thing a guy would sure have to think about."

After dinner I told Eddie I'd pack for him. "I'll do a neater job," I said. "You know men, they're all thumbs."

I went into the bedroom and looked for his little book

that listed where he was going and that sometimes had papers from carnival companies in it saying what they needed, but I couldn't find anything. I packed two pairs of brown pants and three shirts—two yellow and one cinnamon—and then something caught my eye. An envelope tucked up on a closet shelf underneath a spangled vest Eddie had gotten once from a circus ringmaster. He'd worn the vest when he did the song and dance routine when his buddy Chester retired.

I pulled the letter out. It was from a place called Lyndora and it was addressed to Eddie at his old apartment. The envelope had a flower in the corner like it was from a woman. My heart started racing to beat the band. I didn't know whether I wanted to open it or not but I didn't get a chance. I heard Eddie stomping toward the bedroom, so I quick stuck the envelope back. It was all I could think of the next day. I sat at my machine feeding in the nylon for the parachutes even faster than usual and I was one of the fastest feeders they had. I kept saying "Lyndora" to myself. I asked a couple of people if they'd ever heard of a town named Lyndora, if it sounded like a place that was close to Pittsburg, but nobody knew and a couple of the girls asked why I wanted to know so I clammed up.

Nancy was at the apartment door when I got home at 5:30.

"Guess what? I won a prize," she blurted before I had a chance to breathe. "I won a prize for my essay on illusions."

"Your what?"

"My essay on illusions. I told you about it. I wrote it in May and Miss Sandercock sent it in to a contest for kids all over the state. Look, here's a letter. It says I won a war bond."

"A war bond?" I said. "Isn't that something?" I felt grumpy. I just wanted to get into the bedroom and look for the letter with the flower. But Nancy put on her poor woebegone kid look. I knew she'd been moping over the Felker boy. That's how it is with kids. Puppy love. A month later they're gaga over someone else, but you couldn't tell Nancy that. She'd just sass you back or throw around some fancy-sounding saying nobody or their brother understood.

"Well, it's swell that you won a prize," I said, forcing a smile. When you thought about it, it was swell, just bad timing was all.

"I'll read the essay to you," she said, her eyes bright. "It's called 'The Strange World of Illusion.'"

"Illusion, huh?" I wasn't exactly sure what illusion meant. You'd think they had better things to teach the kids at school than a lot of ten-dollar words nobody needed.

"So here goes. 'The alarm clock rings and you jolt awake. You stumble into the bathroom and peek at yourself in the mirror. Oh oh. You look like an old loaf of bread. But wait. Don't be alarmed. This is not the real you, only one of your sides—the just-got-out-of-bed side." She glanced up with her dark eyes.

"Uh huh." It didn't sound like much to me. How could a person look like an old loaf of bread anyway? Plus I hated it when Nancy looked at me with those eyes.

She went on. "You open the medicine cabinet and grope for the toothpaste. You brush your teeth and peek into the mirror again. That's better. Now you look more like the Ipana girl."

The Ipana girl? I wondered if the woman in Lyndora looked like the Ipana girl.

"You wash your hair. It's squeaky clean, and now you feel like the Kreml Shampoo lady." Nancy eyed me again.

"But wait. The shampoo lady's face gets mixed up in your head with the loaf of bread and the Ipana girl. Who are you anyway?"

"Uh, how long is this essay?" I asked. It sounded like all Greek to me. The Ipana girl. The Kreml lady. Bread. I felt dumb, like I must be missing something. It made me nervous, my own kid making me feel dumb.

"Five pages."

Five pages? How could anybody write five pages? It was beyond me. "Well, that's real swell, but why don't you just leave it, and I'll read the rest later."

Her mouth dropped a mile and I felt bad again. I hated

how kids could do that to you. "Uh, well, but winning a war bond, that's swell. I guess you take after me. I was good in English."

"You were?" Her face seemed different lately. Thinner. More like an adult. "I didn't know that. Did you write things?"

"Sure," I said. "I always did real good. One teacher said I had the best penmanship in the class. I made the neatest capital O's and capital I's of anyone."

Nancy looked discombobulated for a minute but then she said, "Oh, yeah. Your handwriting is real neat. A lot better than mine." She looked down at her paper and I noticed her eyelashes. Dark and long, like bugs' legs. Me and Cora, ours were short and light, more like nailbrush bristles. I wished Nancy looked more like the other Sayers girls. She folded the pages and put them in her book bag. She flipped her hair and said she was going to Joanie's. There was something about the way she walked lately. Springier. Ever since she and Eddie'd been practicing a surprise they were cooking up for my birthday.

After she left, I raced into the bedroom and opened the closet door but the letter with the flower wasn't there. The spangled vest was right where it had been the night before, but no letter. I felt on the shelf underneath the vest and looked on the closet floor, squinting to see. I took the clothes off the shelf and ran my fingers through them. Nothing. I searched through the drawers. Eddie must have taken it.

In the kitchen, I got out some Old Crow and 7-Up and mixed myself a drink. I lit a Raleigh, the last one in the pack. I seemed to be going through more cigarettes lately. I finished it, then went down to Doc's to buy more. I was feeling a little woozy so I decided to stay and have a cup of coffee. I sat at the counter stirring milk and sugar into my cup when Genevieve Metzger came in with her daughter Shirley, both dressed to the teeth. They sat in a booth.

"Ralph's out of town on business so Shirley and I are treating ourselves to a night on the town," I heard Genevieve tell Doc. "After dinner we're off to see the new movie at the Strand, 'Four Jills in a Jeep.'"

I sipped my coffee, feeling at loose ends. I thought of asking Doc where Lyndora was but I was afraid he'd ask why I wanted to know. Why couldn't people mind their own business anyway?

I looked at Genevieve and Shirley and thought about something Eddie'd said one day, that I sometimes acted as if I didn't like Nancy all that much. Eddie could be real outspoken. I figured he got it from circus folks. Gypsies. Snake charmers. People who grew up in places that smelled like garlic. I'd said what a thing to say, just because I had to scold her once in a while, every mother did that. Eddie'd said don't get in a huff, I can understand it was tough, gettin' stuck with a kid you didn't ask for, and I'd gone swimmy in the head. Some things you're just not supposed to talk about out loud.

Suddenly now out of the blue I pictured myself back when I was pregnant, walking to work one day, scared Mama might die, and thinking if she did, maybe I'd put the baby in the ragman's truck so it wouldn't be my penance like the reverend said. I wondered what my life would have been like if I'd really done it, then I shook my head to shoo the thought away. I flicked ashes into a black ashtray that had a picture of the cute little Phillip Morris bellhop on it. I picked up a *McCall's* magazine that was laying on the counter and flipped through pages.

Hey, look on the bright side, I told myself. She's lucky she's always had three square meals. Plenty of treats. Pineapple puff. Bread pudding. Tandy Takes. That's more than a lot of kids. Raising a kid can wear anyone to a frazzle, especially when you have bad nerves. I wasn't the only one. I'd heard Mildred and Charlotte from work complain enough times. Kids take a lot out of you. In the magazine, a Kotex ad said it's hard to be all out for victory some days, but if millions can keep going in comfort every day, so can you.

Genevieve was telling a joke, interrupting herself with chuckles as she went along. I couldn't hear it all, just the ending. "My wife? I thought that was *your* wife." Shirley giggled like a kid.

Maybe I should take Nancy out alone once in a while, I

thought. Just the two of us. Have a couple of laughs. I knew some good jokes—I heard them at the factory. Maybe I was too grouchy sometimes. Oh, well, who isn't? I'd make up for it. I'd fuss over her a little more on my birthday. After she and Eddie pulled their surprise. I'd show her I appreciated it.

"Lyndora," I said to myself. It sounded more like a woman's name than a town. I started thinking about a woman named Lyndora. I saw the Ipana girl. I saw the Kreml shampoo lady.

I sneaked another peek at Genevieve. She was talking to Shirley now in a low voice, looking pleased as punch. Of course, it's easier for some folks being a mother. Some folks get all the breaks. I started massaging my neck. Bottom to top. Throat to chin. I tilted my chin up. I reminded myself to get the chin strap out when I went upstairs.

18
NANCY, 1945

On the last day of July, Eddie drove me to Belvedere to meet Mr. Encarnacion, who ran the Magic Midway, a carnival that travelled all over Pennsylvania. The Magic Midway had a side show with a two-headed baby in a jar and a human pincushion—a guy who stuck needles in his arms, slept on nails, and laid his face down in pieces of jagged glass while kids stood on his back. There was a fat lady, a snake charmer, and a belly dancer.

Mr. Encarnacion sat on a folding chair outside a blue trailer, eating a piece of fried chicken from a plate perched on top of an upended garbage can.

"Hey, Armando," Eddie hollered as we got out of the car. "Say hello to Nancy here, world's youngest rubber woman."

Mr. Encarnacion looked up and laughed. He had the whitest teeth I'd ever seen. He was dark skinned and wore a shirt that was open in front, with bristly black hair showing underneath a St. Christopher's medal and a garlic necklace.

"Eddie Jeffers, you old son of a bitch," he yelled. He put the drumstick down on the plate and wiped his hands on his pants. "And say hello to my two new girlfriends here." He stuck his forearm out to show a tattoo of two dancing girls on the biceps. Then he flexed his muscles and the girls' boobs popped out. He and Eddie snickered and I felt my face go hot.

Mr. Encarnacion turned to me. "A rubber woman, huh?" He jiggled the garlic rope at his throat. "Sure, and next thing you're gonna tell me ya got a chicken with teeth, right? A chicken eats corn on the cob, smiles like Bugs Bunny."

Eddie grinned for a second, a hank of hair falling down over his forehead. My mother loved it when Eddie's hair fell down. She thought it made him look like Clark Gable. She loved Clark Gable and got real crabby once when somebody told her Clark had false teeth and bad breath.

"Seein' is believin', right, Armando?" Eddie said.

"I can't argue with that." Mr. Encarnacion squinted at me. "You came all the way over from Marysville, huh?"

I nodded.

"Well, okay, go ahead, do your stuff."

I took off my dungarees and shirt. I had on the spangled outfit underneath that Eddie's circus friend had made for me—a red top with sequins and beads and a red and black bottom with a zigzag pattern like on Superman's chest. I'd loved the outfit the minute I saw it. It had a circus smell to it—makeup or pomade mixed with the smell of animals and popcorn.

Now it felt scratchy against my skin, like a store-bought Halloween costume, and the beads and sequins were suddenly heavy and hot, but I didn't care. I still felt glamorous.

I sat on the ground and curled my feet up around my waist. I crossed my arms behind me and grabbed my feet, pulling them back so from the front it looked like I was just a stump of a person. I unwound, stood and bent forward, touching my nose to the ground, and moving slowly so Mr. Encarnacion would wonder if I'd make it, although I knew I would. Squatting down I crawled into a potato sack a little bit at a time until I was curled up into a ball while Eddie sang "Ac-centuate the Positive," then I rolled. The sack had been Eddie's idea to help me stay curled up and he'd dyed it a bright fuschia to look more carnivaly.

It was blistering hot in the sack and the sequins chafed my skin, but I liked the feeling of being in charge of my own tight little world as Eddie's whispery singing cheered me on. I rolled in one direction for a few feet, then in another. I pretended I was on a curtained stage in a grand theater where Mr. and Mrs. Felker sat in the front row, beaming. I pictured Mrs. Felker turning and bragging to the people around them, "That's our son's fiancee performing, you know. Rhonda is just her stage name. Anyway, pretty soon she's going to be one of the Felker clan."

I crawled out of the sack, straightened up and flung my hair back. Eddie had said to toss my hair, it gave the act a little luster. I'd worried at first what he meant by luster. It sounded dirty, and there was a part of me that still didn't trust Eddie, but then I looked it up in the dictionary and felt better. Finally I did my backbend and walked on all fours in a circle, finishing up in front of Eddie and Mr. Encarnacion. I threw out my arms and beamed, trying to ignore the sledgehammer pounding in my chest, the sweat rolling into my eyes.

Mr. Encarnacion narrowed his eyelids at me as though he was peeking in at fish in a bowl. "Well, now, you've been doing a little practicing, haven't you, young lady?"

I grinned and nodded. The sweat felt like little bugs crawling on me.

"Okay, how's about it?" Eddie asked. "We got a winner here or am I a monkey's uncle?"

Mr. Encarnacion screwed up his mouth. "Well, she's not bad, and I did have a tattooed gal run off with a sailor. But I've been thinking of taking on a guy with no arms, a guy eats with his feet, that's the kind of act the marks go for. I'd be taking more of a chance with a rubber woman."

Eddie scoffed. "Suit yourself, Armando. We'll go put somebody else on Easy Street."

Mr. Encarnacion picked up the piece of chicken, bit off a chunk with his white teeth and chewed. A flap of chicken skin hung out of the corner of his mouth until he sucked it in. "Okay, okay," he said. "What the hell? I'll try her out for a week when we come through Marysville in August. But not for pay, just a tryout to see if the marks go for her."

That was enough for Eddie. He jumped up like he'd been sitting on a tack and pumped Mr. Encarnacion's hand. "You're a lucky son of a bitch, Armando, gettin' the first crack at a classy act like this. One week gratis, that's it. You're not interested, we'll go put somebody else on Easy Street."

Driving home Eddie said, "So you're goin' on the stage, huh, kiddo? Howzit feel?"

"Funny."

"Funny!" He guffawed. "So how's about we do a dress rehearsal at your mom's birthday party? It'll help work off some of the stage fright."

I felt a pinch in my chest. "Oh, geez, Eddie, I don't know. It's her party. It doesn't seem right, my showing off. My mom hates showoffs."

"Waddaya mean?" He shot me a sidewise glance. "I thought we agreed it'd be her birthday surprise. I thought we agreed she'd get a kick out of it."

I looked out the window and thought back to when I was a kid and my mother played Horsey Go Round the Table with me. We'd scramble around the kitchen table on our hands and knees to see who could finish first. She always won. Once Aunt Cora said to her, "Georgia, you know, the mom is supposed to let the kid win." My mother had looked up with a bewildered expression, as though Cora'd accused her of raiding my piggy bank. She let me win after that but you could tell she never enjoyed the game as much.

"Hey, kiddo, ya on another planet someplace?"

I blinked, confused for a minute. "Sorry. I was just thinking I'm not sure my mom will get a kick out of it, after all."

"You two. Cheez." Eddie shook his head. "You're like vinegar and oil, you two."

"It's not just that. I guess I'm . . . uh . . . feeling a little superstitious," I lied. "It might be bad luck to do the routine ahead of time. Maybe I should wait for the Magic Midway."

Eddie pursed his lips and nodded his head at the windshield. "Hmmm. Well, that figures. Showbiz folks are superstitious." He glanced at me. "Guess you're a natural, huh?"

"I guess so."

"Okay, I won't push ya as long as ya don't fink out on me at the Magic Midway. "

"Oh, no, I won't, I promise." That was the truth. I couldn't wait to do my routine for the Magic Midway. The Magic Midway was going to be my ticket out of town.

"So we'll have to come up pronto with a surprise for your mom's shindig. She's gonna wonder what we've been doing with all the rehearsin'."

"Yeah." But I knew Eddie would think of something. We'd come a long way, me and Eddie, from the day he moved in when just a whiff of his Vitalis made me gag.

I got out the writing paper and pulled the copy of Homefront Magazine from my bookbag. I'd swiped the magazine from Doc's the day before, just after Eddie and I got back from Belvedere and I'd started worrying whether Mr. Encarnacion would really take me on. In case he didn't, I wanted a backup escape plan.

I turned to the Victory Canteen page and ran my index finger down the list looking for names of servicemen from cities far enough away so they wouldn't know anybody in Marysville. I didn't want to make a mistake like the Foul Rift story again.

I settled on two soldiers. One was Duane Uhler, from a place called Hatfield, Pennsylvania. He said he worked as a grocery boy and a theater usher and he liked to swim and play the clarinet. My throat went thick as I thought to myself, that would really show Bobby if I married another clarinet player. Duane said what he looked forward to the

139

most was getting back to Hatfield and just doing something simple like putting on a pair of pajamas again.

The other guy was Bruno Sletter from South Philadelphia. He'd been a salesman for Pillsbury flour and he liked to play golf and listen to the Andrews Sisters. He said he'd give anything for a good piece of all-American bread with peanut butter and a glass of cold milk.

Writing to Duane, I tried to picture him playing his clarinet, back arched, eyes squeezed shut, shoulders hunched, trying not to see Bobby instead. I told Duane I was seventeen instead of fifteen and had green eyes and shiny dark hair and I worked at a shirt factory now but I was planning to go to commercial school. I said I might be a secretary and move to a bigger city unless something happened to change my mind. Maybe get married or something. I liked saying that I might do one thing or I might do the other. I told him I loved swimming and clarinet music. The more I wrote, the more I calmed down, as though each word took me one more step away from who I really was.

Then I wrote to Bruno, saying pretty much the same thing, except I told Bruno I loved golf and the Andrews Sisters and that I was amazed at what he said about the peanut butter because I knew if I was on the war front, that would be the very thing I'd miss the most, too.

I reread the letters and decided they needed a fancy quote at the end. I studied my treasury of quotations and found a good one.

"P.S.—Remember what Ralph Waldo Emerson said. Self-trust is the essence of heroism," I wrote on each letter. I grabbed two envelopes and raced toward the post office, spurts and spasms going crazy in my stomach.

We had my mom's party at Aunt Cora's at noon on August eighth. Aunt Cora opened the door looking gorgeous. Ever since she'd got the job modeling girdles for Finkel's Department Store catalog, she had an excuse to primp. Today she wore a coral colored halter top and a white accordion-pleated skirt. The creamy rouge on her cheeks matched her blouse and her silky blond hair was brushed back behind her ears to show off silver earrings that spiraled down her neck like teeny winding staircases.

She gave me a hug, and for a minute I closed my eyes and wanted to be back in Clinton with her, walking with books on our heads and Uncle Walt still off in the European Theater. I opened my eyes and glanced at my uncle to see if he had somehow read my thoughts, but he just smiled and shook a Camel out of a pack.

Aunt Cora had told us he was better. He'd been seeing a counselor who told him keeping busy would be the ticket, so he'd gone back to work at the post office.

"So, how's business?" Eddie asked as he settled down on the sofa.

"Oh, well, can't complain, I guess." Uncle Walt shrugged. "Except they got me stuck in the sorting department." He plunked into a chair. "At least until the old leg is done with its overhaul." He slapped at his khaki pants.

Everyone looked at his leg, then got quiet. The truth was, it didn't look like there was anything wrong with it at all compared to Eddie's shriveled foot.

I cleared my throat. "So tell us about your modeling job, Aunt Cora," I said. "It sounds so glamorous."

"Oh, it's fun. I love it," she gushed, her eyes bright. "You know, I never realized until I went to work for Finkel's that girdles are good for your health."

"Really? How?" my mother asked.

"Well, they keep all your parts in place."

"Isn't that something?" my mother said. "I never thought of that." She tugged at her own two-way stretch underneath her blue two-piece dress. "It makes sense when you think of it, doesn't it?" She looked at Eddie, who just shrugged.

Uncle Walt got a glint in his eye. "I can believe it," he said. "You should hear Cora when she takes one of those buggers—oh, excuse me, ladies—corsets—off. She sounds like a Greyhound bus door opening."

Everybody howled, even Eddie. Aunt Cora didn't mind. She knew she had a good shape, and the joke broke the ice. Uncle Walt sounded like his old self again. Maybe he didn't resent Aunt Cora working, after all, now that he was back on the job himself. I'd heard on the radio that some men came back from the war and griped about their wives holding down good jobs. One guy had even said what was worse, she liked it. That sounded crazy to me. I couldn't figure out if it was a part of the shell shock or if men just needed a lot of boosting in life.

We ate lunch in the dining room: barbecues, ham and cheese sandwiches, deviled eggs, potato salad, pickles and Ritz crackers. Then we sang happy birthday as Aunt Cora marched in from the kitchen with a lemon supreme fluff cake. While we drank coffee, my mom opened her presents. Cora and Walt gave her a cigarette case. I'd bought her a box of handkerchiefs, and Eddie gave her a bottle of perfume in a holder that was shaped like a lady wearing a black corset with a big red silk rose at the bosom.

Then everybody moved back to the living room for our surprise. Eddie pretended he was a master of ceremonies announcing an act at a Stage Door Canteen. He flashed a mile-wide smile, pushed up his yellow shirt sleeves, and rubbed his hands together.

"Well, now, we have a very, very special performance today in honor of Miss Georgia Sayers' birthday," he said. "Just one moment, ladies and gentlemen, and the show will begin."

Eddie and I hot-footed it into the vestibule to get our props and put on a record of Hoagy Carmichael singing "Georgia on My Mind." When he got to the chorus, we high-stepped into the living room singing, along with Hoagy and adding some extras. On the first line, "Georgia, Georgia, the whole day through," Eddie took a clock out of his jacket pocket and held it up and I moved the hands around to show a day going by. The next line, "Just an old sweet song keeps Georgia on my mind," we slapped home-made paper caps on our heads that we'd plastered pictures of my mom all over, and sashayed around in a circle for everyone to get a good look. My mom hooted as loud as one of those papier mâché ladies in front of a fun house.

Eddie had a great time looking devilish like Hoagy. On the next line, "Georgia, Georgia, the sight of you" we put on crazy glasses with crossed eyes painted on them. Aunt Cora snorted. We went on like that through the whole song, with everyone practically dying of laughter.

At the end I was supposed to take a curtsy, but something came over me and I did one of my twists instead. Maybe everybody hooting went to my head and brought out the ham in me. Maybe deep down I wanted to irritate my mother or show off a little, or both. Anyway, I threw myself into a backbend until my hands touched the floor behind me and I did a little pirouette on all fours. Just once around in a circle, real quick. I got up and tossed my hair so it fluffed out.

The whole thing went as fast as a minute. I heard my mom say, "Isn't that awful?" while I was pirouetting, but when I straightened up everybody was smiling. You could tell they thought I was just horsing around. It wouldn't have occurred to them in a hundred years I was going to make my debut at the Magic Midway in a week, except that Eddie told my mom about it when we got home.

"A rubber woman? Well, that doesn't sound very lady-like," she said with a frown. "What will people think?"

"Oh, doll, it's gonna be a lot of fun," Eddie said, throwing an arm around her. "You'll get a big kick out of seeing your little gal on stage. You're gonna be proud of her."

I tried to look cheerful, but I could tell I had an expression like when the sun is too bright.

My mother looked at me for a minute as though I hurt her eyes, too.

19
NANCY, 1945

Mr. Encarnacion said to go to the belly dancer's van to get made up. The belly dancer was named Yvonne. Her face was lumpy like hives but she had live-wire eyes and an hourglass figure. One wall of the trailer was full of pictures of Yvonne dancing, but the other side was covered with swords, all different shapes and sizes.

"Arturo, the sword swallower," she explained with a smile and a flick of her hand. "He's my son."

She sat me down on a narrow couch with a curlicue print cover. Dust specks fluttered up. She pulled some pancake makeup out of a grimy bag, wet a sponge at a little sink, and started on my face.

"So we've been with the carny fifteen years," she told me. "Gus, that's my husband, he's one of the talkers, the guys who announce the shows, and he helps set up rides." Yvonne wore a khaki-colored blouse with little epaulets like WACs, a short tangerine skirt, and perfume. Her breath smelled like exotic food. She smeared some rouge on my cheeks. "Well, now, that looks real pretty," she said. She put lipstick in a shade called Moonswept Red on my mouth and a lot of black makeup around my eyes. I liked her hands on my face. When she finished, she gave me a rabbit's foot.

"For luck," she said. "Arturo always uses it and he hasn't killed himself yet." She laughed and we pinned it onto the side of my tights.

Eddie was waiting outside to take me to the side show tent. "Zowee," he said. "You look like a million bucks." But I felt self-conscious wearing the scratchy outfit and the make-up, and as we walked, my stomach churned. I patted the rabbit's foot, hoping it would work and I'd make it big as Rhonda the Rubber Woman, but something in my bones told me different.

At the sideshow tent, the ticket kid waved us through and people stared at me as we walked by. Eddie casually flipped one of his arms over my shoulders to show he was a part of things, too, not just some ordinary sap walking me down the midway.

I liked the attention. I pictured myself stepping out of a limousine on Market Street and Shirley Metzger rushing up and gushing, "Oh, Rhonda, I saw your latest picture. The one where you did your routine for Roddy McDowell. You were so wonderful. May I have your autograph?" I pictured Bobby standing behind her, arms outstretched, later whispering into my ear, "Oh, Nancy, Nancy, don't ever leave me again. I was so stupid letting you go away. We do stupid things when we're young." I'd smile back sweetly and say, "Well, we'll see. I have a career myself now, you know."

A talker began warming up the crowd. "Step right up, la-deez and gen-tul-men. Behind yon canvas meet Nature's miss-takes and exx-trah-vaganzas. Alice, the World's Fattest Woman. Tips the scale at 468 pounds. Popo, the Two-Headed Baby. Born in Borneo. Scared his mother to an early grave. Rhonda the Rubber Woman. Twists like a Pretzel. Walks on all Fours. The price of admission, la-deez and gen-tul-men: Just ten cents, the tenth part of a dollar."

When he announced "Rhonda the Rubber Woman," my breathing felt shallow and my throat began to ache.

"You're nervous, aincha?" Eddie said.

I nodded, terrified.

"So remember, breathe slow. Deep. Way down. Then do every move re-al slo-ow." Eddie stretched out the words and moved his arms around in slow motion, like a movie getting stuck.

"Okay."

"Remember this is just a start. Next thing you know, it'll be the big top."

I nodded and took a deep breath but it didn't help. I eyed Eddie and wondered how come, if he had such big ideas, he was still a two-bit trinket salesman.

My stage was separated from the two-headed baby and the snake charmer by a flap of canvas on each side. I took off my robe and sat on the stage, rubbing my legs while the talker out front announced the sword swallower, the belly dancer—that was Yvonne—and a new act called Donna and Her Erotic Donkeys.

Next door the snake charmer's music started up. It was the tune kids sing, "Oh, they don't wear pants in the southern part of France." People started coming into the tent but I couldn't look at them. I rubbed my arms and legs over and over, studying them as though somebody had just given them to me.

"Okay, time to start," Eddie yelled and put on a record of "Indian Love Song."

Now I looked out at the crowd for a second but they

were just a blur of hair and T-shirts, cotton candy and sailor suits. A corner of the tent flapped in the warm breeze. The poles that held it up seemed lopsided and wiggly, as though the whole thing could topple down any minute. I was so nervous I was scared I might die of stage fright.

Then I threw myself into the twisting and things got better. A couple of times I heard people say "Ooooh" and during one twist when I had to stick my butt out some guys hooted but other than that it was quiet except for "Indian Love Song."

When I finished, my makeup, wet from the sweat, was dribbling into my eyes and mouth but I tossed my hair and smiled, glad I was still alive.

A couple of people clapped but most just shuffled out, curious to see the next show. Eddie rushed up and said I'd done great. Yvonne, too. "You looked real cute," she said. "The Moonswept Red lipstick really sets off your costume."

My mom hadn't come. "I'm feeling a little under the weather," she'd complained at the last minute. "I think my blood count must be down." But I knew that was an excuse. She always blamed her blood count when she wanted to back out of something.

Every show I thought I spotted Bobby's sandy hair, his green eyes beaming at me from the back of the crowd, although I knew that was impossible. He'd graduated from high school and was playing the clarinet in a combo in the Pocono Mountains for the summer. In the fall, he'd probably go on to college, God knew where. Sometimes I daydreamed about meeting Mrs. Felker on the street and we'd stop and have a heart-to-heart and she'd feel so bad being wrong about me that she'd quick call Bobby on the phone and tell him to rush back. One day I'd walked out to the R.D. and stood across the street from their house hoping she'd come out, but she didn't.

The carnival folks were just what I needed—friendly, with no questions asked. I ate dinner at Yvonne's twice: chicken stew and homemade spaghetti with the biggest meatballs I ever saw. Yvonne loved to cook and she even put up her own spiced peach marmalade. She made all kinds of things you wouldn't think a person could do on a teeny stove in a trailer.

"Pretty soon she's going to be the only belly dancing grandma in the world," Yvonne's husband Gus cracked one day. That's because Arturo was engaged to the age and weight guesser's daughter. But you could tell Gus was real proud of Yvonne, and you could see why, too. She had a way about her as if she knew she could take care of herself. It showed in all kinds of little ways. How she looked you in the eye when you talked like she was really listening instead of worrying what to say back. How she picked up a glass as if it was hers, she wasn't borrowing it from somebody else's cupboard. How she walked like she was teaching people how. Yvonne reminded me a little bit of Aunt Cora.

One night after the shows, Yvonne and I were sitting on the steps of her trailer. It was late and things were winding down. The air seemed magical, warm and full of things that might happen. The string of lights around the edges of the carnival somehow made the world seem safe and exciting at the same time. Thoughts raced through my mind. Thoughts about people who had lived way back when. People in Babylonia and places like that. People who I figured must have sat in the night and looked at the moon and hoped for things like I did. I got a full feeling in my chest and I wanted to cry.

"So what are you going to do if Mr. Encarnacion takes you on?" Yvonne asked. "Quit school or just do the summer circuit? The summer circuit usually goes to October."

I turned toward her. She had a wise look in her eyes.

"Jeez, I haven't had time to think past the tryout week," I whispered.

She nodded, as if she knew.

I stared out at the white moon and listened to the crickets. The snake charmer came out of her van and hung her costume on a clothesline to air out. The carnival lights went off and I felt pings in my throat.

I turned toward Yvonne, wet-eyed. "I'll quit school," I said, too loud, my voice thick. "I'll quit in a minute. I can't wait to get away from this burg."

She leaned toward me and patted me on the back, nodding again. I could feel her breath on my eyelids as I wondered whether the Magic Midway ever played the Poconos.

Driving home, Eddie wasn't his usual bouncy self. He kept sucking in and puffing out his cheeks.

"So do you think Mr. Encarnacion will take me on?" I asked.

He cleared his throat and flipped his bottom lip up over his top one. Finally he said, "Well, if he doesn't, the hell with him. We'll find another carnival. A classier one. Maybe not this year, the season's almost over anyway, but next year for sure. What the hell? A year's practice wouldn't hurt."

I looked at Eddie with his bottom lip flipped up like a monkey, and I knew he knew something I didn't and it wasn't good. I had three days left to my tryout week so I threw myself into my routine. I put extra zip into my twists and strutted around. I liked being a ham as long as people didn't know it was me behind the makeup, and I listened for the hoots and ooohs. I knew I had to zing the marks while I was on stage because the minute I finished they couldn't wait to rush on to the next tent and the next freak.

I lived for every day when Yvonne put on my makeup. I realized after the talk we had in the moonlight she was used to runaway kids begging to sign up in every two-bit town they played, but I wanted her to feel special about me.

I rehearsed asking if she and Gus would take me in when Arturo got married. "He'll move out. You'll probably get lonely for another kid," I'd say. "Hey, you'd have fun playing mother to the world's youngest rubber woman." But I didn't get a chance because Arturo caught a summer cold and had to stay in bed in the trailer for the rest of the week. One thing a sword swallower can't afford to do is to cough during a performance.

After my last performance Eddie came around wearing a grin that smelled of Old Crow and my heart sank. We stood behind the sideshow tents as he asked, "So, kiddo, ya ever catch Yvonne's routine?"

"No." I'd thought about it a couple of times but I knew

I didn't really want to. Anyway, this was no time to talk about Yvonne.

He kicked some sawdust. "Too bad."

"Eddie, you're stalling. What did Mr. Encarnacion say about me?"

He blew out his cheeks and looked up at the sky. "Well, he said he'd take ya on . . . ."

"He did?" I felt my chest swell and my mouth stretch into a grin.

"Wait, wait, wait . . . just hold your horses. He . . . uh . . . said he'd take you on if ya do double duty as a rubber woman and a kootch dancer."

A kootch dancer? The merry-go-round music rang in my ears. I figured Eddie must be fooling around. "A what?" I asked.

He threw his arms out at the midway. "You have to understand Armando's running a business and one thing that's good for business . . . uh . . . the marks like their kootch dancers young and Yvonne is getting up there. Uh, he said maybe the two of you could do a routine together for a while—you and Yvonne—but eventually he'd have to get rid of her."

Eddie must have seen the disbelief in my eyes.

"Well, maybe not get rid of her, she's a feisty old gal, make her a paymaster or something. Anyway, if you're any good, you could take over doin' the dance."

"A hootchy-kootchy dance?" I still thought he must be pulling my leg, teasing me the way he sometimes teased my mother. For a minute I felt sorry for her.

"Oh, well, that's just one thing they call it," he said. "It's more like a belly dance. Hootchy-kootchy. Belly dance. Same difference. Like Yvonne does. You like Yvonne, doncha? The two of you seem to hit it off."

"You're not kidding." My throat swelled up. "You think I should do a belly dance? Take Yvonne's job?" I looked at Eddie for a sign he was teasing. "I'm only fifteen."

"Well, kiddo, the truth is, that's what Mr. Encarnacion likes about ya." Eddie looked down. "What happened, a gypsy girl name of Ramona heard what you was doin' and came around and said hey, she could do twists same as you and the hootchy-kootchy, too, only zippier than Yvonne." He looked up at me but more at my hair. "That's what gave Armando the idea of you doin' double duty. Tell ya the truth, up 'til then he wasn't all that interested. He's been packin' 'em in with Donna and the donkeys. Only reason he's offering now, Ramona gave him the idea. I guess she ain't no prize package in the looks department and he heard you been puttin' more oomph into your routine last couple of days and he knows the marks like 'em young and good-looking."

I stared at Eddie and slumped into a folding chair.

"I didn't think you'd go for it," Eddie said, still talking to my hair. "I tried to reason with him, kiddo. 'Jeez,' I said, 'she's only a kid.' He told me to take it or leave it."

20
GEORGIA, 1945

Everything started going haywire at once. Nancy came home the last night of her tryout week with a face as long as your arm. She didn't say peep, just went in the bathroom, slammed the door, and stayed in long enough to have puppies.

Eddie stayed out all night, and the next day the two of them acted like there was never such a thing as Rhonda the Rubber Woman. I figured Nancy hadn't gone over too good or else she'd got in a snit and quit. Either way, it was fine with me, I'd always thought it was the silliest thing, twisting yourself into all kinds of ungodly shapes. It was embarrassing, your kid being a rubber woman.

The only thing, in September Eddie started going on the road more than before, and if that wasn't bad enough, half the time he was home, Cora was coming around crying on his shoulder over Walt. Just when everyone thought Walt's shell shock was getting better, it took a turn for the worse.

He hit a guy at work for being 4-F, and one night a cop stopped him and Walt said oh, so sorry, ossifer, and slapped the cop on the shoulder and the cop said calm down, buddy, but Walt just yelled why don't you calm down yourself, ossifer, and got louder and louder until they took his driver's license away.

"Eddie, I just don't know what to do," Cora would say, batting her eyes. "I really need a man's point of view," and Eddie'd put his arm around her and say too bad a looker like her had to put up with that kind of guff and then he'd go on for hours about it.

I felt sorry for Cora, but I didn't understand why she had to pick on Eddie. What did Eddie know about shell shock? There were plenty of other men in the world whose shoulders she could cry on. The guys at Finkel's or the regulars at Jolly Jack's. Cora knew more men than you could shake a stick at. The truth was, it got so I hated to see her come. My own sister!

In the end I suppose it didn't matter. One day another letter came from Lyndora, and I knew what it was the minute I saw it. It was the same flowered envelope as before, only this time addressed to me. It was from Eddie. "Hi, sweet stuff," he said "looks like I'm going to be staying in Lyndora for awhile. I got an old friend here, she's a little under the weather and needs some looking after. Sorry so sudden, but this is a special friend, we've been through a lot together. A sweet person like you, I'm sure you understand."

I felt small and worn out. I lit a Raleigh and stared at the handwriting, scribbly, with a lot of loops. I remembered how once Eddie'd introduced me to a black-eyed woman, Madame Olga, who could tell what was in store for you from how you wrote. He said she'd told him he was like a bird, flying high, following the sun. That's why the carny was so perfect for him. He told me she'd do me free, being a friend of his, but I said no. I didn't want to know what was coming.

The letter went on. "Just hang onto the stuff I left, it's not all that much, you know I like to live light."

The apartment felt cold but it was only September. I

looked out the window; the sky was gray and low like a tent. I put some water on for tea and put a teabag into a cup. The cup was shaking in my hand. Outside a drizzly rain began and I watched men who had just got off the late shift at Pritchard's Coal and Ice walking home from work, going to their Beatrices and their Ediths and their Thelmas. Tears started up in my eyes and suddenly one of the men looked like Eddie. I was sure of it. You could see the limp. He'd come back, but then I could see it wasn't Eddie at all, just Sparky Williams acting up, trying to hop between the raindrops.

The phone rang. I jumped and saw that the water had boiled down in the pan, leaving caramel-colored swirls. I turned the burner off and my insides dropped as I lifted the receiver from the hook. Maybe it was Eddie saying he'd just been teasing. Sometimes he could be an awful tease.

"Hello." It wasn't Eddie. It was Joanie calling for Nancy. "She's not here," I snapped and hung up, cranky. I never liked Joanie. She was too sassy and she wore huarachis. Cora'd told me over in Clinton the fast girls wore huarachis. Why couldn't Nancy take up with some of the nicer girls once in a while?

I put more water on to heat and opened a bag of fresh-made doughnuts from the church and took out two, biting into one and putting the other one aside to dunk.

Now that I thought about it, maybe it was Nancy's quitting the twisting that drove Eddie off to Lyndora in the first place, disappointing him after all that work. He figured, who wants to hang around with a kid who isn't even willing to stick with something after all the time he put in?

Maybe I should write Eddie back and ask if Nancy was what drove him off to Lyndora. Goodness, I could understand that. I could tell him I'd talk to her, make her practice, stick with the twisting. After all, I was her mother. I could put my foot down. The problem with me, I was too easy on her. Now that I thought about it, maybe I could even help him train her. Help her on and off with her robe or something. We could have a lot of fun, the three of us. It might be cute, your kid being a rubber woman.

I got up, poured hot water into my cup, and dunked a

piece of doughnut. Sure. A letter would be the polite thing. The least I could do was write and say I was sorry to hear about his friend. I could just hold on to it until he got back.

Then what? I hated writing letters. Practically everybody I knew and their sister wrote to soldiers, but I always got too antsy to sit still, plus I'd go blank trying to think of something cute to say.

I thought about Eddie and some of the good times, having drinks and playing the jukebox over at the Tip Top. Going around to the different carnivals, eating our hot dogs and sno-cones, smiling at the lights and music, we were like the couples you saw in the movies.

I remembered once we played the duck pond game and and I won a pet whistle. He said, "Okay, doll, I'll be your pet. Anytime you want me, whistle." We laughed and laughed. Eddie was such a cutup.

Pouring more hot water over the teabag, I got a little stab of pain in my chest thinking about how things had started going bad. How Eddie'd sometimes go quiet and I'd get all flustered because he usually did the talking and when he didn't I couldn't think of anything to say except some fool thing like it seemed hotter than yesterday, more humid, even though I knew I'd said the same thing three times before. Eddie'd just nod and say yeah.

The tears started up again. Maybe I'd just write a cheery little note. Remind Eddie of all the good times we had, how we'd been through a lot together, too. Make him miss me a little. Suddenly the front door slammed and Nancy walked in calm as you please, strutting down the hallway toward the bedroom.

"I'll thank you to stop slamming that door, young lady," I yelled. "You practically scared me to death."

Nancy looked surprised. I hardly ever yelled. "Okay, go ahead. Thank me. I'll stop slamming it," she said. She had a smirk on her face and I couldn't tell if she was sassing me or not. It didn't matter. It was the last straw. I sat down at the kitchen table and started bawling.

Nancy didn't say anything for a minute, then came over and asked what was wrong and I told her I had a letter from Eddie and he was going to stay in Lyndora for a while.

"What do you mean a while? A couple of weeks or what?"

"I don't know."

"Well, what did he say?" She sat down across from me at the table looking like a human being for a change. I was so glad to have somebody to talk to, I told her she could read the letter for herself.

When she was done I asked, "Don't you think it would be a good idea if I wrote back? Just a cheery little note. Maybe I could even say how you miss him helping you with the Rhonda routine."

She sighed and looked out the window for a minute, then back at the letter. She shook her head and finally said, "You can't write him back. There's no return address."

I decided to call Ethel and Chester, two old friends of Eddie's, people we'd gone to the Tip Top with. Ethel was real friendly on the phone, said she didn't know where Eddie was, these carnies, you can never keep track of them, but maybe Chester knew and, hey, they were coming over to Marysville next Wednesday so why didn't we all go out and have a drink ? I said yes, yes. I could hardly believe my luck. I'd been afraid she'd hang up on me or something, being Eddie's friend.   I figured it was a good sign.

I got my beige and orange shantung suit cleaned, bought some new dress shields, and a tube of hot coral lipstick. I wanted to put my best face forward so Ethel and Chester would tell Eddie how great I looked and he'd miss me.

Cora said I should just be nonchalant and act like Eddie'd probably left the address in the apartment and I'd misplaced it. I should say how sorry I was to hear his friend was under the weather, and then just casually ask had they, by any chance, met her.

"Keep it subtle," she told me. "It wouldn't hurt to be a little more scintillating, too," she said. Cora loved to use big words. She didn't care if people understood what she was talking about or not, and Nancy was getting just like her. She gave me a little joke book and told me to memorize a couple. She gave me a copy of *Life* magazine and said to pick out two things and read them so I could bring them up if there was a lull in the conversation.

"Short things are okay," she said. "Like you could ask 'Did you know General Eisenhower graduated 125th in conduct in a class of 160 at West Point? He got demerits for gabbing too much.'"

I took off work early on Thursday and got my hair set. It looked real cute, little curls all around my face and then a couple drizzling down on my neck. I was a nervous wreck getting dressed but I liked how the hot coral lipstick matched the orange trim on my suit. It looked real smart.

I had just put on my spectator pumps and was about to leave when Nancy came in with a bunch of violets she'd picked. "For good luck," she said. I guess she meant well, she'd been acting nicer lately, but the violets were all wet.

"Oh, for heaven's sake," I complained, "don't get them near my good suit, they're dripping."

Her face dropped. "Sorry," she mumbled, and for a minute I felt bad but then I got cranky at her for putting me on the spot. She always did that, every time I started feeling a little friendly toward her. Plus she knew I hated fresh flowers. You had to find a vase and you had to cut the stalks, they never fit right, then you had to change the water every time you turned around and by then the stems were all slimy. Artificial flowers looked just as good to me, better sometimes, and they lasted. I said I had to rush and hurried out.

Ethel had said to meet them at the Cork 'n Bottle Pub. It was right in town, up on Market Street. I'd never been there. A lot of folks looked down on you for drinking right in town. The Tip Top was different. It was a little ways out and they served food. Plus the waitresses wore snoods. I always said that was a sign of a good place, if the waitresses wore snoods. The Cork 'n Bottle was dark inside and there were just men, talking and laughing. I figured they must have been the crew that was laying the new road out in the township. I wished I'd told Ethel and and Chester I'd meet them outside. The bartender came over to me right away before I had a chance to breathe.

"Afternoon," he said. "Don't think I've seen you in here before. Lookin' fresh as a daisy."

I blushed and said "I uh . . . I uh'm looking for some friends."

"Well, look no more," a guy from the back yelled. "I could use a friend. A bosom buddy." The other guys all snickered and stared.

"I, uh, I think I'll wait for them outside," I said to the bartender, but just then Ethel and Chester came in. I was never so glad to see anybody.

Chester said I was looking good and I said they were, too, but they weren't really. Ethel had on a yellow sleeveless blouse with Scottie dogs on it and pink pedal pushers. The blouse was too tight and she bulged out of it like dough. Chester had on a faded old blue shirt with big perspiration stains shaped like two Liberty Bells, one under each arm.

We ordered a drink and talked about the weather. I asked if they knew Wendell Wilkie's book *One World* had sold faster than any book in history, I read it in *Life*, and they said, no they hadn't known that.

Everyone was quiet for a while, then Chester said, "I would of thought it would be the Bible. I think you must have read that wrong, kiddo."

After we had two drinks each, finally Chester said, "So old Eddie's moved out to Lyndora, huh?" I said I didn't know if he'd moved there exactly, he just said he'd be staying for a while with an old friend.

I said it was stupid of me but I'd misplaced his address, did they by any chance have it, but Chester said no, he figured Eddie'd get in touch when he was ready. We had another round of drinks. I tried to be bright and cheery like Cora'd said so I told one of my jokes.

"Why does an Indian wear feathers?" I asked.

They shook their heads. "Beats me," Chester answered.

"To keep his wig warm," I said and they nudged each other and laughed.

"Whoops, I mean to keep his wigwam," I said, and they laughed even harder.

Chester went over and started chatting with the bartender. Before you knew it the bartender gave us a round on the house. I was getting woozy. It was a hot day and I could feel my hairdo going limp.

Once we were alone Ethel patted me on the arm. "These carnies, they got an old saying, 'I love you, honey, but the season's over.' Eddie, he hung around longer than most."

I guessed that was supposed to be a compliment, but it made me feel worse. Look at how long Chester'd hung around Ethel. What was so wonderful about Ethel with her flabby arms and her pedal pushers? The more we drank, the more down in the dumps I got.

Ethel told me Chester'd said the truth was Eddie had an old girlfriend in Lyndora, someone he'd gone with a long time ago, maybe ten, twelve years. But Eddie'd had itchy feet and the girl got fed up so she married somebody else and Eddie never got over it. Last year her husband was killed in the war and Eddie found out, and called her and one thing led to another.

My chest hurt listening to Ethel but I kept trying to act cheerful. A couple of guys from the back came and sat down with us and started kidding around. I tried to remember my other joke but I couldn't. We all moved over to the bar and had another round. I was so tipsy I couldn't get on the barstool and one of the guys lifted me up and plunked me down, but a minute later I lost my balance and slid off. I didn't hurt myself but I got my suit dirty and started to cry. Chester said it was time to go home.

I couldn't walk very well so Ethel and Chester went with me, one on each side. It was a hot night and there were a lot of people out so I kept trying to act like everything was fine but the truth was the sidewalk felt like one of those trick floors that move up and down in a fun house.

Suddenly I remembered the other joke. I said "Did you hear one about this guy and girl walking along on a country road and the guy says to the girl 'Oh, look at those cows rubbing noses. It makes me want to do the same thing,' and the girl says 'Go ahead, if you like cows.'"

Ethel and Chester howled like that was the funniest thing anybody had ever said, and I felt good, but then

Chester lost his grip on me and I fell down again, only this time I passed out. The last thing I remember before it went black was Genevieve Metzger, wearing a white sundress and white sandals—I never saw such white sandals, there wasn't a spot on them—looking down at me, saying, "My goodness, it's Georgia Sayers."

21
NANCY, 1945

The letter from Bruno came first. When I saw the envelope with my name written on it in big black letters, I got tingly and stared at it for a long time. Somebody taking the time to write my name out always amazed me, as though I had somehow fooled people. I walked into the kitchen, dropped into a chair and opened the envelope.

"How you doing, Nancy? Thanks for writing," it said. "I had a friend who visited a cousin somewhere near Marysville once. He said it rained and he got poison ivy but it was pretty anyway. I'm stationed in the Pacific. I can't tell you where, but it's hot as blazes, and the sky seems bigger than at home. Maybe it's because this place is so spooky. It's like little Jap soldiers are watching us all the time. There's something about those yellow buggers that makes you squirm.

"I'm sure glad to hear you love peanut butter. It's amazing how so many gals who read *Homefront* love it. One gal sent me a box full of chocolate-covered peanut butter candy she'd made herself. Boy, that was a real treat."

I felt irritated. I knew how to make peanut butter candy. Any girl who thought it was a big deal to make peanut butter candy must be pretty jerky.

"'Boogie Woogie Bugle Boy,' yeah, that's a great tune. It's one of my favorites, too. The Andrews Sisters came through and sang it for the company once, and I got to jitterbug with Maxine. That sure was a day to remember.

"Well, I have to sign off. One of the guys got some soap bubbles and we're having a party. It sounds dumb, huh, but it keeps us from going nuts, only over here they call it pineapple crazy."

It was exciting getting the letter, but I couldn't stop thinking about the other girls. I hadn't counted on that. I tried to picture them, and they all came out looking like Shirley Metzger with her blond hair and her nose in the air.

I tried to think of a way to stand out. I considered telling Bruno I had performed for a week as Rhonda the Rubber Woman, but I decided he might think being a carnival contortionist was a little weird. I doodled and smoked a cigarette until I got a better idea.

"Dear Bruno," I wrote. "I was just talking about your letter to my aunt who's a famous model. Did I mention that before? She's gorgeous, and she's teaching me some of her tricks. I might decide to be a model myself someday if I don't go to commercial school. Anyway, my aunt said wasn't it something that you had danced with Maxine. She's always thought I look a little like Maxine myself."

A week later I got a letter from Duane. I liked it better. Duane didn't say peep about any other girls. He just said, "Hello there from the European Theater. It sure was great to hear from a girl who likes clarinet music and always wanted to meet a movie usher. Tell you the truth, sometimes it's a headache cleaning Spearmint off the seats and throwing out the kids who sneak in, but like you say, it's still show business."

As I read, I felt bad about sneaking into the movies with Joanie and Itchy—I'd been hanging out with them again since Bobby dumped me and I got rejected trying to be Rhonda. I decided I wouldn't do it anymore except maybe for Van Johnson.

"Tell you, I've seen enough action to last me a lifetime," Duane went on. "Seems yesterday I was just a kid playing soldier with make-believe machine guns and building bunkers out of piles of hay. I'd count to 50 when I got shot.

Boy, life sure changes. When our company took over one town, a kid yelled, 'Hi yo Silver!'

"I don't know where he got it, but he sure made me homesick and nobody knows yet when we might get sent back. When I do, maybe I'll give you a call, okay? Marysville isn't that far away from Hatfield. Write with more news from the home front, okay?"

I read the letter over and over, especially the part about giving me a call. I pictured Duane sitting in a bunker playing his clarinet, something slow and bluesy, and I tried to make him not look like Bobby. I wrote back saying what fun it would be if Duane got home to Hatfield and called me. What fun was an expression I'd heard Shirley Metzger use. Then I said I was going to send him a surprise, and I hoped he liked peanut butter.

22
JANUARY, 1946

Cora stubbed her cigarette out in a green-tinted glass ashtray that already held four butts, each decorated with a scallop of lipstick, hers a bright red, Georgia's a pale coral. Cora had moved in with Georgia and Nancy five days before Christmas, one day after Walt had beat up a neighbor who was trying to play "Silent Night" on a saxophone.

"God knows I tried to stop him," she told Georgia for the umpteenth time. "I said, come on, honey, it's Christmas, in a couple of days it'll all be over, we'll laugh."

"Oh, sure it would've."

Georgia shoved pork sausages around in a frying pan. Cora thought back. Walt had joked about it at first, saying Jesus, why bother with a horn, why not just scratch a fingernail on a blackboard all day? Who was the guy taking lessons from, Jack Benny?

Then one night he snapped. He'd had a few and was on a stool, stringing lights on the tree. All blue. Cora'd starting using all blue when Walt was overseas to show how she felt without him, and he'd liked the idea so they stuck with it. The guy next door had taken a breather and Bing Crosby was crooning "White Christmas" on the radio, and then suddenly the blare began again.

Walt jumped off the stool wild-eyed and yelled, "Jesus Christ, I'm gonna give that bastard a silent night." He stormed over, pounded on the door, grabbed the saxophone and roughed the guy up with it. Cora ran after him yelling no, don't, Walt, peace on earth, good will toward men and all that, but it didn't work. He slugged her, too. Somebody called the cops and the next day there was a write-up in the paper calling Walt the Saxophone Scrooge. Meanwhile he'd disappeared. Cora didn't have any idea where he'd gone.

The smell of the pork fat sizzling made Cora's mouth water, but she knew by the time Georgia finished with them, the sausages would be black and hard as old turds. Georgia was deathly afraid of pink meat, thought it gave you polio. In the old days Cora would have made a snide remark, but not today. Today there was too much heartache.

She studied the butts. "Lipstick traces," she thought. "Romantic places." She sang in a throaty whisper Georgia couldn't hear above the sizzle of the grease, "These foolish things remind me of you" and tears started up in her eyes. Walt had shown up in Marysville on New Year's Day. He'd known where she'd be. He apologized, said he missed her and begged her to come back but she'd said she didn't know. The truth was she missed him, too, something awful, but she had to sort things out.

"It was the damn war," she said all of a sudden. "That's what it was. Walt couldn't shake it. It does terrible things to men, Georgia. War."

"Oh, I know," Georgia answered. "I've heard stories."

Cora had seen from the day he got home Walt was different. Refusing to wear his civvies, drinking with the other vets, getting into arguments at work. He hated being a cripple, hated having to work as a sorter until his leg healed. Then one day a woman in his department asked if he killed any Japs overseas and he exploded, yelling wasn't that great, he'd been over there getting his leg ripped open, seeing his buddies killed left and right, arms and legs flying all over the fucking front, and now he's supposed to work alongside a goddamn fool who sat on her fat ass the whole time, doesn't even know there aren't any Japs in Italy. His supervisor'd tried to smooth it over, saying the woman meant well, but that just made Walt even more furious, so he quit and told Cora good riddance, he'd find a better job. But he never tried, and he stopped going to see the V.A. counselor.

The window rattled from the winter wind. It's almost February already, Cora thought. She looked up. "Nancy coming?"

Georgia stiffened, "Nah, she's eating over at Joanie's. Or somebody's. I can't keep track."

"Bobby soxers. They think if they're not together every minute, they're gonna miss something," Cora joked, but privately she felt uneasy. Things weren't the same between her and Nancy. Part of the problem was if Cora wasn't off at work, Nancy was out gallivanting with her friends. Even when they tried to clown around, they'd talk too loud or their laughs would stop too abruptly and Cora noticed Nancy was getting a bold and weary look to her. Cora had thought a couple of times of giving Nancy a hug and saying, "Hey, don't let it get you down, living with a couple of sad sacks like me and your mom; remember, everything is temporary," but she realized it sounded corny and she was too heartbroken to come up with anything wiser, so she just let it drop.

Georgia took the sausages out of the pan, put them on a plate, and broke four eggs into the sizzling grease. Cora watched the yolks splatter and spread. She sighed again, then looked at the clock. Five on the button. "Time for a seven and seven for me," she said. "Want a Coke?"

"Yeah." Georgia'd gone on the wagon after the day she passed out on the street. Cora fixed herself a drink, heavy on the Seagram's, light on the 7-Up. She opened a Coke for Georgia and poured it into a Little Orphan Annie mug.

Georgia lifted the eggs out of the pan with a spatula, put them on two dinner plates, added the sausages and poured the pan fat down the sink.

"Hey, don't do that," Cora grumbled. "You can take that fat to the butcher's and get red points."

"Oh, I don't save fat," Georgia answered, putting the plates on the table and taking a sip of her Coke. "It's too messy. All those greasy jars. We don't cook enough to have much." She grimaced at the butts, dumped them out, and ran hot water over the ashtray.

Cora sighed. She'd learned all the statistics when Walt was overseas. A pound of fat had enough glycerine in it to make fifty 30-caliber bullets or six 75-millimeter shells. She'd saved every ounce of bacon fat, every tin can, every lipstick tube. The saving somehow made her seem like a soldier, too, fighting alongside Walt in a way.

She suddenly felt irritated at Georgia. Walt would have saved fat. He had a temper, sure, but at least he thought about a few things in the world except himself.

Georgia tore off a piece of bread and tried to dip it into her egg, but the yolk was as hard as a dandelion heart. "It's hard to get them right," she said.

"Mmm." Cora picked at her food. Once after work she'd driven over to their apartment in Clinton but Walt wasn't there. The place was a mess. Piles of clothes all over. Moldy food and a bitter beer smell. She sat and cried, then on her way out she ran into a neighbor—not the saxophone one—and the neighbor said she heard Walt was staying with another vet over on Dixie Cup Road.

"What time are we going?" Georgia asked, cutting a piece of sausage into five neat pieces. Cora was taking Georgia to Finkel's annual recognition party. It used to be a dinner, but this year because of war shortages it was just going to be drinks, dessert and dancing. Whoever'd sold the most corsets and brassieres during the past year got a handshake from one of the mucky mucks and a round of applause from the others.

"Oh, we should leave about 7:00. Get there by 7:30." Cora mixed another drink.

"Do you think my rhinestone earrings would be too dressy?"

"Nah. There'll be a lot of ritzy-fitz people trying to show off. You know models. They'll be all dolled up."

"I thought I'd wear my blue wool. It looks rich, don't you think?"

"Yeah. It'll look cute." Cora cut into an egg. It slipped away. Walt would probably say, hey, you should save this for the scrap rubber drive. She wished Georgia weren't so boring. Most of the time Walt treated her good. It was just once in a while he'd go off the deep end but then he'd apologize and say, "Jeez, I don't know what got into me, I love you so much, you're so beautiful, I'm so lucky."

And he'd look so handsome and sincere. Like Gary Cooper in *Sergeant York*. Like Jimmy Stewart in *It's a Wonderful Life*. Cora's heart would melt. She'd cry, sag against him, and he'd take her in his big arms and whisper, "That's my girl." She'd feel a thrill ordinary people couldn't know. It was too special, being the girl the tough guy always comes back to, the girl he needs.

Georgia was ready by 6:30. "So will the ritzy-fitz people act stuck-up?" she asked in a small voice. "I hate stuck-up people. Do I look all right? Uh . . . and . . . uh . . . where did you put the joke book?"

"You look great," Cora replied. "Nah, they won't be stuck-up, they know what I've been going through, but the joke book won't help. The people at Finkel's already heard them all." Georgia paced from room to room with a tissue, wiping invisible splotches off the woodwork. She asked did Cora think if she put her chin strap on for a few minutes it would ruin her hairdo and Cora said "Nah" so Georgia put it on and circled the rooms again, looking like an accident victim.

Cora was leaning forward against the basin making up her eyes when Georgia showed up in the bathroom doorway with her rhinestone earrings and her chin strap, looking so ridiculous Cora smudged her mascara. She wanted to yell oh, for Christ sake, go have a drink, but she didn't, out of pity. Georgia smelled like Tabu, and she was holding the perfume bottle Eddie'd given her for her birthday, the one shaped like a woman wearing a red corset with black lace. Since Eddie'd left, she walked around holding the perfume bottle a lot. Or sometimes staring at the belongings he'd left.

"What do they usually talk about, the people at Finkel's?" she asked, and Cora was feeling just irritable enough to say "Oh, the same stuff as everyone."

Practically as soon as Cora and Georgia walked in, a bunch of salesmen swarmed around them like bees going for honey.

"Hey, Cora, I didn't recognize you for a minute with your clothes on," one joked.

"Hey, Cora, if I told you you had a great body, would you hold it against me?" another one cracked.

Cora just laughed and wisecracked back, "I told my sister there'd be a lot of wits here. I forgot to say half-wits." Cora knew how to handle men. Eventually their wives came around and claimed them anyway. Watching them go, Cora joked to Georgia that, with the rubber shortage, there was no way anyone could make corsets broad enough for some of those backsides.

Georgia giggled and whispered, "Oh, Cora, you're awful!"

Cora drank a Manhattan, Georgia sipped punch with pieces of mixed fruit floating in it and then they sat down for dessert at a table with some girls who worked in the bindery.

The president announced that Finkel's had done pretty well in 1945, even with the rubber cutback. One thing that had helped, they'd put more into brassieres. You can use wires and stays, so you don't need so much rubber. Then he read the names of the salesmen who'd gone over their quotas and asked for a special hand for their advertising man who had written the slogan "Formfit, for the support you need during these hectic days of added responsibility." Everyone clapped and a few guys hooted.

After the ceremony, nobody at Cora and Georgia's table said anything for a minute while everyone eyed one another's hands to see who had wedding rings and who didn't. Then a waiter wheeled the desserts around and everybody took one and dug in. One of the men started talking politics.

Cora looked around the room. There wasn't a guy in it who was anywhere near as handsome as Walt. Anywhere near as exciting. You could take the head off one and put it on another and it wouldn't make any difference.

Across the table Earl Speck, the company bookkeeper, asked Georgia, "So what do you think of the presidential candidates?" Georgia's face went empty for a minute. "Well, uh . . . some of the girls I work with . . . uh . . . like Dewey," she managed. "I like his mustache myself. It's always so neat. I like a man with a neat mustache."

Another thing, Georgia was beginning to drive Cora to distraction. For a while they'd got along okay. They commiserated, but you couldn't mope around and stare at somebody's left-over underwear forever. You had to have a little spunk in life.

Teddy Donatelli and His Rhythm Boys struck up the band as Teddy announced, "Now you men be sure to take turns asking the ladies to dance, so many of them have husbands or boyfriends off in the service." Hah, Cora thought, glancing around the room again, spare me the favor. Some of the other women apparently felt the same way because they jumped up and danced with one another. Georgia danced with Earl Speck, but she looked scared. She wasn't much of a dancer.

On the fast numbers like "Chattanooga Choo Choo" and "Pistol Packin' Mama," the women's ballerina skirts swirled out like parachutes. Georgia, back at the table now, sat smiling at the dancers, her face flushed from the excitement. Earl Speck leaned toward her with puppy dog eyes and a grin.

Cora watched them and swirled a swizzle stick in the air, thinking about something she hadn't quite figured out yet.

Later on the way home she suggested, "How about stopping at the Tip Top for a drink?"

"Okay, but just a Coke for me," Georgia answered.

The two sat smoking, sipping their drinks and staring at the dull shine on the mahogany bar. The tavern was empty for a Saturday night, and the emptiness cut into Cora's heart like a scalpel. She couldn't bear the thought of endless empty nights ahead, nights without Walt.

Georgia slipped off her coat and shoes and her clip-on rhinestone earrings. "Oh, boy, it's nice to relax."

Cora narrowed her eyes and thought back to Mama whispering, "When I go, Cora, promise me you'll keep an eye on Georgia. You know I worry about her." Cora, teary-eyed, had picked up Mama's gnarled hand and promised, but now suddenly she felt a fury at the obligation that shocked her.

She ordered another drink and turned to Georgia. "You know, I've been thinking about me and Walt. I've been thinking about the way we've been through things together. It's the same with his vet buddies. They've been through things together. That's what life is about, really."

Georgia blinked and looked confused. Her innocent expression infuriated Cora. "The trouble with you, Georgia, you're not deep, you don't go through things with people."

Georgia's face went flatter, then she laughed weakly. "Oh, Cora, you've had one too many. What does Walt say? Tee many martoonies?"

That irked Cora even more. Her voice rose. "No, I haven't had tee many martoonies. I've been thinking about Walt and the other vets. How they have something ordinary people don't have. Stuff they won't even talk about to any-one else. Ties. Ties. That's what it is." Cora looked Georgia in the eye.

Georgia cleared her throat and swallowed.

"Well, me and Walt, we have our ties, too. We've been through things. Some good. Some bad. Better. Worse. Same as the vets. That's what life is about, don't you see? Going through things. Deep things. Ties."

Georgia swiveled her Coke glass in a circle on the table and blinked. Her eyelashes fluttered like trapped bugs.

23
NANCY, MARCH, 1946

In February, Aunt Cora moved back to Clinton, back to Uncle Walt after he promised to see the VA counselor again. "We have our ups and downs, sure," she explained the afternoon she left, "but, to tell you the truth, I think we both like it that way." She blew a smoke ring into a slant of dusty sun that pierced our living room window. "I've always headed for the roller coaster, you know. The merry-go-round is too tame for me."

My mom and I moved to a cheaper apartment out near Matlock's Stables. It smelled like horses and had worn linoleum floors in a swirly cream and green pattern that looked like different colors of mold. The worst part, though, we weren't able to run down to Doc's anymore whenever we couldn't stand one another's company.

Everything my mom did irritated me. The way she smacked her food. Her phony smile. Her chin. The strap she'd bought didn't work and she was getting a double chin that looked ridiculous on a little 5-foot 2-inch person who was skinny everywhere else. The thing that drove me the craziest, though, was the way she let her sentences drift off like a person's breath on a cold day. "I thought I'd . . . " "Let's see, where did . . . " "I guess it's time . . . " I wanted to scream, "Finish your stupid sentence."

I started crying at the slightest thing. There was a built-in cabinet in the bathroom somebody had started carving a name onto. "M-a-r" it said. One day I couldn't stand looking at the M-a-r another second. What was it supposed to be? Mary or Marion or Marvin or what? What kind of a person would start to carve a name and stop? I tore a picture of Van Johnson out of an issue of *Photoplay* and pasted it over the M-a-r as though my life depended on it, but the next day my mom tore the picture off cleaning. When I saw Van was gone and M-a-r was back I sat on the john and busted out crying.

The only good thing was my mother was going to some kind of meetings at Mildred's, a woman from work, and that gave me time to myself to write more black and bitter poems.

One afternoon in March, my mom stood in the bedroom in her slip. "Uh, Cora and Walt are coming up tonight," she said. "We're going over to the covered dish dinner at the church."

She opened a jar of Mum and rubbed it under her arms like she was scouring, "Incidentally, they're bringing a guest along. Earl. I met him the time I went to that . . . uh . . . function with Cora."

"The Finkel's banquet?"

"Yeah. The Finkel's banquet. You remember, right?"

I nodded. It was the day after the Finkel's banquet Aunt Cora started talking about going back to Walt. "He needs me," she'd explained. "This time I just need to lay down a few more rules." You could tell by the sparkle in her eyes, she couldn't wait to go.

My mother put on a dusty rose crepe dress with a neckline that was scalloped like the top part of a heart. You could see her brassiere straps.

"That doesn't look like the kind of dress you should wear to a covered dish supper at the church," I grumbled. Why did she still have to have a good shape anyway? Why couldn't she look more like Kate Smith?

She looked down at the dress. "Well, my heavens, what a thing to say. This is a sweetheart neckline. It's all the style in the . . . You see it in all the . . . "

"All the what?" I snapped.

She looked bewildered, as though I'd said something in French. She grabbed a Raleigh and lit it. "You see . . . uh . . . sweetheart necklines in all the . . . uh . . . magazines."

"Maybe for a party but not for a covered dish supper at the church," I grumbled.

My mother closed her eyes and took a drag on her Raleigh. The tip of it burned orange. "Oh, I don't know. These days people . . . uh . . . dress up more," she said, but I knew she wasn't dressing for the covered dish supper. She was dressing for this Earl. I didn't like him already.

I grabbed my book bag from my drawer, took out some letters from Duane and sat on the bed running my fingers around the red, white, and blue borders of the onion-skin envelopes. Duane was the only bright spot in my life. I had eight letters from him, their creases worn soft from being folded and unfolded so many times. I'd stopped writing to Bruno. He didn't seem like the kind of guy who was going to propose, and anyway, I liked Duane better. We had a lot in common. We both loved cherry Cokes, and Benny Goodman, and Duane had loved my peanut butter candy.

I reread his last letter. "It's only a matter of time now," he wrote. Most of the boys in his company had already been sent home, but the married guys had come first.

I pictured going to meet Duane at his house in Hatfield. He said it had a green roof and a big lawn, and I saw him coming to greet me at the door. His cocker spaniel Crackers would be yapping at his legs. We'd go inside and his parents would say how lovely to meet me, they'd always wanted a daughter. They'd look just like Andy Hardy's mom and dad. Then Duane would put some records on, we'd dance, and he'd whisper in my ear, "This is what I fought for." The only problem, when we started to dance, Duane began to sing scat and when I pulled back to smile at him, he looked like Bobby.

My mother came back into the bedroom. "For heaven's sake, get that dirty book bag off the bedspread." She looked exasperated. "They'll be here any minute."

"I thought it was a free country," I mumbled. "I thought you could put your book bag on your own bed." I shoved the letters back into the bag as my mom flounced off. "Anyway I didn't realize you were going to entertain in the bedroom," I shouted. I took my mother's hairbrush off the dresser, picked out a handful of blond hairs, slouched into the bathroom, and set them in the middle of the sink. Back in the bedroom, I opened her sweater drawer and twisted the top button off a cardigan.

Earl wore glasses, had chipmunk cheeks, and a belly that hung out over his pants like melted wax. He was carrying a paper bag.

"This is Earl," my mom said to me. "He's a book-keeper."

He blinked at me and said "Hi." One of his eyes seemed to wander.

"Hello," I grunted.

"So the ball and chain here wants a drink before we go," Walt announced, squeezing Aunt Cora's waist. She flashed him a flirty smile.

"He uses me as his excuse," she laughed. You could tell they were feeling lovey-dovey about one another again. I thought back to the day she left. "He knows I can get along on my own if I have to now," she'd said with a sly smile. "That's going to make a difference."

"Oh, sure," my mom answered. "Drinks." She wasn't used to being a hostess. "Let me see. I'll get some . . . I think we have some . . . "

"Actually, I brought a little something," Earl piped up. He held out the paper bag and opened his mouth into a lower case letter "o." I guessed it was supposed to be a smile but it was more round, sort of a miniature of the rest of Earl's shape.

"Well, my heavens, thank you." She opened the bag and pulled out a bottle of Seagram's Seven and a package of swizzle sticks.

"Let's see, I'll get the glasses and some . . . uh . . . Nancy, why don't you open the swizzle sticks? I'll get the glasses and . . . uh . . . ice. I guess ice would be nice."

"Oh, that's rich," Earl declared. "Ice would be nice. That's cute." He smiled his little round smile again. It looked like he was eyeing my mother's brassiere straps.

I picked up the swizzle sticks, tore off the cellophane and when I saw what was inside I wanted to puke. Each stick was a different sideway silhouette of an African lady getting older and droopier as she went along. The first one was young with a flat tummy and boobs like fresh tomatoes, but by the last one her belly and her backside drooped like potato sacks and her breasts hung like fried eggs.

I felt a buzz in my head and smacked the swizzle sticks down on the kitchen counter.

"Oh, boy, get a load of these, Earl," Uncle Walt said, picking up the fried egg stick. "See what we have to look forward to. The pin-up gals twenty years later."

Earl chuckled.

I slouched into the bedroom and stared out the window at Matlock's Stables. I wanted to be like my aunt and Yvonne and Clarissa. And Miss Sandercock. I wanted to get that look in my eye like I knew where I was going, but I was terrified I was destined to end up like my mom.

"Cheers," Aunt Cora sang out from the kitchen.

Mr. Matlock was riding one of the horses around the corral, his shoulders bouncing as they went.

"Right. Here's mud in your cup." My mom's voice was so thin and cheery and innocent. Tears rolled down my cheeks as I watched Mr. Matlock ride the horse around and around, going over and over the same path. Why couldn't he take the horse a different way for once?

When I heard the door close, I snatched my book bag from my bureau again and pulled out a Christmas card from Yvonne. I stared at the return address in Philadelphia as a clap of thunder shattered the quiet, and a sudden spring downpour began.

I grabbed my box of writing paper, knowing I couldn't stand to stay in the apartment with my mother through the summer even if I had to be a kootch dancer to get away. If I was going to be Georgia Sayers' slut of a daughter, I might as well go all the way, with spangles and sequins, and strut around in a spotlight on a carnival stage while a talker out front coaxed the marks into paying to see nature's mistakes and extrah-vah-ganzas.

I sat at the kitchen table and wrote, making up a juicy story that got better as I went along. I told Yvonne I had to join the Magic Midway because my mother had a new boyfriend and was kicking me out.

"He has something called shell shock," I wrote. "He goes along acting like a normal human being and then all of a sudden he tries to slug everybody in sight. Me. My mom." I told her he'd beat up a guy over Christmas who was just trying to play "Silent Night" on the saxophone, and he'd said he was going to get me next. I told her I begged my mom to leave him but she wouldn't. She loved him. She said she always headed for the roller coaster in life, and if I didn't like it, I could lump it and get out.

"Please write me back right away," I told Yvonne. "I'll do a kootch dance. I'll sell hot dogs, sno-cones, collect tickets, anything, if you'll just take me. I don't have anywhere else to turn."

I finished the letter and paced around the apartment, reading it over. It sounded good. She couldn't turn me down. I got myself an Orange Crush from the refrigerator, sat down at the table again and daydreamed about how nice it would be, me and Yvonne and Gus in a cute trailer somewhere, Yvonne making spiced peach preserves, Gus oiling a squeak in the door and me telling funny stories about my days and quoting clever quotes.

I swigged the last of my Orange Crush and spun out of the apartment, hot-footing it past the Matlock's lawn, down Carlton Road, and across the boarded-up service station on Lower Market Street.

Just as I turned the corner onto Broadway, I spotted Mrs. Felker walking toward me across the street, maybe a block away. I felt my insides rise up out of me. I tried to think of all I'd said in the letters I'd written to her and never sent, letters telling how I was a girl she and Bobby could be proud of, but the words got all mixed up.

I stood stiff as a pole, hoping for a miracle, hoping she'd run up to me and say, "Oh, Nancy, I'm so glad to see you, Bobby misses you so much." But instead she all of a sudden stopped, looked into her purse and turned back.

She must have seen me and decided to give me a good snub. I wheeled around and I ran into Mr. Repsher, the mailman. When he saw my letter he offered to take it for me.

"Oh, sure, thanks." I handed the envelope to him, fingers quivering.

"By the way," he said, rooting around in his pouch, "I got a letter for you from Fort Gordon, Georgia. Looks like that soldier boy you write to is back in the good 'ol U. S. of A."

Fort Gordon? Duane? Duane was in Georgia? I grabbed Yvonne's letter back out of Mr. Repsher's hand and said, "Oh, Mr. Repsher I'll take this back. I just changed my mind about something."

24
NANCY, MARCH-JUNE, 1946

"It's not Hatfield but it's sure a lot more like home than Salerno," Duane wrote. "It feels great walking on good American dirt." I felt a throb in my legs and looked at the pavement. A bright vapor rose in the sun from puddles of rain water as though Duane was sending me a special hello through the good American dirt.

"Our company commander says we're supposed to get sent up to Fort Dix any day. Hey, if I get that close, I'll come and visit you in Marysville."

I sucked in my breath. I couldn't let Duane come to Marysville. I couldn't let him meet my mother or find out I wasn't eighteen and planning to go to commercial school, just a kid who had roller-skated through the lobby of the Colonial Hotel wearing a Lone Ranger mask and got rejected trying out to be Rhonda the Rubber Woman.

I stumbled home, past the newspaper store, past the shoe repair shop, my muscles aching, my underarms suddenly sticky. I had to find a way to get to Duane first. How far was Fort Dix anyway? Where could I get money? And what about all the lies? I had to come up with some kind of excuse for the lies—at least the ones I could remember.

That night I dreamed I visited Duane in Fort Dix. He had splotchy pink cheeks and bright eyes, and his family was there. They took me out to dinner in a place called the Pump Room that had pink table covers and white napkins. Real cloth.

"It's soooo nice to meet you," his mom said. She was heavyset with gray corkscrew curls. "We've heard soooo much about you." She put her hand on my arm and her fingers turned into monster claws. Her face became Mrs. Felker's.

"We've heard just tons of things about you. But tell us about your mother. She must worry about you coming all alone to a place like Fort Dix."

"Oh, yes, she worries about me a lot. You know

moms." I laughed like I'd heard Shirley Metzger do, trying to get a little tinkle into it.

Duane's father's head grew big and bobbed around. "I hope your father is a Mason," he said between bobs.

"Oh, yes, yes, he sure is a Mason." I pictured a guy wearing an Arabian hat with a tassel, or maybe that was an Elk. I started to sweat. I wanted to say oops, I forgot, my dad is dead, but somehow sitting with Duane's family in the Pump Room with a real cloth napkin on my lap, even a dead dad didn't seem respectable enough.

"I'm in the Eastern Star," Mrs. Uhler announced. "Last month I hosted a luncheon for forty girls." My hand had disappeared underneath her claw. "Does your mother host luncheons?"

"Oh, yes. Yes. She loves to host luncheons." My arm was throbbing with pain.

"Oh, good." Mrs. Uhler smiled. "I hope she's teaching you some of her secrets." Her breath came at me like a hot wind.

"Oh, yes, she loves to teach me her secrets," I stammered as Duane rode around the table on a unicycle beaming at me.

I woke up sweating and I looked over at my mother in bed with her cold cream and spongy curlers. I knew it was hopeless. I sat at the kitchen table and wrote a letter to Duane saying I was sorry but I'd just got engaged to a boy from home, a boy who played the clarinet just like him. I said I was sorry this was so sudden, but it didn't seem right to send him a Dear John letter when he was overseas, I thought I should wait until he was back on good American dirt.

I stayed at the kitchen table for hours staring out through the branches of a budding elm tree at a black starless sky, listening to crickets.

In the morning I rushed out to the post office to mail the letter to Duane along with the letter I'd written earlier to Yvonne.

"Look," my mother cried, poking a jittery hand in my

face to show off a dinky diamond. It was a windy April day and I'd just come in from a movie.

I was astonished. In my craziest daydreams I'd never pictured my mother married. I glanced at Earl, who sat in the living room like a newly purchased overstuffed chair.

"Well, so when's the big day?" I untied my scarf and stuffed it in the jacket of my pea coat.

"June." My mother laughed, breathless, her eyes big as pies. "I always wanted to be a June bride." The four leaf clover pin she wore on her white bunny sweater throbbed with the excited pounding of her heart.

That was all I needed to make some plans of my own. Later that night in bed, I thought it all out. I'd finish my junior year in June, and I'd already skipped the third grade, so why not the twelfth? I'd probably learn more in a big city anyway than in a two-bit school in the sticks.

The best thing was, I could leave now without guilt. I didn't have to picture my mother slumped alone in this shabby apartment that smelled like horses, chain-smoking her cigarettes, blowing on her coffee and staring at the cracked linoleum.

My mother sat at the kitchen table, leafing through a *Bride's* magazine. It was a week since she'd got engaged. I sauntered in, poured some juice, got out the bag of doughnuts and plunked down on a chair across from her.

"Oh, by the way, I'm thinking of moving to Philly when you get married."

She set the magazine down. "Philly, huh?" She looked at me as if daisies were sprouting out of my ears. "Well, if that's what you want . . . " Glancing at the newspaper, she opened to the want ads. She and Earl were looking for a new apartment.

"Yeah." I reached for a doughnut and tried to sound casual. "You know what they say. 'Leave thy house, O youth, and seek out alien shores.'"

"Where would you stay?" She looked serious.

"Maybe the Y. A lot of girls stay there since the war. Or I might call Yvonne, the woman from the Magic Midway. You remember, she had me over to dinner a couple of times."

My mother nodded and I could tell she didn't remember. "She lives in Philly and we got along pretty well. Maybe I'll give her a call and see if I could stay with her." I didn't mention I'd sent a letter to Yvonne a month ago and I hadn't heard back yet.

My mom picked up the paper. "Well, that would be good, a grown-up to stay with." She brightened. "I guess you always had itchy feet. I guess you might as well get it out of your . . . ah . . . "

"System. Yeah." I was glad she was being so agreeable, but somehow little disappointed, too.

"What about school?" she asked. "Don't you have another year of school?"

"Well, yeah, but in Philly you can finish high school at night," I lied, although for all I knew, maybe you could. School was the last thing on my mind.

"Is that right?" My mother gave me a small, slightly surprised smile, as though she was pleased I was making things so easy for her.

"Well, I suppose that would be as good a time . . . " Her sentence drifted off. She set the paper down. "Well, lucky, there's plenty of time to talk about that later."

"Yeah. Lucky." I took a bite of my doughnut, chewing it slowly. I felt a little numb.

My mother got married on June eighth at the Good Shepherd Baptist Church. She wore a three-quarter length white dress with a chiffon top and a blue satin sash and a little skull cap that had white and silver sequins with a mesh veil. She looked gorgeous, a little bit like June Allyson but with wispier hair.

Reverend Mackey performed the ceremony in a tiny courtyard behind the church. "We come to celebrate the sanctity of marriage," Reverend Mackey droned. Mrs. Mackey stood behind him wearing a lemon yellow dress shaped like a hot air balloon.

I glared at the reverend and muttered to myself, "Clodpole. Addlepated. Barmy in the brain."

"The scripture says it is not good that man should be alone . . . " I watched my mother's shoulders bob as she stared expressionless at the reverend. "Bone of my bones, flesh of my flesh . . . " Earl blinked and his mouth moved. I went stiff just thinking about my mother's and Earl's flesh.

After the ceremony everyone threw rice and hugged the bride. My mom smelled like Joy perfume, and the sweet scent of her followed me as I walked back to stand with the others. I smiled in the sun but somehow the aroma of the Joy made me sad and teary.

"So they're gonna hear those bedsprings rattle in Niagara Falls tonight, huh, Earl?" one of the men joked.

"Hey, Georgia, watch it, you're gonna be walking bow-legged tomorrow," another cracked.

I wanted to scream. "Is that all you can say about my mom? Sex stuff? Don't you understand, all this sex stuff is driving me crazy?"

I excused myself and ran into the church basement where I sat on the john and cried until I heard the cars drive away. Upstairs the organist began to practice, "I Come to the Garden Alone." I looked at the peanut-colored stall door and a voice inside me said, "Are you sure it's the sex? Are you really sure? Suppose your mom came in right now and gave you a hug and said, 'Oh, Nance, I know I'm a loose woman, an adulteress. I know I have no shame. But look what I got for it. I got you.'"

I laughed a jagged little laugh. "Oh, sure," I said to the dank church basement. "And then she'll tell me, 'Oh, incidentally, I found a million dollars in the crawl space under the apartment. Here, take half of it and have a good time in Philly.'" I padded out of the stall, splashed cold water on my splotched face and walked home.

25
NANCY, 1946

I stood outside the Palm Gardens, a Clinton nightclub they'd turned into a sort of Stage Door Canteen during the war. Bobby played the clarinet there every Friday night in a combo. I'd got the bus to Clinton, telling my mother I wanted say goodbye to Aunt Cora and Uncle Walt before I moved to Philly, but the real reason was I wanted to sneak a last peek at Bobby.

The door to the Palm Gardens was padded with gold-colored plastic. Black metal pineapples attached to each side held thin tubes of flashing neon that stretched up and across the top in arches. I stared at the pulsing neon and started to think things I'd been trying to forget: the feel of Bobby's ribs against my chest, his lips on my ears. I almost turned, as though the garish neon was warning me away, but the need to see him once more was too strong. I pushed open the door and stepped inside. The air was bitter and smoky. Soldiers stood around in tight knots drinking Cokes and 7-Up. Bright-eyed young girls wearing sloppy joe sweaters smiled and snapped their fingers to the music. Nobody asked me for an I.D. or even noticed me walk in.

A huge dusty palm tree separated the bar from the canteen. I edged past the fake palm leaves to get a better look at the combo. The musicians swayed with bent knees on a small bandstand as they played "Why Doncha Do Right?" A blue and gold banner behind them announced "Live Jive Every Friday."

When I spotted Bobby, my knees went rubbery. He was wearing a canary yellow shirt and olive green pants. His eyes were closed, and his back was arched as he rotated his clarinet in a slow circle, an expression on his face that looked like pain but I knew was something else. I knew he was really feeling a fullness in his heart so sweet it seemed too wonderful to last. I'd seen that same look on his face, and I'd felt the same sweet richness during the days we couldn't keep our hands off one another.

I inched closer to the stage in the grainy light past a tiny dance floor clotted with couples who could hardly move but you could tell they didn't care. There was an edge in the air—an eat-drink-and-be-merry mood that I recognized from Jolly Jack's. Soon I was alongside the bandstand and, as though he knew it, Bobby opened his eyes. They widened, seeing me, and they stayed on me until the end of the song, when he whispered something to the piano player who stood up and announced an intermission.

Bobby jumped down, smiled, and put a hand on my elbow. I felt a thrill that started in my stomach, traveled up and made my throat tingle.

"Let's go outside," he whispered and led me into a grassy clearing alongside the parking lot. Standing with his hands on my arms, he studied my face.

"Nancy, I'm so glad to see you," he whispered finally.

I smiled back, a goofy smile, ecstatic at the warm feel of his hands.

He pulled me closer and gave me a short gentle kiss. "I missed you," he murmured into my hair.

"Oh, I missed you, too," I gushed, and sagged against him, feeling the energy drain out the soles of my feet.

Just then a sailor and a girl, half dancing, half hugging, whirled into the clearing. The girl giggled. Bobby pulled away from me, frowning as the couple twirled past toward a knot of pine trees nearby. He cleared his throat in an exaggerated way, the same way he had the day he'd brushed me off.

I remembered why I'd come and cleared my own throat, as if to show him this time I was the one who had an announcement.

"I . . . ah . . . thought I should say goodbye," I murmured. "You might have heard, my mom got married, and I decided to move to Philadelphia."

Bobby's head jerked. "Philadelphia?" His face looked somber, puzzled with that Buster Keaton expression that made me love him all the more.

"Yeah, I think I'm ready for the big city." My voice sounded fuzzy. "I've had enough of small towns."

Bobby frowned. "What about school? Don't you have another year?" The faint rings around his eyes made him look so sophisticated, I shivered.

"Yeah, well, I already skipped one grade and I don't think I missed anything, so why not just skip another?" My sentence had too many esses in it, like I was hissing at the night.

Bobby lowered his eyebrows and put on a fatherly expression, or at least what I imagined a fatherly expression would be like. "I don't think you should quit school. I think you'd regret it later." I liked him scolding me, as though it showed he cared.

"Nah. I can type. I always get the highest grades in typing. I'm a real whiz. That's all a girl needs these days, to be able to type."

"You can do a lot more than type." Bobby's eyes looked straight at me.

I shrugged. "Anyway, my mom and Earl don't want me around." I tried to sound casual. "They're a couple of lovebirds. The last thing they want around is an overgrown kid."

Bobby moved closer. "Couldn't you move back with your Aunt Cora? At least you wouldn't be so far away."

My heart leapt. He cared how far away I was.

"Nah, she's got her hands full with my uncle. My uncle came back from the war with shell shock. Besides, I thought you were going to college. I thought you were going to move away from Marysville yourself."

Bobby sighed. He raised a hand and ran the pads of his fingers across my temples and down my cheeks. "I'm just going to Clinton State. I won't be moving away. And I'll still play with the combo. That's what I really love, you know." He pulled me to him again, so tight I could feel his heartbeat.

"Nancy, don't go," he groaned.

"Parting is such sweet sorrow, huh?" I quipped, but the minute I said the words I went limp and moaned, "I don't want to go. Why do you think I came here? You told me once, 'It seems like we belong together. You and me.' It still seems that way to me."

Suddenly he stiffened and dropped his arms. "I know I did, but there's something else." He looked confused, hunched his shoulders, and turned toward the Palm

Gardens. The flashing neon from the door lit his face in quick purple spurts.

"What? Tell me."

"I can't."

I stepped back. "I know what it is. Your mother doesn't approve of me because I'm Georgia Sayers' girl. She doesn't want you running around with the daughter of the town slut."

"No." Bobby looked shocked.

"Don't say no." By now my voice sounded like a wasp caught in a lamp. If that wasn't it, if it wasn't his mother turning him against me, that meant he'd decided on his own I wasn't good enough for him, and I couldn't bear that.

"Nancy, it's not that. Believe me." His face twisted in the purple flashes of neon.

"Then what is it?" I kept my eyes on his face, damned if I was going to make it easy for him.

"Listen . . ." A drum roll from inside drowned out his sentence. He glanced at the building. "I have to go in. Will you wait for me until I finish playing?"

I hesitated, but he looked so earnest I couldn't refuse, so I nodded. He gave me a quick squeeze on the arm and hurried inside. A group of giggling girls with curls piled up on top of their heads edged in beside him, making googoo eyes at him as I ran my fingers over my arm where he'd touched it.

I stared up at the stars, hoping they might give me a sign whether I should stay or go. The sailor and his girlfriend rustled leaves from behind the cluster of pine trees as the moon clouded over. I went weak, afraid I was setting myself up for another brush-off. "Beetle brain, foggy in the crumpet," I muttered to myself, wondering if somehow all my mother's helplessness and neediness and desperation had seeped into me through the air we shared in the apartment. I pressed my lips together. At least I was one step ahead; I was getting out.

I trudged down the cindered pathway that led up to the Palm Garden from the highway, listening to the stones crackle underneath my feet and feeling the purple neon pulse on my back until I reached the bus stop.

26

NANCY, 1946

"Take care of yourself," my mother said, walking me to the car, wearing a new champagne colored housecoat, flashing a sunny smile. "Be sure to eat breakfast. And . . . uh . . . let's see . . . you got your umbrella?"

"Yeah."

Earl was driving me to Philadelphia early on a Saturday morning in his two-tone tan and maroon Pontiac. My mother had backed out at the last minute because she had to go and wait at the apartment they'd rented up on Fourth Street for a bed to be delivered. She lit up whenever she talked about the apartment. "Wait 'til the girls see the Hotpoint stove and the Kelvinator," she'd brag.

"Good. Well, don't forget to write." She turned to Earl. "And you be sure to drive careful. I don't want to lose my honey."

"Don't worry," he said, beaming at her concern.

She looked at me again, started toward me, then stopped. She reached out and put a hand on my shoulder. A bird squawked behind her. "Well . . . uh . . . don't forget to wash behind your ears." Her blue eyes became serious for a second, or maybe just blank. Sometimes it was hard to tell.

"Nah." I reached out to put my hand on her shoulder but she dropped hers at the same time and our arms banged against one another in mid-air.

My mother bounced. "Well, remember to write us a letter."

"Yeah, I'll remember."

It was so early, there was a mist over everything. I couldn't remember ever seeing the world so gray. Teensy drops of moisture covered the car and the grass and the roofs of the houses. Sheets of mist rose from the ground and puffed out into wet clouds, turning everything a kind of grainy gray—the pavement, the Delaware River, even the cows in the pastures.

Earl didn't talk. The quiet made everything seem

grayer, and for a while I sat there with the terrible feeling that Earl was the devil in disguise and he was driving me into the valley of death.

Then Earl burped and said "Ooops, a little extra taste of breakfast there," and laughed nervously. I realized how silly I'd been. The devil would never disguise himself as Earl. I edged closer to my door.

I pretended to fall asleep and Earl put on the radio, first to a program called Hymns of All Churches and then the Breakfast Club. After that a man came on telling women who still worked in factories it was time to go home and turn their kitchens into cozy corners of sanity in a crazy world. It seemed like men had an awful lot of advice for women that women didn't want.

I stayed cramped in the same position for the whole trip as we rode past misty hills in two-bit towns with windows still dark from the night. A program came on with Eddie Duchin playing the piano with his magic fingers and the music made me think of Bobby. I daydreamed he'd been so brokenhearted not to find me at the Palm Garden that night, he'd decided to move to Philly himself and was already wandering the streets searching for me. I pictured myself strolling down Market Street—I knew that was the main street from a map—and suddenly I spotted Bobby running toward me, crying, "I knew you'd come this way. I've prayed to God to send you," and we fell into each other's arms, kissing and laughing.

Before I knew it, Earl was driving into Philadelphia. I perked up as he wove through city streets, full of cars honking horns and buses stirring up clouds of blue smoke and people bustling every which way. I still didn't let on I was awake, but as I peeked out, I felt excitement throb in my fingers. By now the mist was gone and the sun was shining on the cars and buildings bright as butter.

Earl pulled up outside the Y and helped me in with my bags. His shirt was scrunched up in the back from the long ride so that you could see the pale skin of his back above the baggy trousers. Inside, he put the bags down on the tile floor by the desk. A girl with blood-red fingernails and a velvet hair ribbon to match was handing a key to the clerk, who took it absent-mindedly as he brushed crumbs off a newspaper.

"So . . . uh . . . do you have your money?" Earl asked.

I nodded. I had cashed in my war bond, and my mother and Aunt Cora had given me going-away money. I had $75 in all.

"Yeah, it's in my sock," I said. My shoe felt tight as I thought about it. The girl with the fingernails ran smiling to a group of sailors huddled by the door.

Earl gave me a lower case "o." "Well, don't take any wooden nickels."

"I won't. And thanks for the ride."

"Sure thing. Write to your mom, now."

"Yeah."

He walked out, his red and black shirt still riding up above his belt. I felt tight around the temples, like once when I had tried on my mother's chin strap as though it was a head band, like Tonto's.

27
NANCY, 1946

My room was small. The narrow bed had a white chenille bedspread with a sort of orangey stain on one side that would have driven my mom nuts but didn't bother me. I just tried not to look at it. There was a cardboard wardrobe painted like wood, a set of drawers, and little table with a swirly yellow Formica top by the window. Some thumbtacks on the wall had bits of paper peeking out from around them like sunbursts. A banner pasted to the wall behind the bed said Khaki Wacky. The room smelled like Lysol.

I unpacked and went out and bought a *Philadelphia Inquirer* and a box of Good & Plenties. Back in the room, I sat on the bed, eating the candy and looking through want ads. I circled the typing jobs that sounded good, like at The Merry Go Round Record Store and Woolworth's, and skipped the ones that sounded boring like at Wyeth Laboratories and I-T-E Circuit Breaker Company.

Tiptoeing out into the hallway to call some of the places, I went tongue-tied wondering what kinds of questions they'd ask. I found a phone book tucked into a shelf underneath the wall phone and started to look up Yvonne's name when a girl closed a door down the hall and walked toward me. She had a big head shaped like an eggplant with curly red hair, and a huge belly, as though the bulging belly was supposed to somehow offset the head. I thought what a peculiar place for a pregnant girl, the Y. She smiled and said hello. I said hello back and flipped the phone book closed quick, as though she'd caught me doing something illegal. I pretended to read the newspaper until she got on the elevator, then looked in the telephone book again but Yvonne and Gus weren't listed.

In my room I stared out at the city, then opened a drawer, took out a manila envelope full of poems and spread the papers around on the bedspread. The air was so still, it seemed like time was stopping and my arms and legs felt like cement. I got scared, afraid if I didn't move I'd disappear.

At the desk downstairs, I picked up a Philadelphia map and started wandering the streets. The air was mild and the sky was a perfect blue. My spirits lifted. I was wearing my loafers with new pennies tucked into them for luck. I'd washed my hair with beer to make it shine, and I felt sophisticated as I watched people scurry to what I was sure must be exotic places. I felt a giddiness I'd never known before. All of a sudden I realized it was because I was free to be anybody in the world. Nobody in Philly had to know I was Georgia Sayers's daughter. This is what I've been waiting for, I thought.

I passed City Hall and turned left on Market Street toward the Delaware. I knew it was silly to hope Bobby would be waiting for me by the river but a part of me hoped it anyway. As I walked I realized I was also drawn to the river for another reason. The first time I'd seen the Delaware was just after Grandma died. I was six. My mother and I took a bus to Clinton to visit Aunt Cora and

Uncle Walt. I remember the bus whizzed by the Rutt Ridge Silk Factory, where my mother worked, then past roadside bars with signs that showed cocktails with cherries on top: Daisy's Paradise Club, Lizzie's Tittle Tattle, The Dew Drop Inn. Later there were junkyards and houses with no sidewalks in front, just grass.

Suddenly we turned a corner, and out of the blue, there was the Delaware. I'd gasped. It was the most beautiful thing I'd ever seen, and I felt my heart beat like a rhumba as we drove for miles and miles past homes made of gray wood with porches built right out over the water and little boats tied up alongside. I'd thought to myself I'd follow the Delaware someday to a place that would be the answer to all my dreams.

Further along on Market Street, near Independence Square, I stopped at a small park and settled on a bench. A mother lounged on the grass, dipping a tiny spoon into a jar of strained bananas while her baby nestled in her lap, his little mouth opening and closing like a baby bird, his eyes fixed on her face. He was so helpless and dependent on her, tears sprang to my eyes.

A guy wearing blue jeans and a navy blue turtle neck shirt walked up and sat down on the bench alongside me. His brown hair was shiny and tousled and he wore tortoise shell glasses. Flashing a smile, he looked me up and down.

I blushed and turned away.

"So . . . " he said, jutting his chin at my map, "you leaving home? Or just vacationing in the City of Brotherly Love?" His eyes had a bold look and his smile widened, showing large teeth.

I felt myself redden even more. How did he know?

"I . . . uh . . . ah . . . just graduated from high school," I lied. "I decided it would be interesting to see what life was like in Philly."

"Well, you came to the right place." Another smile. "There's plenty of life in Philly." He took a lazy look around the square, as if he owned it, then turned back to me. "Where you from?" he asked.

I dropped my eyes to my lap, then peeked up and smiled, the way you saw Chinese brides do in newsreels.

"Uh . . . from upstate P.A." I mumbled, nervously. "I just moved here from upstate P.A."

"Ah, upstate P.A." He looked up at the sky and took a slow deep breath.

"So where you staying?" he asked.

"At the Y."

"Mmm hmmm. The good ol' Y. The citadel of sad stories."

What did he mean? What was the matter with the Y? Then I thought about the girl with the blood-red fingernails and the pregnant girl with the eggplant head.

"If only the walls could talk, huh?" I quipped.

He smiled again, sunnier now, as if he meant it this time. "So . . . I'm Clark. I work just over there." He waved a hand toward some brick buildings behind us and shifted in his seat to face me. "I'm an artist, a free spirit, a part of the avant garde. You want a personal tour of the city with a bona fide member of the avant garde?"

I looked him in the face. "Sounds to me more like I should be on my guard."

He laughed out loud and said, "Touché."

I laughed too. "I'm Nancy, and I'd love a personal tour."

I knew it was risky, but a part of me said, go ahead. If they find you somewhere staring up from ragwort weeds, they'll be sorry. I pictured my mom wringing her hands and whining to Earl, "I should have paid more attention to her. I should have cuddled her in my lap and fed her strained bananas. I should have hugged her and promised I'd make sure the reverend kept his filthy mechanical hand off of her." I envisioned Bobby sobbing, "I shouldn't have let her go," the rings around his eyes as black and sad as soot.

Clark walked me through an alleyway to the back of a small brick building where he said he had a studio. He opened the door to a powder blue Plymouth.

"I'll treat you to a picnic lunch in Fairmount Park," he said as I slipped in.

We stopped at a delicatessen where Clark bought two corned beef sandwiches and a pack of beer, then drove out to the park and settled on the grass by the Schuylkill River.

Fairmount Park was the biggest place I'd ever seen, with enough different kinds of bushes and trees for a forest.

Clark handed me a beer. "A little drink before lunch," he explained. "Does wonders for the psyche."

Psyche. What a debonair word. Clark was what Aunt Cora would call a real man of the world.

We sipped beer while Clark told me he was a free-lance commercial artist and he could work whenever he pleased. I said that sounded fantastic. The sun shone in slants through the branches of a tree, making reddish stripes on his hair.

"So how about you, are you going to get a job or what?" Clark unwrapped his sandwich.

"I'm going to look for a typing job," I said as I unwrapped my own fat sandwich and tried to figure out how to eat it. "I'm a demon typist. I was top in my class. My stepfather was saying just this morning driving me down, I'm lucky I'm a demon typist."

Clark smiled. "Well, I figured you were a girl with talent," he said. "So you got recommendations?" He took a huge bite out of his sandwich.

"Recommendations? No. I never thought of that. I figured they'd just give me a test or something." I eyed my sandwich again. There was no way I could open my mouth that wide. I started nibbling across it.

"Well, a smart girl like you, you want a reference, I'll give you one. What the hell? Just put my name down, say you did some typing for me. I'll tell them you're a demon typist."

He grinned, his teeth big as a horse's. "Maybe you can do me a favor sometime."

"A little quid pro quo, huh?" I'd just learned the phrase a week ago and was thrilled with a chance to use it.

By the time Clark took me back to the Y, I figured it was kind of a sign that I'd met somebody so debonair—an artist, a member of the avant garde. It was a sign I did the right thing, moving to Philadelphia.

The next night Clark took me to a party in an apartment with dim lights and the sweet aroma of incense. I recognized the scent from the Magic Midway where the snake charmer had burned it in her trailer. I brightened, thinking I knew more about the world than I realized.

He introduced me to a group where a guy named Jeffrey was babbling, "So my favorite scene is where he's watching 'La Traviata.' They're singing the Drinking Song and he's in the audience on the verge of tremors."

"Yeah, yeah," a fat girl with eye makeup butted in. "The camera shifts back and forth from the guys guzzling onstage to him practically collapsing from wanting a drink."

"Brilliant movie-making," Jeffrey said. "Brilliant." He turned to me. "So, we're talking about *The Lost Weekend.* What did you think of it?"

"I . . . uh . . . well, I thought it was brilliant movie-making, too," I stammered. "I was telling my stepfather just the other day I thought it was brilliant. Plus I always like Ray Milland." That wasn't true. Ray Milland wasn't enough of a dreamboat for me, too much chin and forehead, but it seemed like the thing to say.

I'd never been around such brainy people. They talked about writers I'd never heard of. Bertrand Russell. Phillip Wylie. John Hersey. They knew about classical music and jazz and laughed at everything.

I was careful to listen more than I talked but a couple of times I dropped a quote. "A rose is a rose is a rose, huh?" or "The truth shall make you free, right?" Once when something really flew over my head, I gushed, "My stepfather, he's real smart, he feels the same way." I felt sneaky bragging about Earl but I liked being able to say I had a stepfather. Stepfather. Even the word seemed to make me more important.

Later Clark and I sat on a sofa watching some of the others dance, Clark's hand resting on the cushion between us.

"Boy, your friends are sure deep thinkers, aren't they? They're real debonair."

He gave me a smile. "I suppose so. I like them fresh from upstate P.A. myself." He patted my hand and I thought to myself, Clark was just the kind of guy who could take my mind off Bobby.

The next week without any trouble at all, I found a typing job at an ad agency and I thought, hey, this is just a beginning. Maybe I'll turn out to know just where I'm going in life after all. Clark took me to his apartment for a drink to celebrate. There was big room in front with pictures from magazines plastered all over the walls showing advertisements he had illustrated. Ekco Pressure Cookers. Cuticura for Baby Chafing. Ajax Hard Rubber Combs.

He mixed me a rum and Coke and told me he and his friends were bohemians and atheists. He said the trouble with most people, they didn't think things through or appreciate culture. Most people were philistines. That confused me because I thought philistines were a tribe in the Bible, but I kept my mouth shut.

Clark told me he saw a head shrinker once a week. "I'm extremely neurotic. Most of my friends are, too." The reason he was so neurotic, he explained, was that his father had committed suicide. "That's not the kind of trauma you get over, you know. It's not the kind of kick in the gut you can forgive."

"Oh, I understand," I said.

"I thought you would, smart girl like you." He poured another drink and told me that his father had never felt he was successful enough in life, and Clark blamed his mother for pressuring his dad too much. He said it was criminal the way people ruined one another's lives.

"Oh, I think so, too." I lit a Pall Mall, waited a couple of seconds, then asked, "Do you think I'm extremely neurotic?" I hoped he'd say yes.

Clark squinted. "Mmmm. I'd say you have more of an inferiority complex." I felt disappointed.

He saw my face and grabbed my hand. "But we'll work on changing that," he whispered, leaning forward kissing me on the mouth. It was different than with Bobby. With Bobby, a kiss was like a flood of sunlight, but with Clark it was more crackly, like heat lightning.

But I was thrilled that he liked me enough to say we'd work on changing things. That was just what I wanted: to change things. Sometimes at night in my room at the Y, I'd curl up in bed and watch the neon sign flash outside. I'd feel as though I was deep down alone, and Clark was a bright ray of light I needed to help me find a place for myself in the world.

I asked for another rum and Coke and tried to think of a way to impress him. I downed the drink, took a deep breath and said, "I don't have a father either, you know."

"Really?" He looked at me, interested.

I lowered my eyes. "It was terrible. He went hunting in the woods with friends, and he decided to go in deeper—my father was always the most adventurous—and nobody ever saw him again. The police combed the woods for weeks but never found him. They figured he must have got lost and starved and animals ate him."

"Ugh. How grisly." Clark's eyes widened. I could tell he was impressed.

"My mother got hysterical and after that she was never the same again." I looked up, trying to make my eyes teary, trying to give a small, sad smile, but I felt a raw ache in my throat. I was furious with myself. Why couldn't I just tell the truth? What would be so horrible if for once in my life I just told the truth?

28
NANCY, 1946

Randolph Street in North Philadelphia was lined with narrow rundown brown stone apartments. Number 127 smelled like pot roast. As I stood staring at the peeling paint on the door, I wondered if Yvonne was somewhere inside cooking up dinner. I ran my finger over the list of names scribbled on dingy cards tucked into a tarnished metal plaque alongside the door, but there was no Gus Montana.

I felt half glad and half disappointed. I worried whether Clark was really going to be that ray of light for me. When

I was with him I'd think yes, but later in my room at the Y, I'd wonder. He could be sweet as you please and then suddenly he'd turn and ridicule you. I'd decided if I found Yvonne, that would mean I should ask to stay with her and go back to the carny, and if I didn't, it would mean I was supposed to stick with Clark and become a part of the avant garde. All I knew for sure was I wasn't wise enough to decide on my own.

"Who ya want, dearie?" a gravelly voice called from upstairs.

I lifted my head and saw a woman in curlers leaning out a second story window, one plump red hand dangling alongside a geranium plant that was all stems.

"I'm looking for Yvonne and Gus Montana," I replied.

The woman chewed on the inside of her cheek for a minute. "Ah, the carnies. Yvonne and Gus. They moved away, dearie. Pret near a year ago now, I'd say. Hard to remember, they was gone so much."

"Do you know where they moved to?"

"Nah. Prolly somewhere here in North Philly." She waved her pudgy hand.

"Well, thank you." I felt small and lost.

I turned and walked down Randolph Street. A radio was playing "Coming in on a Wing and a Prayer" from one of the houses. I felt strange, like the atoms, neurons, and other things that hold a person's body together were pulling loose inside me.

Clark and I were at his apartment drinking rum and Cokes. We'd just got back from a party at an old guy's house who wore a black beret and was married to a six-foot redhead who'd been a WAC and played the guitar while she sang "The Rising of the Moon."

I sat on the edge of the studio couch. "Uh, do you remember a couple of weeks ago when I told you about my father?" My voice came out in a quick burst, like I was winded. "That he was lost in the woods?"

"Do I remember?" Clark laughed.

I felt myself redden. "I . . . uh . . . made up the story."

"Now, why doesn't that surprise me?" he teased. I should have been irritated, but I was too anxious to get the truth out, and there was nobody else I could tell who wouldn't look down their nose at me.

I took another swig of rum. "The truth is I have no idea who my father is at all."

"Really?" Clark's voice rose.

"Yeah, really." I felt old and weary. Running my fingers along the Japanesey patterns on the couch cover, I blurted out practically my whole life story. I told him how the kids used to tease, "Hey, it's Harry, Dick, and Tom, havin' fun with Nancy's mom." I told him about Eddie, Mr. Encarnacion and the Magic Midway, Yvonne, Earl. Everything except Bobby. Bobby was too important.

When I finished, Clark gave a soft whistle. "Well, that explains a lot including why you'd . . . " He looked toward the shuttered window for a second . . . "uh, well, among other things, why you'd live at a dump like the Y."

He put an arm over my shoulders. "Jesus, Nance, that's tough. I knew a guy in college who was a bastard. It really ate at him, not knowing who his father was. He turned out to be an alcoholic."

I jerked and for a minute I pictured myself sprawled out in a gutter with stringy hair, a bottle in one grimy hand.

"So all those years what did you say if somebody asked about your dad?" Clark took his glasses off, breathed on them, and wiped them on his shirttail. He looked odd without his glasses, like his face wasn't finished.

"I made up lies, like the one about him getting eaten in the woods." This was the first time I'd ever admitted to all the lies. It felt good. The rum had helped. "I made up lies and then went to bed and cried about it."

"Oooh, boy. Nancy, Nancy. The trouble with you is you're too damn repressed."

"You mean depressed," I said, confused.

"No, not depressed. Everyone is depressed. Repressed. And you should tell your mother to fuck off."

I gasped, not from the word, Clark used it all the time, but from what he was saying.

"Oh, Clark . . . don't . . . " I couldn't finish. I wasn't even sure what I wanted to say. My chin started to wobble.

"Okay, okay, sorry." Clark took my hand. "I sometimes forget you're not battle-hardened yet." He ran his finger over my trembling knuckles. "So tell me more."

"Well sometimes if a kid asked me about my dad and I didn't care about the kid I'd say can you keep a secret and the kid would say sure and I'd say, so can I." Clark howled and hugged me.

"I still say you need to tell your mother to fuck the fuck off. Tell her from now on you can just fuck your life up yourself." We both roared.

"Frankly, my dear, that might not even be enough. From what I can see, you're a real hardship case in the repression department," he said seriously. "Telling good ol' mom off might be just the start. I bet a head shrinker would tell you to look for good ol' dad. If I were you that's what I'd want to do. Meet good ole' dad."

I sputtered, "My father?"

"Oui. Si. Fa-ther. As in what I lack myself."

I thought about the men I used to look at in Marysville and wonder about and gag over. I remembered for awhile I'd thought it might be Reverend Mackey. On Sundays I'd sit in church and stare at him through the sea of ladies' hats, all silk tulips and colored cherries, watching him wave his arms around like he was about to take off. He'd warn that the Devil was loose from the bowels of the earth, and it was up to us to drive him away or burn in hell. Then, when he'd look around, to be sure everyone was good and scared, I'd want to yell, "Are you my dad, Reverend Mackey? Are you the one?"

Now looking at Clark, my heart started pounding so hard I felt it in my ears. "What would I say? What would I do?" I picked a round glass paperweight off the floor and clutched it in my hands. It felt heavy as the world.

"I don't know. 'Long time, no see,' maybe."

"Clark, it's not funny."

"I know it isn't." His eyes became serious again. "So what's with all the can-you-keep-a-secret jokes?"

I felt like a photograph that's out of focus. "I don't know," I whispered.

29

NANCY, 1946

It was October first but there was an Indian summer. Walking to work, I eyed men rushing this way and that with suit jackets flipped over their shoulders, hooked to their thumbs. I looked for someone with almond-brown eyes and feathery eyebrows, someone with an egg-shaped face whose shoulders jutted forward like mine, as though he was in more of a hurry than the others to get someplace.

I had a new aim in life: looking for my dad. He could be any one of them, I figured. Any one of them could have lived in Marysville once. Or gone to the Pocono Mountains for a vacation, stopped to see the slate quarries, and wandered into town. It was as though Clark had unleashed a longing that had always been inside me. All I'd needed was for him to say: let it out.

At the office, Marilyn, the red-haired receptionist, said, "There's a special meeting in the conference room right away."

I stopped cold. "Me too?" Most of the bigwigs at the agency never even looked at me.

"Yep, everybody," Marilyn said, tossing her head.

"Wow." Self-conscious, I followed the carpeted hall to the conference room. Everyone was there, from Jo-Jo, the crippled mail boy, to Mr. Feygelman, the agency president.

I couldn't stop thinking about my dad as I stared at Mr. Feygelman's gray hair and wondered if it was ever brown. I peeked at Mr. Madison. Mr. Madison was a dreamboat. Light-skinned with freckles, he reminded me of Van Johnson. I studied my arms for freckles, and I found a couple of little caramel colored ones. I wondered if Aunt Cora would tell me anything. Maybe if I went home for a weekend I could just casually ask, "Incidentally, do you remember anything about my dad? I was just wondering."

"Good morning," Mr. Feygelman said. There were columns of figures on the blackboard and he went into a long-winded speech about economics and competition. The agency had lost a big client, and some of us would have to be let go, right away, that day. There just wasn't enough work for some of us anymore, including guess who.

Back at my desk, my supervisor, Mr. Constable, said, "I'm sorry, Nancy." Mr. Constable had huge pores and smelled like tomato juice. "Why don't you finish up this typing and just leave at lunchtime. We'll send your last check to you."

"Oh, sure," I said with a smile, as though leaving at lunchtime was just another work assignment. My stomach felt like it was full of jumping beans, but I didn't want to let on, it didn't seem citified. Mr. Constable looked relieved.

At eleven forty-five I packed my belongings: a half-eaten bag of pretzels, a pair of sunglasses with a bent stem, a Kotex wrapped in toilet paper from the Y.

I walked out with Glenda, another typist who'd been let go. She wasn't worried, her husband was getting her a better job at the company where he worked anyway. She said she'd already called him to come pick her up and blow some of her last paycheck on lunch.

There was a warm breeze blowing up from the river and cumulus clouds were gathering in the sky. They looked like dumplings plumping up in boiling water, and they reminded me of my grandma cooking Sunday dinner. I got an ache in my throat.

"Good luck, Nancy," Glenda hollered as she clacked across the street in her high heels.

"You, too," I yelled, but I didn't mean it. Glenda had enough good luck. I looked in my wallet. $8.27. I might as well blow some of it on lunch myself. I walked across the street to Lucas' Pie and Lunch, and ordered a ham and cheese sandwich and a root beer.

The lunch counter was horseshoe-shaped. I liked long counters with mirrors better where you could eye people without staring right at them. I liked to watch elegant-looking people eat, figuring I could learn from them. With the horseshoe-shaped counters, you were stuck looking at whoever sat across from you. It could be any old slob. I worked hard trying to keep up with Clark and his crowd, read the newspapers at the public library and looked up words in my desk dictionary. It had been a huge thrill to me to have my very own dictionary; suddenly my heart dropped, realizing I wouldn't have it anymore.

Maybe my getting laid off was a warning from God, I thought. Maybe God was telling me I was getting too big for my britches. Or, as my mom would say, bridges. Maybe God was saying who did I think I was, trying to move to a big-time city like Philly, thinking I could get in with a hotshot like Clark, thinking I could look for my dad and get a look in my eye like Aunt Cora.

The waitress brought my root beer. I looked across the counter and wondered if the woman with her eyebrows plucked and half circles penciled in above them had ever been fired. What about the man with the egg salad on his chin or the woman who was all in green—green crepe dress, green purse, green crocheted beret? Probably not. I'd never known anybody else who was fired. Oh, well, Glenda, but she didn't count. She had a husband to get her another job.

My sandwich came so I unfolded my napkin and laid it neatly in my lap. I bit into the sandwich, then wiped my greasy fingers on the napkin. The sandwich tasted delicious, the crunchy buttery toast, the thick hot creamy cheese, as though it was a small reward for all my misery. Bite, wipe, bite, wipe. At least there were some things in life you could count on.

Suddenly somebody came in and a gust of wind blew my napkin off my lap onto the counter in front of the lady in green. Nobody else's napkin blew off, just mine. It sat there with my greasy finger marks on it. It made me so sad I started to cry. I looked in my purse for a hanky but I couldn't find one, so I took the toilet paper off the Kotex and pretended to blow my nose with it.

Back at the Y, I sat on the bed and pulled out my letters from home. One was from Aunt Cora, written in August. It was on powder blue paper and said, "Hi, kiddo. The big news here is I'm pregnant. Me and a couple of million other war wives. I'm six months along, and all is well. I had to take a leave of absence at work, but I'll go back. I'm not the type to sit around the house crocheting afghans.

"Walt's doing great, acting like a doting dad already.

He's working full time so we can sock a little away for the blessed event. Plus he helps out weekends at a mortuary on his mail route. The VA counselor convinced him keeping busy would be the ticket. So far, so good."

I put down the letter and thought about the year I'd lived with Aunt Cora. I pictured us walking with books on our heads and huddled over *Readers' Digest*, building word power. I remembered how she'd said you had to take something for yourself in life, you only go around once, and I wanted to, but it seemed so hard. I needed more confidence. Clark was probably right, finding my dad would be the answer. A father's love would clear the cobwebs out of my brain and make me smart and witty and suddenly I'd know exactly what to take in life and how to take it.

I opened a letter from my mom. She sounded more grown-up in letters. You couldn't hear the little girl voice or see the cheery smile saying, "See me. Aren't I cute?" Her penmanship was neat as a row of tulips.

"We went to a banquet at the Order of the Rainbow last night. Vera Buzzard was installed as Worthy Advisor. You remember Vera. She looks real good. The doctor gives her water pills.

"Mildred has been giving pep talks to the girls at work who started like me back before the war. She says we have to consolidate to keep our jobs. Consolidate. How's that for a $10 word? Anyway, plants all around have been laying off everybody and their sister with the boys coming home. But I'm not worried. Mr. Hildebrant wouldn't let me go. He always calls me Georgia Sunshine. Plus we're making stockings again and I'm back on seams and I'm the best seamer they have."

I let the letter flutter to my lap. Even my mom could hold onto a job. I felt my eyelids twitch, opened them hard, and glanced down.

"I just got back from Mildred's this afternoon. Her neighbor was there with her twins. Two sweet little blonds. They're so cute, growing like tops."

"Topsy," I said, loud as a gunshot. "Growing like Topsy." And how come all the sweet little kids had to be blonds anyway? I slammed the letter down.

I closed my eyes, wondering if my mom ever bragged about how cute I was. I wondered if my father ever saw me and thought I was cute. I pictured storming to Marysville and sitting my mom down and saying I wanted to know once and for all who my father was, without worrying that she'd bounce and cry and say what a thing to ask your mother.

I got up, walked to the window and gazed out at the city. It looked huge and cold and made me feel small and pitiful. I shuffled back to the bed and arranged my letters, spreading them around on the bed as though that might make things turn out better. It was so quiet, it seemed like the world had come to an end.

Out in the hallway, I called Clark.

"Hi, chum. What's up?" he said.

"Bad news." I felt tears swell in my eyes again.

"Oh oh."

"I got fired." The tears streaked down my cheeks. It was like saying I'd been arrested. "They lost an account and they had to let some of us go."

I was glad Clark couldn't see my tears. "It's just a little setback, I know. Uh . . . what's the saying? Don't take life too seriously or you'll never get out of it alive?" One thing, at least.

He chuckled. "Atta girl. That's the spirit."

"Sure." My nose started running. "Uh, speaking of spirits . . . "

"So come on over. We'll have a snort together."

"Oh, Clark, thanks." One thing about Clark, you could count on him to help when you were down. His crowd was all like that, friendlier when you were blue.

He opened his door, brushed my cheeks with his lips, and handed me a drink.

In his studio, a girl with a big nose sat eating a sweet roll. "How," she said, putting her hand up like an Indian. "I was in the neighborhood. No hanky panky. Honest."

"Nancy, you remember Betsy," Clark said. "From McElhatton's Pub, couple of weeks ago." All I remembered was that she had gotten soused and run out into the intersection singing at the top of her lungs, "Love is a Many Splintered Thing."

"So what next?" Clark asked, his green eyes looking pale in the afternoon light.

"Oh, I don't know." I sighed. "Maybe I should go home for a while."

"Good God, no, that would be the worst thing, going home sniveling." He put his arm around me. "Come on, kiddo, show some backbone."

"Listen, don't let it get you down," Betsy said, her cheek bulging with sweet roll. "Lots of people get fired. I got fired once."

"Really?" I looked at Betsy closer. Her dark eyes sloped down at the corners like they might slide off her face.

"Yeah, it happens," she said. "People boss you around. It gets to you. Plenty of people get fired. Probably the smartest people."

I felt the drink going to my head. "Huh, you know, I think I read that somewhere," I said. "The smartest people, they don't always fit in. They march to a different drummer, right?" I realized getting laid off at Ad Land with Glenda wasn't quite the same thing, but it was close.

"Well, look, gals," Clark said, "enchanting as all this chitchat is, I have a deadline, so how's about you two come back at five, and we'll get plastered."

Outside it was warming up. People sat in the park across the street with their faces turned up, happy for a dose of sun before the cold weather set in.

Betsy asked if I wanted to go to her place and I said sure, feeling friendlier toward her, two girls who'd been fired.

Her apartment was L-shaped with two wide doors opening to a kitchenette along one wall.

Betsy got out two Cokes and a box of Cheez-Its. Taking a swig of her Coke, she said, "Uh, look, I got an idea. If you want to stay with me for a while, you're welcome. You can just pay whatever you can afford until you get back on your feet."

"Really? Oh, gee, I don't know." It made me sad to think I had to get back on my feet. I was only sixteen.

"Well, it's up to you. You're welcome. Think it over." The apartment looked so inviting, with a bright rug and a bathroom of its own, I perked up. Clark had been telling me I should get out of a dump like the Y just to show I had a little respect for myself.

"So Clark tells me you got mom problems," Betsy continued. "Welcome to the club."

"You too?"

"Yeah," she said. "My mom is a socialite, always gallivanting. You name it, she's there, everywhere but home." She started ticking off all the things that were wrong with her mom, but I wasn't listening.

I was thinking maybe getting fired meant I was supposed to move in with Betsy. Maybe it was fate. Two girls who'd been fired. Girls with mom problems.

I took another sip of Coke. Imagine living with a socialite's daughter, I thought to myself. I could probably learn a lot from Betsy.

"Uh, listen, maybe I will take you up on your offer. Uh . . . to move in with you."

"Oh, hey, terrif," Betsy said, her eyes brightening, as if there was a little kid behind all her sophisticated ways.

"Yeah? Really? Great. Thanks a lot."

I leaned back on the sofa and thought boy, my luck is finally changing. I even found another job in three days at a place called Cranston's Claim Service. They handled claims for insurance companies, but mostly tried to figure out ways the company wouldn't have to pay.

I wrote letters home, telling everyone I had a glamorous new job and had moved in with a socialite's daughter. By the time Aunt Cora's baby was born in November—a little girl, Barbara—I was earning $16 a week, enough to pay Betsy half the rent, and we got along great. Sometimes she stayed at her boyfriend Jake's, and if her mom called I was supposed to say she was at the library. It was fun living with another liar.

She gave me a book called *Generation of Vipers* by a guy named Philip Wylie that was all about moms. The book said moms were vain and vicious, pretending to be angels but carrying swords. One thing I'll never forget, it said moms were forever reminding you that they're moms, acting like martyrs but their urine would etch glass. It took me a while to figure that line out but after I did, I loved it and I used it every chance I had.

"They ought to make you get a license to be a mom," Betsy said one night as we sat at the little kitchenette table, eating pizza. "They make you pass a test to drive a car but any moron can have a kid and ruin its life."

"You're right," I agreed, watching Betsy drop a string of cheese into her mouth. I pictured the girl at the Y with the eggplant head and the belly big as a bathtub. What kind of a life was her kid going to have? "There ought to be a law against having a kid any old time you feel like it."

Once we got into the swing of it, Betsy and I could find a way to blame practically any problem on our moms. I felt debonair hanging out with Clark and Betsy. I loved being a bohemian. I loved it that Clark and Betsy and their friends looked down their noses at all the bigwig kinds of people who used to look down their noses at me.

I went home for two days at Thanksgiving and hated every minute of it. My mother and Earl's new apartment didn't have an extra bedroom so I had to sleep on a cot on a closed-in porch. We were supposed to go to Aunt Cora's for Thanksgiving dinner but my mom caught a cold and Aunt Cora was afraid she'd give it to little Barbara, so my mom and Earl and I went to a diner in Wind Gap instead, where my mother coughed on my mashed potatoes and Earl ordered a steak instead of turkey and slathered butter all over the top of it. It was disgusting.

At least I talked to my aunt on the phone for a couple of minutes, but it wasn't the same between us as before. It started off okay. She asked, "How's life treating you in the big city?" but a couple of times in the middle of my sentence, she'd say "Oops, Barbara just curled her itty bitty hand around my finger." Or "Oooh, she just smiled the sweetest little smile. Walt kids that it's gas but I don't believe it." I twisted the cord of the phone around my wrist and said I couldn't wait to see the baby when I came home for Christmas, but it wasn't true. I was jealous already. I couldn't wait to get back to Philadelphia.

Clark decided that I was probably neurotic after all; my problem wasn't just an inferiority complex. I was glad. At night I'd lie on the sofa bed in Betsy's apartment and whisper to the dark, "Neurotic. Neurotic. I'm Nancy and I'm neurotic."

Clark said I was stuck in the past and I wouldn't be able to be a normal grown-up until I found my father and also unleashed all the rage I secretly felt at my mother.

I tried to envision finding my dad. I daydreamed of him sitting on a cliff, with a breeze behind him tousling his dark hair, his eyebrows knitted together like Tyrone Power's. I'd run up to him and he'd say, is it you, is it really you, and I'd nod and he'd light up and whisper, "Thank God. Now my life is complete." But then in my real dreams, it would turn out different. In one dream I found him on Skid Row, wearing cardboard shoes tied on with a string. Another time he was an elevator operator with a five o'clock shadow. When I announced myself, he said, "Who? Why in the world would I want to meet you?" And he swung the door shut in my face.

Betsy got drunk pretty regularly. She got me a fake I.D. and introduced me to Bloody Marys. I loved them. They had the funniest name I'd ever heard, and I liked that they didn't seem like real drinks, more like little snacks. Tomato juice and celery sticks.

One Wednesday night in December, Betsy and her boyfriend Jake and Clark and I went to a club called Blondie's Eleventh Hour, where a Negro woman played jazz and a stand-up comedian in a too-tight suit told jokes.

"My wife keeps imitating Teddy Roosevelt," he said. "She runs from store to store yelling 'Charge.'" "The meanest thing you can do to a woman is to lock her in a room with a thousand hats and no mirror." The audience laughed straggly, lukewarm laughs but the comedian kept smiling and babbling on as though he was a wind-up doll.

During intermission, Betsy got the bright idea I should run up on stage and do my Rhonda act. She always said it was the craziest thing she'd ever seen and when I'd shown it to Clark, the night I'd poured out practically my whole life story to him, he'd grinned and said, "Nancy, whoops, Rhonda, you're priceless, one of a kind."

I'd beamed.

"Go on," he said now, with a glint in his eyes. "You're a hell of a lot better than that two-bit comedian. It'll be fun."

"Do you think so?" I was jittery. Betsy had given me a pep pill before we came. She took them all the time and said they gave you confidence. I needed all the confidence I could get with Clark. He could go along being sweet and then I'd say something I thought was clever and he'd laugh and tease, "Oh, this young blood." I couldn't be sure if that was supposed to be a compliment or an insult. Another thing. We necked a little once in a while but he'd never tried anything funny and I couldn't help worrying there was something wrong with me. Betsy'd just said, "Oh, that's Clark. He wants to hold off until you're panting for it. He's like that with all the girls." I had thought to myself, well, this is one girl who can wait until hell freezes over, but then later I realized I wasn't so sure. Sometimes I wanted Clark to pick me up and carry me off like Rhett Butler had with Scarlet O'Hara so I could wake up the next morning madly in love with him instead of still writing love poems about Bobby.

Right now, though, sitting in Blondie's Eleventh Hour Club, I felt more confident than I could ever remember feeling before. "In the Mood" started up on the jukebox and I felt a rush of energy.

"Hey, why not?" I thought. I looked down at my swirly gray skirt and black sweater and stockings and thought it was too bad I didn't have my Rhonda costume on underneath but I scooted up to the stage anyway. I grabbed the microphone and announced, "We have an extra act tonight." I loved the audience staring at me. "A debut act that I think you'll enjoy." I flashed a wide smile. "Here's Rhonda the Rubber Woman."

And with that, I hurled myself into a backbend and walked around on all fours in a quick circle. My skirt swirled up and landed in folds somewhere around my midsection but by now I didn't care. Somebody hooted. I stood up, shaking my hair and then bent forward, planted my hands flat on the floor and lowered my nose to touch them. I went slow, inch by inch with everyone wondering if I'd make it.

When I finally did, a man yelled "Yo, Rhonda," and I heard coins hit the floor of the stage.

They like me, I thought. Maybe Clark was right. Maybe I am priceless. I bet I could do my Rhonda act right here in Philadelphia, right on a stage in Blondie's Eleventh Hour Club. I pictured my photograph out front, alongside the Negro woman's.

I sat on the floor, hitched my skirt up to my thighs and started curling into a ball. I heard Betsy snicker and felt my muscles stretch and strain, but I knew they'd do whatever I told them. I loved it.

"It was a such riot when the comedian came back and you didn't notice," Betsy gurgled the next afternoon as we were in the kitchenette drinking cocoa.

"Yeah." I giggled. I'd been finishing my curl up, ready to roll into a ball, when I noticed pant legs close to my right cheek, cheap pants with metallic threads in them. Then he'd leaned down and slanting the microphone toward me. "Would you mind, miss? You have all night to make a fool of yourself. They're only paying me for another fifteen minutes." Everyone had howled, and I'd laughed and unwound myself, and pranced back to my seat. I didn't mind the comedian ridiculing me; I knew I'd put on a good act. Betsy'd been right. The pep pill did give me a lot of confidence.

"Good show," Clark announced and gave me a pat on my backside. We all ordered another round of Bloody Marys.

But now as I stared out the window watching the tangerine sunset, I wasn't sure the whole thing had been such a riot, after all. I thought of something Clark had read to me from a psychology book: "We so-called love children are too quick to go bad. We're too quick to believe nobody will ever love us anyway so what do a few slips matter?" Maybe that writer was right. You started to let things slip and before you knew it you were the kind of girl who'd go all the way with a guy and give free shows in public and take too many pep pills and who knew what you'd do after that?

The phone interrupted my thoughts.

I jerked and turned to Betsy. "Ah, it's probably Paramount Pictures," I teased. "Why don't you answer and say you're my manager, and whatever they offer, Rhonda has to think about it."

Betsy grinned and picked up the receiver. "Heh-lo," she said in a British accent.

She listened, then handed the phone to me. "It's for you. It's a teary-sounding lady."

I felt my stomach clutch as I got on the phone.

"Nancy, it's Cora. A terrible thing happened." Her voice broke. "Earl had a heart attack this morning. He died. Come home quick."

31
NANCY, 1946

The day of the funeral, a dreary misty rain covered the whole town. During the ceremony at the graveyard, my mother screamed, "My honey," every couple of minutes even after the reverend said Earl finally had found everlasting peace. Once she lurched from her folding chair toward the grave as if she might jump in. Uncle Walt and two of the pallbearers—men from Earl's work—rushed to hold her back, then returned to huddling underneath the edge of the tan canopy with their fingers laced together in front of their crotches.

I tried to help the only way I could think to do. I leaned over from my chair and whispered to her, "Sunset and evening star, and one clear call for me. May there be no moaning of the bar when I put out to sea." That stopped her. She looked at me for a minute like she was trying to see through a tunnel. "That's from Tennyson," I muttered. "The Crossing of the Bar." I'd memorized it just that morning and I'd thought it sounded deep and hoped my mother would listen to the no moaning part, hoped it might inspire her to let up, but it didn't. She blinked, swallowed, and started yelling "My honey" again.

By night, fog hung in the streets, and the yellow headlights of passing cars seemed to come out of the mist like creatures from another planet. I sat on a wooden rocking chair in the sunporch of the apartment on Fourth Street holding two books Clark had loaned me in my lap. My mom was deep asleep in her bed from pills Dr. Di Salvo had given her for her nerves. Aunt Cora and Uncle Walt had gone home to Clinton but my aunt had promised to come back first thing in the morning.

I opened one of the books. It was about a guy called Immanuel Kant who Clark had said was brilliant. I turned to the first page and started reading.

"Kant's philosophy presupposes a radical distinction between de facto and de jure questions," it said. What? I skipped to the next page. "For Kant, the fundamental question of the critic of reason was how are a priori synthetic judgments possible."

I closed the book, got up and walked to the door of my mother's bedroom. Her arms and legs were limp, flung out like a rag doll's over the double bed. She looked like a little kid, as though any second she'd stick her thumb in her mouth and grope for a teddy bear. For a minute I felt jealous. My mom would never have to worry about whether or not she understood Immanuel Kant. I wished I had a cigarette. I wished I had a Bloody Mary.

I tiptoed to the kitchen, heated some milk in a pan, got out the tin of hot chocolate and opened the other book. *The Portable Dorothy Parker.* Standing by the stove, I flipped the pages to some verses in the back and read one.

> "Oh, life is a glorious cycle of song,
> A medley of extemporanea;
> And love is a thing that can never go wrong;
> And I am Marie of Roumania."

I smiled. She was being sarcastic. She wasn't really Marie of Roumania. She didn't really believe love could never go wrong. I sat down and turned to another verse.

"One perfect rose he sent me since we met.
All tenderly his messenger he chose.
Sweet-hearted, pure, with scented dew still wet.
One perfect rose.
Why is it no one ever sent me yet
One perfect limousine do you suppose?
Oh, no, it's always just my luck to get
One perfect rose."

"One Perfect Rose" was even funnier. It started out like the other one, flowery, and then it got bitter. I stared at the cover of the book. Dorothy Parker. She was like me. I could hardly believe it.

The milk started boiling and as I got up to turn it off, I thought, "I could write verses like that. I could be cute and funny and sarcastic." I hugged the book, so thrilled with Dorothy Parker I couldn't wait to call Clark and tell him.

The kitchen clock said eleven forty-eight. He'd still be up so I went into the hallway and dialed his number but there was no answer. I paced back and forth between the sunporch and the kitchen. I couldn't wait to get back to Philly and start writing cute sarcastic verses. I could see it now. *The Portable Nancy Sayers.* A couple of stories. A few clever verses. How long could that take? Maybe my father would see it and come looking for me, he'd be so proud.

A light wind had started up outside, whooshing and rustling in the night like ghosts. Teeth chattering and flesh creeping, I pulled down the blinds and slipped underneath the plaid wool blanket on the cot and tried to fall to sleep.

I jerked awake to the sound of my mother moving in the kitchen. Strips of thin morning light slipped through the slats of the venetian blinds, and I smelled coffee. That seemed like a good sign, but I still felt edgy. How would we get through the day?

I eased off the squeaky cot, reached for my purse, and groped for the pep pills Betsy had wrapped for me. She said I'd probably need all the confidence I could get and she was right.

In the kitchen, my mother looked groggy. She was sitting at the table in her champagne-colored housecoat with a peach-colored cardigan sweater over it.

"Ah, you made some coffee." I hardly breathed. "Good."

"Yeah." She held a half eaten piece of shoofly pie in her hand.

"I'm . . . uh . . . bathroom," I muttered, giving a weak little wave.

I peeked at the clock. Only seven-thirty.

In the bathroom, I took a pep pill, washed my face and hands, and brushed my teeth then carefully wiped the water spots off the spigot.

Taking a deep breath, I padded back to the kitchen and glanced at the clock again. Seven thirty-five. I swallowed, "So Aunt Cora's coming at eight, right?"

"Yeah." I noticed my mother was working on her second piece of shoofly pie.

"That looks good," I said. My voice was thick and fuzzy. "One of the girls from work brought it, huh?"

"Yeah." She looked up at me with empty eyes. The wind had died down; the world seemed still and lifeless outside.

I took a coffee cup from the cupboard and glanced at my mother's back. Her hair was matted and bunched up so you could see her pink neck. It looked so innocent and helpless, suddenly the back of her neck seemed like the saddest thing in the world.

"If you're still a little sleepy, you can go on back to bed," I said. "I'll clean up here."

"Nah, I'll do it." My mother started to get up when the doorbell rang. It was Mildred, and I was so happy to see her.

She gave me a hug. "Nice thing about being one of the mucky-mucks at the plant, you can take a day off without groveling and jumping through hoops."

I smiled. I couldn't imagine Mildred groveling or jumping through anybody's hoops.

We sat down with my mother at the little maple table and sipped coffee and babbled about the floral arrangements at the funeral, which ones were the biggest, the most colorful, which had flowers you didn't usually see this time of year, whatever we could think of. I surprised myself, having so many opinions about flowers. The pill must be working.

A little after eight, Mildred said, "Georgia, let's take a walk. It's a nice, still day, and real warm for December. It'll be good for you."

My mother looked bewildered, then got up like a wind-up toy on a low battery.

Aunt Cora dashed in at 8:25, carrying Barbara in a bundle of pink flannel blankets. The baby was wrapped up so tight, she looked like a little packaged coconut with eyes.

"I ran into Georgia and Mildred down on Broadway," my aunt said, rolling her eyes.

After putting Barabara down for a nap, she poured herself a cup of coffee and plopped down on a chair with a sigh. She looked me in the face. "Nancy, I'm glad to have some time alone with you."

"Oh, me, too," I said, but I sucked in my breath, afraid of what was coming next. "I might as well get to the point. I think you should move home with your mother. She needs you."

"What does she need me for?" I whimpered, "I'm just a kid. Can't she move in with you?"

My aunt sighed. "I think it's better for her to keep a place of her own." She cupped her right hand, swept some shoofly pie crumbs into it and dropped them into her saucer.

"How come?"

She cleared her throat. "I have Walt. I have Barbara. Our lives are different."

"You mean my mom isn't good enough for you?" I felt

flushed, amazed at myself for sassing Aunt Cora, and even more amazed at sticking up for my mother.

Aunt Cora looked up sharply, "Well, of course, that's not what I mean."

I knew my aunt had her hands full with my uncle and the baby. I knew Uncle Walt ridiculed my mother, and it wouldn't really work. This wasn't the way I wanted to be talking to Aunt Cora, but I had to stand up for myself. It was what she'd told me to do that day at the park.

"There are people in Philly just like me," I said. My voice sounded whiny. "They understand me. They're smart and funny. They read books. Immanuel Kant. Dorothy Parker."

Aunt Cora pulled a Kleenex out of her skirt pocket, wiped her eyes and blew her nose.

"Nancy, I know you haven't had an easy time of it. But neither has Georgia, and she is your mother."

"She doesn't even like me," I yelped, tears starting up. I kept hearing Clark warn me not to let them talk me into anything. "She hardly even pays any attention to me except if I put the tuna fish cans on the wrong shelf or I forget to walk on hankies after she waxes the floor."

My aunt took a sip of her coffee and frowned. "Sometimes she doesn't know what to say. Georgia is . . . simple. I think she's a little afraid of you. All she wants is for you to be friendly and cheerful. That doesn't seem to me to be too much to ask."

I shifted in my chair, feeling sorry for my mom, and then for myself, as tears slipped into my mouth.

My aunt came around the table and put her arms around me.

I took a deep breath. "You know, my mom never even told me a word about my dad." My voice quivered. "Who he is. Where he lives. Anything."

I felt my aunt stiffen. I looked up. She'd closed her eyes as though she hoped that might shut me up, but I couldn't stop. It'd taken too much nerve to get started. "Everywhere I go, people ask about my dad. What am I supposed to say?"

Aunt Cora sighed again, slumping into the chair. "I don't know. I was young," she said. "All I know is he was married. He had a family. He was somebody your mother met at work."

"Married? My father was married? To somebody else?"

"Yes, I'm afraid so, but that's all I know." She took a deep drag on her cigarette and exhaled a huge cloud of smoke.

The back door opened and a rush of cold air swept in. I felt a wave of shame, and when Mildred walked into the kitchen with my mother, I couldn't face them.

"I . . . uh . . . think I'll go for a walk myself," I muttered, and slouched to the sunroom to grab my jacket.

Aunt Cora's words rattled in my brain as I lunged down Broadway. My father was married. He had a family. Now I wished she hadn't told me. It ruined everything. I thought of my fantasy that I'd find him sitting on a cliff with a breeze behind him tousling his dark hair, handsome as Tyrone Power, overjoyed to see me. I shoved my hands deep into my jacket pocket. I didn't want to think of my dad with a wife. A wife wouldn't be overjoyed to see me,

I walked faster, looking back as though somebody was closing in on me. The air was still moist but my throat felt parched as I headed toward Pysher's Pond. Wet leaves squished under my saddle shoes. I reached the damp gray bench, sat down, and stared up at the bare limbs of the trees twitching in the breeze.

I couldn't sit still and got up, starting toward the eucalyptus grove at the Old Welsh Church, when a voice behind me said "Nancy?" A tiny sweet voice. I turned.

It was Sylvia Staples.

"Sylvia," I said, so glad to see her, I rushed up and gave her a hug. She looked better. She'd had a perm and her hair was parted in the middle and fastened on each side above the ears with barrettes shaped like corn on the cob; then it fluffed out in curly little clouds like puffed sleeves.

"Well, how are you? Gee, I'm glad to see you. I mean, I'm really glad to see you." I'd always felt bad about the way I'd snubbed Sylvia after I started hanging around with Joanie. Maybe it meant something, running into her now. Maybe we could become good friends again. Except, of course, I wouldn't be in Marysville very long. Aunt Cora's words raced through my brain, " . . . I think you should move back home with your mother."

"I'm sorry to hear about your mother's husband," Sylvia said.

"Oh, thanks. Poor Earl." I glanced in the direction of the cemetery, shook my head and shivered.

"So how do you like the big city?" Sylvia asked.

"Oh, I love it." I couldn't stop babbling.

"And how about you? Anything new at your house?" I was bouncing and energy seemed to be building inside me.

"Yeah, Clarissa went off to Allensburg to a commercial school. My mom got arthritis. She don't get around so good, so I quit school to help take care of my brothers." She was wearing a washed-out looking yellow sweater underneath a blue plaid jumper with straps that were too long and one of them hung down over her upper arm.

"You quit school? Oh, Sylvia, no." The thought of her having to quit school suddenly seemed like the saddest thing I could think of. It wasn't fair, Sylvia having to quit school, having to wear a jumper that didn't fit while Clarissa got to go off to commercial school. Why was life so damned unfair?

"Well, you quit, too," she said.

"Oops, you're right. I did." I laughed but I knew with me it was different. I was off in Philly hanging out with bright witty people who were part of the avant garde. I reached over and picked up the loose jumper strap and set it back on Sylvia's shoulder.

"It fell down." I smiled awkwardly.

"Oh, thanks." She glanced at me, "Maybe you could come and see me tomorrow." Her voice was sweet and inviting. "I could buy some Tandy Takes. I remember you loved them. You could tell me all about your life in Philadelphia."

"Oh, that would be great," I gushed. I wanted to make up to Sylvia for the way I'd used her, making friends just to get back at my mom. I wanted to make it up to her that she had to quit school. Maybe I'd dedicate one of my poems to her, one of the poems in *The Portable Nancy Sayers.* "That would be really great," I said. "I'll come over early in the afternoon."

"Okay, good. So I'll see you tomorrow."

As she rambled off in the wet leaves, the strap of her jumper fell down again. I stomped away to the eucalyptus grove behind the Old Welsh Church, climbed on the band-stand and twisted until I ached.

Late that afternoon, some of the girls from the factory stopped by with a meat loaf and a macaroni and cheese casserole. They stayed awhile and talked shop and I could see the color creep back into my mother's cheeks. Charlotte said some plants were laying off women to give jobs to men who weren't vets. Mildred said no fair, they had to protest.

I thought of a magazine article I'd read that said women had spread their wings during the war, even those who didn't work in defense plants. And they said women were more independent now. I wouldn't in a million years have thought of my mom in the same breath as an independent woman, but I could tell she felt good being part of this group, and by dinner time she'd perked up.

Aunt Cora was heating up the macaroni and cheese when Barbara woke up crying, fluttering her tiny fists in the air.

"Pick her up for a minute until I finish here," Aunt Cora said.

My mother looked scared, but she reached down, tucked her right hand behind Barbara's wobbly head, and slowly lifted the baby up with the other. She cradled the bundle of blankets in her arms and watched Barbara move her tiny wet mouth in quick puckering motions. Then she looked me in the face and said, "Isn't that cute? Just like when you were a baby."

I gasped and stared back. I couldn't say a word.

32
NANCY, 1946

By the time Bobby called at 8:30 that night, things were going real well. During dinner, I'd told a couple of Philadelphia stories and everybody'd snickered. Aunt Cora hadn't said another word about me moving home. Mildred had stopped by to say, hey, let's all take a ride out to Amish country on Friday, and my mother's dull eyes had brightened. She loved Amish country. "The girls look so sweet," she'd once said when we'd taken a drive there with Eddie, "like angels on earth. I'd like to be Amish myself if I wasn't Baptist. I think I'd look cute in a bonnet, and I wouldn't have to put my hair up every night."

When Bobby telephoned to ask if he could come over Tuesday morning to pay his respects to my mother and take me out for a ride, I began to think things might work out all right after all.

"Well, it's nice your friend wants to come pay his respects," my mother said the next morning, tearing a piece of waxed paper off the roll to wrap up the remains of the shoofly pie. "That's a sign of a nice boy."

"My friend is a nice boy," I said, giving her a shy smile. The kitchen clock said eight forty-five. He was coming at nine. I'd already taken a pep pill. In fact, I'd been up since five studying myself in the bathroom mirror. I'd pulled my hair back from my face, and made spit curls along my temples. Then I rubbed on some of my mother's Pink Perfection rouge. Back in the sunroom, I started to read through my lists of quotations, then picked up *The Portable Dorothy Parker.*

Now my mother and I were in the kitchen where I was washing dishes; so many different people had come to visit over the weekend.

"I forget, where does he live again? Your friend?" she asked.

"Out in the R. D."

Her jaw tightened. "I don't trust people from the R.D.," she said in her little voice.

I put down a plate. "You said that once before. I don't understand. There are good people in the R.D. Some of the best people live there."

She looked at her tiny hands. "Was that the boy who was peeking in the door with you that day?"

She was talking about the day Eddie moved in and when I was sick and ran into Bobby at the park.

"Mother, that was years ago. You've met Bobby since then. Look, maybe you're not up to company. You don't have to talk to Bobby right now if you don't want to. He'll understand."

Just then the bell rang. I looked at her, unsure what to do.

She gave me a trace of a smile. "Oh, sure I'm up to talking. I guess my nerves were just working overtime there for a minute." One of her hands fluttered toward me, like a little hummingbird.

I grinned back at her, thankful. This was the way mothers and daughters were supposed to be, looking each other in the eye, talking things out. I raced to the door.

Bobby looked wonderful, with his hair a little ruffled, as though he had dressed in a hurry, as though he couldn't wait to see me. He handed my mother a cake box closed with a silver sticker that said "From Katy's Kitchen."

She flashed him a wide smile and said, "Well, that's so thoughtful." She looked at me. "Isn't that thoughtful, Nancy?" You wouldn't have known she was upset a minute ago.

I nodded.

"If there's . . . uh . . . anything I can help you with . . . around the house, let me know," Bobby said. "I'll be in town over Christmas."

"Oh, well, isn't that thoughtful?" My mom beamed.

"So you're going to be okay now?" I asked, sounding worried and sincere, but now I couldn't be sure if I was putting it on for Bobby or if it was real.

"Oh, yeah. Mildred's coming over later, and meantime, I've got lots to do. I have to change the sheets and wash and starch some blouses." She picked up a list from the table. "Let's see. I have to dust the leaves on the ivy plants, put some Sani-Flush in the . . . " She stopped, "Oh, well, there's just lots. You know what they say. No rest for the idle."

The sun was a dazzling winter white, as if it was saying, "Look, I'm giving you a special day." Walking alongside Bobby toward the curb, I thought to myself, this is nice, Bobby coming to pick me up at home, chatting with my mother. Of course, it was easier with a mom who was a grieving widow than it would have been back in the days when she was still a slut and a scarlet woman.

He opened the passenger door of his stepfather Barney's pea green Buick, and helped me in. "I thought we might take a drive over to Wind Gap." I looked up at him, giddy. I wanted to pull him in beside me right there on Fourth Street, wanted to feel him against me, wanted the warmth of his breath on my neck. I felt shameless.

"If you like, we can stop at the diner for coffee," he said.

"That sounds perfect," I murmured, suddenly full of confidence from the diet pill and the wispy curls that I knew set off my eyes. I felt bright and pretty.

As we rode along, side by side in the car, it was like we were in a bubble together, just me and Bobby, set apart from the world.

He gave me a sidewise glance. "I missed you."

"Oh, I missed you, too," I gushed, then caught myself. I wasn't going to invite another brush-off. "But I've been busy in Philly, you know. Parties. I went to a nightclub last week. Blondie's Eleventh Hour Club. You would have liked it. The people in Philly are so debonair." I decided not to mention I'd gotten drunk and done my Rhonda act and the comedian had to heckle me off the stage.

"I'm sure they are," he said in a quiet voice.

Nobody spoke for a minute.

"So you're switching colleges, huh?" I asked.

He sighed. "Yeah, they have a better music program at Hamlin. I've decided that's what I really want to do in life. I know it'll disappoint Barney, partly because it will take me away, but the music really pulls me to it."

"Oh, I think he'll understand," I said. "He seems like an understanding man."

He slowed the car down and I noticed we were on Wind Gap Junction Road. He turned to me. "So do you. You really pull me to you."

He parked the car and we flew into one another's arms. He kissed me so long and hard I went dizzy. He nuzzled my neck and he brushed my ear with his lips. I folded my arms tight around his warm neck.

Then suddenly he pulled away and lowered the car window on his side. The cold air was like a slap in the face.

He didn't say anything and I felt my heart sink. I figured he was asking himself what he was doing in broad daylight with a girl who was only good for one thing. My face burned with shame at the way he had left me gasping. I decided I might as well shock him even more.

I swallowed and said, "You know, I've been talking with my Philadelphia friends about looking for my father. I'm thinking of looking for him."

He whirled toward me, his face twisted.

"I have no idea who he is, you know." I felt ashamed admitting I was a bastard, but what did it matter? He probably knew anyway. Everybody else did. At least I could show him I was getting worldly and debonair about it. "My mother has never said peep to me about him, and Clark, one of my friends from Philadelphia—Clark is the smartest person I've ever met—he said I'll never feel like a real person unless I find him. Clark says a girl's relationship with her father is the most important."

Bobby looked me full in the face. "You might not like what you learn."

"Oh, sure. I understand that," I responded, but all of a sudden I didn't feel confident and debonair anymore. I felt sweaty and soiled. Suddenly shocking Bobby didn't seem as wonderful an idea as it had a minute ago.

He kept looking at me, then turned and gazed out of the open car window on his side. Unexpectedly, he opened his door. "Give me a minute. There's something I have to tell you. I need to think how to say it." And just like that, he walked away and stood on the other side of the road, staring at a huge live oak tree with a meadow behind it. A flock of blackbirds whooshed by and headed toward a cluster of deep green hills in the distance.

I felt my shoulders collapse. He was probably trying to figure out a nice way of saying I wasn't good enough for him. He thought he should be kind because poor Earl had died and I was stuck back with my mom again. I closed my eyes and watched yellowish blobs build and break and build again. That's me, I thought, a big yellowish blob, building and breaking, building and breaking.

I looked out the car window at Bobby who was kicking at an exposed root of the live oak tree. Partly I wanted to run to him and partly I wanted to slip away into the field of weeds on my side of the road. I stared out at a field and that's when it came to me, in a quick blazing flash, like a sun spot.

Why in the world should I look for my father? What did my father ever do for me except to cause me grief? And what's worse, if I started to search for my dad, I'd end up just like my mother, like a fish on a hook, counting on a man to make me happy.

I was so startled at this realization, I felt my brain start to push the thought into a little corner, as though it was too big to feel all at once.

I looked up at the sky and wondered if I was trying to make a bargain with God. I'd give up on my father if he'd let me have Bobby. But then something stirred in me, some old fury at a faceless man who had ruined my life for too many years, and I knew I wasn't trying to make a deal. Tears pricked at the back of my eyes.

The air in the car was too close. I opened my door and stepped out, exhausted, as though I had done something that took tremendous effort. The damp weeds smelled slightly minty and the hills in the distance were a glistening blur as tears began to form on my lashes.

Bobby turned, walked back and put his hands on my shoulders. Our breath made warm puffs of air between us as he brushed his fingers over the wispy curls that framed my forehead.

"First the coffee," he said. "Then I'll tell you what I have to tell you. Promise."

I thought to myself, maybe I'll get another chance. Maybe if I'm pretty and witty and debonair at the diner, he'll decide I'm good enough for him, after all.

We sipped coffee while Bobby told me about the combo he was going to sit in with that afternoon in the Poconos. He said the piano player had once worked for a band that played for Frank Sinatra back in his Hoboken days.

"Really?" My voice came out like a squawk, a little like Henry Aldrich. "Wow," I said, "that's really something." I hadn't realized Bobby was becoming such a big timer. I'd have to bone up on music.

"Yeah." His eyes took on a mischievous look. He grinned, "This guy was at the performance when Frank first sang, 'I'll Walk Alone' and a girl in the audience screamed, 'I'll wok wid ya, Frankie.'

I giggled. He looked so adorable my throat ached.

I recited a Dorothy Parker poem.

Bobby laughed and said, "It's clever, but I like your own poems as well." He put his hand on the table near mine. "Are you still writing them?"

I lowered my eyes. "No, not lately, I've been busy, there's so much to do in Philadelphia. But I'll get back to it. I was thinking just this morning I should get back to it."

Bobby just nodded and kept looking at me, his hand still alongside mine.

"Anyway, speaking of music," I said, wondering what he was thinking, "I listen to it all the time. I love music. You should ask my roommate, Betsy."

He kept looking at me. "Good," he said.

Be pretty and witty, I reminded myself,

Outside in the car, Bobby turned on the ignition, then turned it off again.

He sucked in his breath. "I thought I could just go off and never have to tell you this. You might never have to know, but I can't do that."

"What?" My heart sank.

"I know who your father is."

I gasped. "What? You know what?" I blinked, bewildered. I looked around me as though my father had turned up outside the diner all of a sudden. I looked back at Bobby. Behind him, I could see the waitress in the diner cleaning off the table we'd sat at.

"We . . . uh . . . " Bobby's gaze fell. "We have the same father."

"What?"

"You and I. We have the same father." He glanced up, looking miserable. "I learned it the day you came to the Fourth of July picnic at our house. That's why I had to break off with you."

Barney wasn't Bobby's real father. So if it was true, that meant he didn't dump me because I was a slut. He didn't brush me off because I wasn't cute or witty enough. He was just trying to be honorable or whatever it is people are when they decide to break their own heart just to do the right thing. The waitress came back to our table with a rag and wiped away every trace that we'd been there.

Bobby stared at the steering wheel, muscles moving underneath his clenched jaw.

But wait again. If I was his sister, then there wasn't anything I could do to win him back. At least if it was just that I was a slut, I could change. I could show him I was different. My head hurt and I rubbed my temples.

A minute passed silently.

"Who is he?" My voice sounded like a wind in the distance.

"His name is Carl Markell. He used to repair machines at the Rutt Ridge Stocking Factory. He was married to my mother when we still lived out in the R.D. She told me all this the day after you came to the Fourth of July picnic at our house. Before that, she had your mother mixed up with somebody else."

"But how does she know your father . . . my mother . . . ?" I couldn't say the words.

"She doesn't know absolutely. But she'd heard gossip that he was carrying on with one of the girls at the stocking factory. Then when your mother had a baby, she put two and two together."

"But she can't be really sure. Maybe it was just a coincidence. Maybe he carried on with somebody else and she went off someplace to have a baby." I thought of the eggplant girl at the Philadelphia Y.

"Or maybe whoever he carried on with didn't have a baby at all." I was trying to figure out a way to show Bobby that the whole thing might be just a terrible misunderstanding.

Bobby shook his head. "No, she can't be sure, but she told me that day at our house she was startled at how much you looked like him. Around the eyebrows, she said. And a way you have of moving your shoulders when you walk." Bobby's voice sounded far away.

I felt sweaty and light-headed. I stared at a power line coming out of the diner. "But, then that means the only person who knows for sure is my mother."

He nodded and bit his lips. It looked like he had tears in his eyes.

"What was he like?" I asked.

"Charming. Unreliable." Bobby groaned and took me in his arms.

When he dropped me off at the apartment, he said he'd come back for me at 7:00 after his jam session was over and we'd talk about what to do.

"Will you be all right until then?" he asked.

I nodded. "I'm going to visit a girlfriend. That'll keep me busy."

"Good." He brushed my chin with his fingers and drove away.

33
NANCY, 1946

I slunk into the apartment and found a note from my mother on the kitchen table saying she'd gone to Mildred's. Thank God. I poured a glass of water, rushed to the sunporch, snatched another pill from my purse and gulped it down. I sat on the cot, staring out at the white winter sky, waiting for the pill to work, but my blood was racing through my veins. I got up and pounded my fists on the wall until the whole sunporch shook. I wondered if Clark would know what to do. If he didn't, at least he could ask his shrink. I needed to talk to someone who knew about the world to tell me what to do. I headed for the phone, but just then the apartment door opened and I heard my mother's footsteps, light and nervous. I wanted to run. I knew if I faced her, it would mean trouble.

"My favorite was the little kid with the short pants and the suspenders. The one who did the pig." It was Mildred's voice. Good. I wouldn't explode in front of Mildred.

"Nancy, you here?" my mom called.

I wanted to scream, "What do you mean here? Do you mean like a normal person who didn't have to spend her life feeling guilty about being born? Because if that's what you mean, no, I'm not here."

"Nancy?" She called again in her baby girl voice, as if she knew I was hiding.

I sighed. "Yes," I yelled back, my voice hissing. I moved like a zombie to the living room door.

"We just saw the cutest thing on television. Kids making bird and animal sounds." My mother looked like a kid with who'd just found a four-leaf clover. "Mildred bought herself a television for Christmas. There are only six of them in town."

I looked at Mildred. She was large and bony with thick dyed red hair.

I felt something lift in my head, almost like waves. It made me feel floaty, but calmer. I felt a little more confident that I could handle things after all.

"They were so cute," my mother went on. "They came up to the microphone one at a time. I liked the one that went tweet-eek, tweet-eek. Wasn't he a riot, Mildred?" And then she laughed her loud laugh and that did it.

Pictures of my mother laughing her big laugh through the years zipped across my brain like the flip-it movies you could buy at the five and dime. I heard a hum in my ears.

"Well, while you were out having a high old time, I was

busy trying to figure out how I could get in touch with a certain Mister Carl Markell." For a minute, I wasn't sure if I said the words or thought them.

My mother bounced so I must have said them.

"Where did you hear that name?" She went white.

My stomach heaved. So it was true. All the calmness I thought had been gathering in me went whoosh.

"Why didn't you ever tell me who my father was?" I felt if I didn't scream now I'd end up trying to choke her. My arms flailed, my heart stabbing at me like a jackhammer.

"Nancy, what a way to talk to your mother." My mom looked shocked and hurt, but I could see a flash of anger in her face, too.

"Couldn't you just have sat me down and said his name was Carl Markell and he worked at the stocking factory and he was married to another woman and you were sorry things weren't different? Couldn't you at least have done that? Is that too much to ask?"

"Nancy . . . " My mother said in an odd voice, half-hurt, and half-scolding, "this is no time to talk about things like that."

"The problem with you is there's never a time to talk about things like that." I screamed, the cords pulling in my throat. "You're just what they say. None are so blind as those who will not see."

My mother stood as if she was paralyzed. Out of the corner of my eye I could see a look of horror on Mildred's face.

But I couldn't stop. "I just learned that Carl Markell is Bobby Felker's father." My voice was a hoarse cry. "He's Bobby's father and he's my father, and I love Bobby and Bobby loves me and look at the mess we're in all because of you." My arms slashed the air wildly. "What kind of a mother would let me go out on dates with my own brother?"

"Bobby? Carl?" My mother's chin practically fell to the floor.

"Don't act so damn innocent. Don't you realize you've ruined my life, trying to act so damn innocent all the time when everybody knows different?"

My mother went white as a ghost and grabbed Mildred

225

by the arm. I knew I'd gone too far. I leaned against the wall and slid down to the floor.

Nobody spoke. I stared at the waxed floor boards as my mother edged toward me.

Her voice came out high and sobby. "You could be a little more thankful after all I've sacrificed for you." You could tell she was trying to holler but was too upset to do it right. "I could have just put you in the rag man's truck." Now her voice broke. "I thought about it." Then she burst into tears.

I didn't move a muscle, just sat there with my eyes fixed on the wood planks as what she had just said sank in.

I heard Mildred move towards her. "Listen, Georgia, it's an upsetting time," she said in a low husky voice. "I think both of you could do with one of your nerve pills."

The sunporch windows were dark when I awoke feeling like my insides had been scooped out. I moaned, remembering where I was and what had happened. I tiptoed to the door to peek at the kitchen clock. Six twenty-five.

I could hear my mother's gurgly breathing that told me she was deep asleep in her room.

I tiptoed to the bathroom, washed my face, and brushed my teeth. Slipping on my jacket, I hurried outside where I stood on the pavement alongside the house shivering in the chilly night air as I waited for Bobby.

I should call Sylvia, I thought, looking up at the half-moon. I turned toward the house for a minute, but then I shuddered and knew I couldn't go back in. I'd apologize to Sylvia in the morning. I'd go to see her first thing.

I stared at a puddle of moonlight. A car backfired in the distance and a window slammed nearby. I realized that whatever else was going to happen, things would never be the same between me and my mother again.

Maybe it was just as well. Maybe she'd face up to life more now. Maybe I'd really done my mother a favor in disguise. Oh, the timing might have been a little bad, but overall, maybe it was a healthy thing for both of us. That's what Clark would say. He'd say it was a healthy catharsis, that it would clear the air. But then my mother's face popped up, crying, "You could be a little more grateful. I could have put you in the rag man's truck."

By the time Bobby pulled up in the Buick, I knew what I wanted to do. His face shone white in a slash of moonlight. "Your house?" That didn't fit in at all with what I wanted to say. "There's no one home. They're out 'til midnight. It'll be all right."

"Oh, okay." I nodded and sat back on the scratchy car seat, feeling like a criminal he was going to harbor.

"I have a plan," he said as he closed the door to his house behind us. The rooms smelled piney, like Christmas.

"You do?" My heart leapt.

"We can go away together."

"We can? That's what you want, too?" I had already decided I didn't care if we were half brother and half sister, I still wanted Bobby more than anything else in the world. What difference did it make anyway? We felt the same about each other as we had the day before. The only difference was he'd said some words. The sun and moon still rose and set. Birds still cooed the same songs. I'd pictured us on the road, Bobby playing with his combo, me sitting at a table and polishing up my little books of verses.

We gazed at one another, standing close together in the vestibule. He smelled a little boozy as he put an arm around my shoulder and led me into the house. We passed underneath a sprig of mistletoe and he stopped and kissed me, a soft tender kiss.

We settled on the sofa, where he sat sideways, facing me, pulling his knee up so it rested on the cushion between us. "I think I can get on with the combo I sat in with this afternoon. We might be on the road a lot. I'm not sure we'd have much money."

"Oh, Bobby, I don't care about money. I don't care about being on the road. I'd love being on the road with you."

He looked toward the fireplace for a second, then back toward me. "I'd want us to get married."

"Married? Can we?" My voice came out like a little girl

asking if it was all right to cross the street, and for a minute, my eyes drifted to the photographs above the fireplace. Barney and Mrs. Felker at their wedding. Snapshots of the five boys clowning.

"What I mean is, is it legal?" I asked.

"Probably not. But who will know? Once we're away from Marysville, we can do anything we want." I spread my hands on his chest to feel the pumping of his heart, as if I needed to convince myself he was real. "You're right. What does it matter? I'm already illegal. Just being alive I'm illegal."

"No," he said. "Just being alive, you're making me very happy."

He reached forward and gently pulled me to him. We eased together down onto the sofa and I closed my eyes.

34
NANCY, 1946

My mother was in the kitchen ironing a pink bunny sweater when I got up.

"I'm going into work for a few hours. One of the girls is picking me up."

"I see." I'd just walked into the kitchen, still in my pajamas. "Well, maybe it'll be good for you."

"Yeah. That's what Mildred said." She didn't look up, just concentrated on the ironing as though it was the most important thing she'd ever done.

"Is there . . . uh . . . anything you want me to do?" It was chilly in the kitchen but my palms felt sweaty.

"No, just don't put the salt shaker next to the sink again. The salt was all globby last night."

"Oh, okay. I'm sorry. I won't." Maybe I was wrong. Maybe things wouldn't be any different between me and my mother after all. Maybe she'd just pretend yesterday never happened and I'd try to go along with it because I didn't know what else to do. But I did know that I had to get away. All that pretending day after day was too exhausting. It took too much out of your life. I started out for Sylvia's. The day was gray and gusty, and my ears stung from the wind. When I thought of Bobby my heart would go warm with love, but then as I remembered all the things I'd yelled at my mother it would go hard and chilly, and a minute after that, I'd be filled with fury at her for driving me to it. And underneath it all, there was guilt so strong it made my knees feel loose and my ears burn.

I passed the Marysville School, noticed there were bunches of kids standing outside, hunched together, and wondered what was up. School should have already started. I recognized Mary Bobst and Jennie Miller in one of the groups and strayed over.

"Oh, Nancy, I didn't know you were back," Mary said.

"Just for a week."

"Did you hear about Sylvia?"

"Sylvia?"

"It was terrible. She died. There was a terrible accident."

Every speck of blood in me dropped to my feet.

"Yesterday afternoon. About three o'clock," Jennie interrupted. "Everyone in school, that's all they're talking about. The teachers said we don't have to go to class if we're too upset."

"What happened?" I felt faint.

"Her brother did it," Mary said.

"What?"

"He was running with the shears and he fell on her."

"She was stooped down cleaning the yard," Jennie butted in. "She wanted to prune some twigs off a bush."

"He tripped on a root beer bottle. Florence Butz said the shears went right through her heart."

I stood paralyzed, thinking, if I'd gone to Sylvia's yesterday like I was supposed to, I could have grabbed her brother before he reached her. I could have taken her the shears myself. She wouldn't have been pruning the twigs off a bush anyway. She'd have been sitting at the rickety kitchen table drinking milk and eating Tandy Takes with me. But, no, I was too busy telling my mother how much she'd ruined my miserable life.

35
GEORGIA, 1946

I knew Nancy would blow up one day. You don't have to have an I.Q. the size of a German tank to know some things. I could see it behind her eyes practically from the day she was born. At least I learned I could put her off if I bounced and looked hurt and whatnot. If I said, "What a thing to ask your mother," and turned away, I could keep her in line. It wasn't that I didn't have bad nerves to begin with, I was always flighty, I just put it on a little more with Nancy. You have to do what you can when you're not a genius and you get flustered easy and say things that don't always follow what everybody's talking about.

Sure, I haven't been a perfect mother, didn't cross all the I's and T's, but who does? And I was so young when I had her. When you're that young, a baby seems like a toy and then before you know it, it gets a personality and turns out different than you and starts writing poems and essays and sassing you. Kids don't grow up the way they used to, minding their elders.

One thing, though, I truly didn't know about Bobby, and I feel real sorry for her over that. I had no idea Bobby was Carl's boy. The only reason I scolded about folks from the R.D. was because it seemed like a bad luck place to me after Carl. I didn't like to think about the R.D. after Carl.

Oh, I know Nancy would say what kind of a mother was I that I didn't even try to find out who Carl was married to, but things were different then. Everybody didn't tell everybody and their uncle all their business. I know these days you're supposed to say any fool thing that comes into your head. I've had my fill of Nancy spouting, "Ye shall know the truth." Well, I haven't noticed that the truth always makes you feel like you've been named queen for a day.

I remember just after Eddie took off for western P.A., I put on a couple of pounds and Cora didn't waste a minute making Kate Smith jokes, kidding that it was for my own good. Well, between you and me and the post office, I'd say it was more that Cora was all worked up over Walt and his episodes and feeling mean and nasty and who else was there to take it out on? That was a little truth I could have done just fine without, thank you. I don't understand why people can't just let a smile be their umbrella.

Anyway I did get one idea this morning when I was ironing and Nancy came into the kitchen and we both went tongue-tied. An idea that might help her out some. I suppose I owe her something after all those years of acting like a distant cousin. She didn't realize I was more afraid of her than anything. Plus she's being nicer lately and I notice her eyes go scared sometimes like she can use a little help in life.

Another thing, when she was out with Bobby yesterday I went in to straighten up the sunporch and found a poem on the table by the cot.

I picked it up. "Come with me and I'll show you my heart," it said. "On the way we'll dance through secret back roads of my mind . . . " After that I get it mixed up but it said something cute about kissing in the sun and then it went sad, saying people will tell you beware, don't go there, but it ended up cute again, saying something like, look, the moon still shines.

I figured it was a love poem for Bobby and it made me cry. It reminded me of how I felt about Carl, and then that made me cry even harder, thinking about Carl instead of Earl. Poor Earl. We only had six months together, and we were real happy. Earl was proud of me. He'd tell everybody he never thought he'd end up married to a looker like me. But at least he went happy. I made him a happy man. That's more than a lot of people can say in life.

The love poem gave me an idea of something I could do for Nancy and Bobby. I'd have to tell a little white lie, but so what if it helped them out for awhile. Puppy love. It never lasts anyway. Six months from now they'll both be gaga over somebody else. The main problem would be getting the words out straight. It wouldn't be easy talking about a thing I spent half my life pretending never happened, but I could practice. A little practice wouldn't hurt to help out my own kid.

36
NANCY, 1947

I stumbled home, crawled up on the cot, curled into a ball and cried for two days.

Nothing anybody said or did could help. Aunt Cora tried. Bobby tried, even my mother. She sat on the edge of the cot and put an arm around my shoulder, so light it could have been made of little bird bones, and said, "You can't go on crying forever. Sylvia wouldn't want it." She said the living had to get on with life; look at her, she was trying.

Finally she called in Dr. Di Salvo, who shone a flashlight into my eyes and listened to my heart, even though I couldn't believe there was still a heart left in me, and announced, "A bit of a breakdown, I'm afraid."

After that everything went foggy. I knew Bobby came every day and held my hand but the rest of him seemed far away and hazy. I kept seeing a skinny girl with puffy curls knocking at the sunporch window, calling in a muffled voice, "Nancy . . . Nancy . . .Come out to see me, Nancy." The only thing that kept me going was remembering how I'd reached over and put Sylvia's jumper strap back on her shoulder. At least I'd touched her. I pictured it over and over in my head. It wasn't much but it was the only decent thing I could think of that I'd done.

"If I'd only been there," I whimpered to Bobby one day, and he said, "Please don't think that. Life is a million ifs." He sat on the rocker by the cot. "If I hadn't told you about your father, you would have been there. I might just as well blame myself, but what good would it do? If Sylvia had gotten up that morning ten minutes earlier or ten minutes later. If her telephone had rung or if the mailman had stopped by or if her brother had decided to ride his bike or climb a tree or skin a cat . . . "

I nodded and tried to memorize his words so I could recite them to myself when I was alone at night, but even though I went through the whole list—the telephone, the mailman, the bicycle, the tree, the cat—when I finished I still felt sick to my stomach and croaked to the dark, "If only I'd been there."

Christmas came and went. My mother and I tried to ignore it. Just a Christmas carol on the radio could send us running for our nerve pills. We had our own bottles, side by side in the medicine cabinet next to the Pond's Cold Cream and the Cuticura. Most of the time I was asleep, dead to the world asleep. It was just as well because awake, my brain was like a pinball machine. I'd try to think straight but my thoughts would hit snags, scooting off in other directions. Backwards. Sideways. Clack. Crash. And I'd give up.

On New Year's Day I put on a gray skirt and a rose-colored sweater and sat in the living room. Bobby nestled by me on the plaid couch. "I've decided not to go to Hamlin," he said. "I'm going to quit college and stay in Marysville with you."

I started to cry. Bobby and I together was something too big to think about. I couldn't even decide what kind of an egg I wanted for breakfast, or if I wanted breakfast at all.

He squeezed my hand, "Oh, Nancy, the last thing I want to do is make you cry."

"Then don't stay," I bubbled. I didn't look at him, just stared at the braided rag rug on the floor.

His voice was quiet. "I don't believe you mean that." I felt his breath on my cheek as he looked at me.

Bobby gently took my hand. "You'll get well soon, and then we'll go ahead with our plans." His green eyes looked so sincere I felt he must not be seeing me right, he must have me mixed up with some other girl.

"No," I said, loud. "I want you to go to Hamlin." As

bewildered as I was, I knew I couldn't stand the guilt of ruining Bobby's life. I knew Mrs. Felker would be horrified at the thought of him going off with me, and he'd think for a while he didn't care, it was enough that we loved each other, but eventually he'd turn bitter and who could blame him?

He jerked back, surprised at the harshness of my voice.

"Bobby," I whispered, putting my hand on his knee, "I can't think of anything as complicated as going away together now." I felt the warmth of his leg through his corduroy pants and wanted to keep my fingertips there forever. "I'm not up to it. I'll get better faster if you go."

He turned my hand over, staring at my palm as though he was trying to read it. After a while he sighed, "I understand." The next week he told me he'd signed up at Hamlin but that he'd write to me every day and come to see me every weekend, and he did.

My mother went back to work but Mildred and Aunt Cora took turns bringing us dinner most afternoons. They'd knock on the door around five o'clock with a casserole and stories about the rest of the world. My mother and I sat at the kitchen table and listened to them like two puppy dogs trying to learn a trick. Weekends, my mother spent hours dusting her little porcelain figurines with a teeny red-handled paint brush, going over and over each Scotty dog, bunny and kitten to be sure she got every speck of dust.

At the end of January, I went back to school. Miss Sandercock came to the apartment twice a week to help me catch up, so I could graduate with the rest of the class. It wasn't hard. I threw myself into my school work the way my mother went at sticky floors and splotchy chrome. I read and read. *Look Homeward Angel*. *Pride and Prejudice*. *Jane Eyre*. I wrote two book reports a week. My favorites were sob stories, novels where everything looked hopeless but worked out in the end.

One day Miss Sandercock asked if I ever thought of going to college.

"Well, maybe after I fly to Jupiter and Mars," I joked.

She told me there were colleges that didn't cost an arm

and a leg, and I could probably get a scholarship to one of them.

I looked at her, feeling like Alice eying Wonderland but later that week I went to the library and copied down a list of colleges in Pennsylvania.

Bobby's letters helped keep me going. "I watched the sunrise today and saw your eyes in the morning light," he'd say. "I dreamt last night we danced together while Artie Shaw played 'Begin the Beguine.'" Reading his letters helped me feel more like a real person instead of a shadowy silhouette, someone with eyes and a heartbeat.

I'd made him promise not to talk about going off together until June, when I graduated from high school and he finished his first semester at Hamlin. "If it's meant to be, we'll love each other just as much then," I'd whispered and he'd kissed me until I thought he might pull all the breath out of me.

There were other little pinpricks of light. One cold February morning, out of the blue I got up early and wrote a poem about a girl who spilled the beans on the reverend with wandering hands. The girl in the poem sounded like the kind of person people would remember for doing something important.

Later that day I answered a Christmas note I'd gotten from Clark with a letter that stretched to six pages and the next Sunday morning, he called.

"It sounds like you've gone through a real nightmare up there." It was good to hear his voice. Clark was someone who could understand.

"I have."

"Are you seeing a shrink?"

"No. The doctor gave me nerve pills."

He sighed. "When are you coming back?"

"I don't know if I am."

"Hmmmm. Well, listen, don't let them talk you into anything. I worry about you up there, getting sucked into some small-town rut you'll live to hate."

"I know. I won't." I twirled the phone cord around my finger and decided not to say Bobby and I were thinking of going away together. Clark would just say we were drawn

235

together because we were related. But with me and Bobby I knew it was different. I knew it was true love.

"Besides, I miss you," he said. "I really mean it. Who else do I know who can touch her nose to the floor and roll into a ball and curl?"

I realized I missed Clark, too. I began to feel witty and debonair again, as though Clark brought out a certain spunk and spark in me. Plus, he wasn't being sarcastic. He was being sweet, although I supposed that was pretty much the way you had to be to someone who was getting over a nervous breakdown. Still, Philadelphia started to seem exciting and full of promises again.

"Uh, look, Nancy, I hope you realize that you have some tough work ahead. The breakdown was your body's way of telling you to stop and take a look at your life and all the grudges and guilt that drove you to it."

"I know."

"Another thing, I know you've been through a real hell up there, but that doesn't mean you shouldn't try to meet your father." Clark's voice was somber now. "It might help you to understand yourself in ways you haven't even thought about. And who knows. He may be thrilled to find out he has a girl after three boys."

"I have no interest in thrilling my father." I pulled the telephone cord tight in my fist.

"Hmmm. Well, I can understand that," Clark said. "God, I wish I were there to help you talk this mess out."

"Oh, Clark, I do, too. I get so confused." And I realized I meant it, and after I hung up, that confused me even more.

By May, I knew I was getting itchy feet again. There was something about spring. You've been cooped up all winter and suddenly you walk out one day and a warm breeze brushes your cheek and you want to waltz down the street. Next thing you know, there are baby leaves on the trees and a flower pokes up through the old slushy snow, looking so pretty it practically breaks your heart.

Plus in the spring Dr. DiSalvo took me off the nerve pills and the nightmares started. I'd be stuck on a high narrow bridge in black space, so narrow I could only walk one foot in front of the other, as fierce rapids churned and roared far underneath me.   A cold wind would blow up from the water and call "Nancy, come to us, Nancy," as ghosts in gray robes floated by.   I'd wake up with sweat on my chest and race into the bathroom, turn on the light and stare at myself in the mirror to be sure I was real.

Sometimes in the morning I'd watch my mom sit at the maple table smacking doughnuts and looking innocent and I'd want her to stop so much I'd go rigid holding back the tears.   All day long at school I'd hear her smacking doughnuts until by the time I got back home, I'd want to scream at her, "Why didn't you just put me in the rag man's truck if you wanted to?   Somebody would have adopted me and raised me in a normal family and I could be a hot shot like Shirley Metzger and wear real velvet dresses and marry Bobby and everybody would say, look, aren't they cute instead of ugh, how disgusting.   Why didn't you just go ahead and put me in the truck?"

Sylvia was all mixed up in it, too.   Just about the time I'd go weak with rage at how miserable my life was, I'd think Sylvia would be happy just to be alive, and I'd scold myself for being so evil and selfish and promise to try harder to forgive even if I couldn't forget.   I carried around little scraps of paper saying, "Only the brave know how to forgive." "Without forgiveness, life is governed by an endless cycle of resentment." "To err is human, to forgive divine."   The quotations got me through the day, but they didn't help the nights.

37
NANCY, 1947

In mid-May my mother pulled all our summer clothes out of garment bags like she did every May, and on Decoration Day we got dolled up and went to a celebration

Mildred threw at a resort in the Poconos. Cora and Walt were there, too, plus a couple Mildred knew from Keller's Creek, a town near Clinton.

My mother wore an organdy V-necked dress and I had on a melon-colored cotton dress with a gathered skirt and a scoop neckline. We put on our summer shoes and my mom said, "We should wear gloves. We haven't been out for a while. We need to put our best face forward."

I was thrilled to be going to the Poconos. It would give me a chance to picture what it would be like being on the road with Bobby. I knew lots of combos played there.

Uncle Walt and Aunt Cora picked us up at three o'clock. "We tossed to see who'd drive," Uncle Walt cracked with a grin as he pulled up and we climbed into the DeSoto. "You lucked out. I won. Cora's driving is picking up, though," he went on. "These days she's getting twenty miles to the fender."

Aunt Cora looked more gorgeous than ever. She was back modeling part time at Finkel's now.

We drove toward forests full of green pines past neat pastel houses perched in fields that looked as if they stretched to the end of the world. Traveling up the mountain road, we passed small wood cabins curled around a lake, as blue and shiny as a satin ribbon. Roadside signs announced the resorts up ahead: Pocono Pines, Bear Creek, Promised Land.

By the time Uncle Walt pulled up in front of Sugar Notch, my heart leapt with joy picturing me and Bobby, walking arm in arm through the grounds full of hollyhocks and lilac trees and weeping willows that encircled the small hotel.

Inside, the lobby had a brick-colored tile floor and a milk can full of pussy willows on a polished wooden counter. A man with a name tag on his lapel that said "Kenneth McBright, Assistant Manager" showed us to the restaurant, but as we followed behind him, I peeked back at a curved staircase that I figured must lead up to the rooms and I daydreamed of Bobby and me snuggled together underneath a fresh-smelling starched sheet as the moon smiled in at us through the window.

Mildred and the others were at a table in a small room all decked out with red, white, and blue balloons. On the table were two platters, each with a mound of soft yellow cheese in the center, then a circle of radishes cut to look like flowers, a circle of green olives, bologna slices, and around the rim, an edging of Ritz crackers overlapping one another. There were lots of hellos and bustling about. Aunt Cora recited "Flanders Field" and all our eyes got bright with tears until Uncle Walt said, "Well, look at this sorry bunch of crybabies," and we laughed and started wolfing down the fried chicken, scalloped potatoes, and coleslaw.

Aunt Cora straightened an American flag on a toothpick in Uncle Walt's lapel and he turned, flashing her a brilliant smile. I thought back to one day when she'd brought us dinner. "Walt's doing real great," she'd said. "He has his ups and downs, of course. He has his Bela Lugosi days. But most days he's Gary Cooper, my own matinee idol." Then she got serious. "At first I thought it was the VA counseling that was helping, then I thought it was probably Barbara. I'm sure it was partly both of those, but in the end it was something even more important that made the difference." She took waxed paper off the top of the bowl and looked me in the eye. She put a hand on my arm as if she wanted to be sure I heard what she said. "I used to suspect this but now I'm sure of it. In the end, it's that he knows I can get along on my own now if I have to."

Mr. McBright came around our table, hopping from person to person, asking if everything was all right. He was a stocky man with thick gray hair and two steep peaks in the center of his upper lip, like bridge spires. When he got to my mother's place, he spotted her name card and said, "Georgia, what a pretty name. I was born in Georgia. The state, that is." He laughed.

My mother looked up at him smiling and you could see the red start to creep up her neck like a thermometer.

Then he left.

"Hey, you two should take a vacation together, you deserve it." Cora sipped her Scotch and water. "If you want a chaperon, count me in."

My mother and I both laughed but I felt my spine go

stiff and my mom looked uncomfortable, too. She was probably thinking the same thing I was. Now that we were growing stronger, we were getting on one another's nerves again. We tried to pretend it was different, we specialized in fake smiles. Some days I'd try to convince myself that maybe if two people gave each other enough fake smiles, one day they'd become real.

But other times I'd find myself just weary and resentful.

Everyone got up and headed for the lobby but I walked outside and sat on a huge veranda that wrapped around three sides of the hotel.

I watched the sun do a rhumba on the porch floor, but I was really picturing me and Bobby at the Jersey shore. Atlantic City.

He'd be on stage with a combo on the Steel Pier, playing, "I Only Have Eyes For You" as I stood by the bandstand wearing the same lilac sweater and swirly black skirt I wore on our first date.

When the set ended, Bobby would jump down and we would dance together as the juke-box played "I'll Get By," moving as much to the rhythm of our heartbeats as to the music.

My mother's voice brought me back to real life. "Nancy, you should see the cute rooms," she called, stepping out onto the veranda with my aunt and Mr. McBright. "The beds have flowered chintz counterpanes and they use Sani-Flush in the bathrooms just like home," my mother said.

I chuckled to myself. She swore by Sani-Flush and she used it twice a week to avoid unsightly toilet bowl stains. She liked the ad for Sani-Flush in *Good Housekeeping* that showed two women looking disgusted, one whispering to the other, "Some things are inexcusable." She liked that nobody would ever whisper about Georgia Sayers' toilet bowl.

My mom looked at Mr. McBright. "I always say that's a sign of a good place, if the bathrooms are clean. Even though I'm just a widow now, I still keep a nice clean house."

Mr. McBright's face took on a half-surprised, half-pleased expression, and I thought to myself, my mother sounds almost brazen. Then I realized why. She was finally respectable. More and more I'd noticed she would mention poor Earl, her poor late husband, even in conversations where Earl didn't exactly fit. More and more she seemed to find reasons to say things were hard when you were a widow but you had to go on. Being a widow seemed to give my mother a kind of confidence she'd never had before. "Have you seen the parlor behind the lobby?" Mr. McBright asked, his eyebrows arching. "We have a television there. Not too many hotels have them, you know."

"Television?" My mother's eyes grew huge. He might as well have said they were giving out hundred dollar bills. She turned to me and my aunt.

"You go ahead, Georgia," Aunt Cora said. "I'll wait out here on the veranda with Nancy."

When they were out of sight, my aunt smoothed her white accordion pleated skirt, then asked, "How are you doing, Nancy? Really."

I stared down at a bed of roses in the garden, watching a red beetle lug a tiny piece of twig across the dirt.

After a long minute, I answered, "I can't stay in Marysville. I have to go."

Aunt Cora's mouth twitched. "I know." Her blue eyes looked at me straight in a way my mother never could. "Your mother knows, too."

"She does?"

"Yeah. She calls it wanderlust. She said she'll probably move in with Mildred anyway. She's gone gaga over television, and she likes Mildred's women's group."

I glanced up at Cora. Maybe that was another thing giving my mother confidence, getting in more with the girls at work. I noticed all of them spoke their minds more lately instead of waiting to see what somebody's husband had to say.

"Or who knows?" Aunt Cora rolled her eyes toward the hotel lobby. "Maybe she'll marry again. With Georgia, anything can happen."

"Why didn't you tell me she didn't care if I went?" My voice sounded whiny again and I couldn't help feeling bitter, thinking of all my sleepless nights, the terrifying dreams, the guilt.

My aunt wet her lips. "I thought about it. Nancy, I know you're fighting demons. I know I might have lightened the load for you." She reached out and touched my hand. "But in the end I knew you needed to make your own decision. I learned that from going through the past year with Walt."

My gaze traveled back to the beetle. I knew my aunt was right. I thought of telling her Bobby and I might go away together. I wondered if that would shock her but decided that it probably wouldn't. She'd probably just shrug and say, "Stranger things have happened." The beetle stopped, zig-zagged for a minute, then went on again without the twig. I wondered if he was sorry to lose it or if the twig had just got stuck to him by mistake.

I watched a slice of sun jiggling on the veranda floor. "It's easy for you to say with Georgia anything can happen. She's only your sister. But when she's your mother . . . ."

Tears pricked my eyes. "Some days I feel so furious I just shake and then she looks at me with that baby girl expression and I know it's . . . hopeless. I suppose it's a terrible thing to say, but all that damned cheerfulness makes me so sour by comparison, sometimes I want to scream."

"Oh, Nancy, I know." Aunt Cora said huskily. "I remember when we were little. We'd get into mischief like any kids, but if we ever got caught, Georgia would run to Daddy and hug his legs and say I made her do it."

She laughed quietly. "That was usually true. But Daddy would give Georgia a hug, and then ask if I wanted my mouth washed out with soap and I'd say yes just to shock him." A light breeze ruffled her hair. "If I had to put up with a mouthful of Lux suds to get a little attention, that's what I'd do."

I looked in my aunt's eyes and realized she was telling me she'd had to learn how to deal with my mother, and I had to find my own way. I thought of saying if I didn't run away with Bobby I might go back to Philadelphia and see a shrink or go to college, but I knew how she'd just say,

"Seeing a shrink wouldn't hurt. Going to college definitely wouldn't hurt either."

Aunt Cora slipped closer to me and gave me a hug just as we heard Uncle Walt's deep laugh and watched my mother and Mr. McBright step back onto the porch.

"Listen, kiddo,"Aunt Cora said, "anytime you want to talk, call or write or come and stay with me, I'll always have time for you, you hear? We have a special connection, you and me. Remember the good old days pouring over the thesaurus and the joke books? Remember the pelvic tilt exercises and hip thrusts?" My aunt flipped her right hip up a tiny bit, the way models are taught to do to help clothes hang better. I flipped my hip up to match and we both giggled, but I noticed her eyelashes were damp.

A young couple drove up to the hotel entrance in a fire-engine red Chevrolet coupe. My uncle, who was standing there with Mr. McBright now, put his hand up to his mouth as if he was letting him in on a secret, but his voice was loud as brass.   o

"Well, you know what they say," he bellowed, "in a cigarette it's taste, in a whiskey it's age, but in a coupe it's impossible."

Mr. McBright laughed and headed for the car.

My mom made a beeline for me and my aunt. "Such a nice man," she said, her face flushed. "And he looked at me special. I could tell. You didn't have to be blind to see it."

We watched Mr. McBright greet the young couple and escort them inside.

"I wonder what it would be like to live in a cute place like this" My mom's voice was high. "I wonder what it would be like being married to an assistant manager of a nice resort."

Aunt Cora looked sidewise at me and I faked a smile.

"Not that I'm interested, of course," my mother went on. "Being a widow. And he's probably married anyway."

Mildred came into view at end of the lawn, the late afternoon sun behind her. She waved and walked toward us.

"In which case," Aunt Cora said, "it might be more interesting to wonder what it would be like to be an assistant manager of a nice resort." She gave my mom a wise smile. "You start with a can of Sani-Flush and a cheery smile and who knows where it'll lead."

My mother looked confused for a minute and wet her lips. Then her eyes brightened. "That's right," she said, her voice rising, "I bet someday there will be girl assistant managers."

Aunt Cora and I burst out laughing as Mildred came up and asked what was so funny.

"Life," Aunt Cora said.

"Right. Life," I echoed, and the four of us stood on the veranda together, watching our shadows lengthen in the blazing sun.

38
NANCY, 1947

Bobby drove me to the bus station. I looked back at Marysville as we pulled out, watching the neat rows of pastel houses slide away like stage scenery. I twisted to see behind me until the whole town became a gray smudge in the distance.

I stared at Bobby's profile as he drove. His sandy hair was longer than it used to be and some wisps curled up in the back at the curve of his neck. He drummed his fingers lightly on the wheel. I wanted to go away with him more than I wanted to breathe, wanted to say, "Oh, Bobby, forget it. It was silly, thinking I needed a week in Philadelphia. Let's just turn around and go off together right now."

Instead I closed my eyes and watched pinwheels spin and disappear and felt my eyelids flutter.

Bobby broke the silence. "I worry it's the guy there you're really going to see."

"Oh, Bobby, no, it's not the guy at all. That's one thing you don't have to worry about." That was true. My heart didn't turn somersaults over Clark, but I couldn't help thinking to myself there was something about what Clark represented that made my blood race—a kind of life where you might do neurotic things like put on your Rhonda act in a nightclub, that made you want to try new things and find new ways to laugh at the insanity in the world.

I looked out my car window. Houses with gray fences and overgrown yards raced by. Shades were pulled down halfway, making windows look like sleepy eyes.

I was going to stay with Betsy, but what I was really looking forward to was having the time alone to sit in Fairmount Park, stare at the Schuylkill River and try to write out everything I wanted to tell myself.

"It's only a week," I reminded Bobby. "And when you drive down next Friday to pick me up, you can meet the whole crazy mixed-up bunch for yourself."

He gave me a sidewise glance, and I knew what he was thinking. How would I introduce him. This is my boyfriend. And, oh, by the way, he's also my brother? That would certainly put us in the avant garde. Or would I just blurt, "Meet Bobby, the two of us are running off together next week." Bobby has a gig playing clarinet with a combo in Scranton, then in Pittsburg, and after that who knows? And I may go to college, a class here, a class there. We're thinking of getting married.

At the station we stood side by side underneath a hazy sun, arms around one another. The air was warm and still.

"Oh, before I go, I just remembered. My mother gave me a note. She told me to read it after I got to the station." I pulled a blue envelope from my skirt pocket. Inside there was a single piece of blue scented writing paper. I unfolded it.

"Dear Nancy," it said. "I haven't been able to find a way to say this. You know I'm not too good with words. But I wanted you to know this Carl Markell that you told me about isn't your father. Carl Markell must have run around with one of the other girls at the factory. Your father was somebody else, a real good man, but he died before he got a chance to know you. It was an automobile accident out on Wind Gap Junction Road. It was very sad. It made me too sad to think about it. That's why I never said anything before, but I wanted you to know now so you and Bobby can go on with your lives."

Bobby and I looked at each other and gasped. We read the letter again then we hugged and twirled around in a circle. All of a sudden I started to laugh and cry at the same time. I pulled back and stared at Bobby. "She made this up. If you'd seen her face the day I mentioned the name Carl Markell, you'd know she made this up."

I looked back at the neat rows of handwriting and a tear streamed down my cheek. After all those years, she finally made up a story about my father.

"But it still gives us an out," Bobby said, his cheeks pink with excitement. "And what's better, we have it in writing. People can suspect anything they want. We have a letter that says we're not related."

I smiled but my voice seemed to be bunched up in my throat. After a minute you could see Bobby's face change, too, as he realized that we would always know the truth. We stood quietly and watched a young boy kick a can along the pavement across the street.

When my bus arrived, Bobby helped me settle into a seat and stashed my suitcase in the overhead luggage compartment. He slipped into the seat next to me for a second, gave me a wide smile and said, "Okay, here's looking at you, kid," then pressed my hand and left. I watched him walk back to the Buick, moving with smooth, sure steps,

The bus pulled out and I read the note from my mother over and over. Bobby was right. Even if it wasn't true, Bobby could tell his mother it was, and she might suspect different but she'd never really know. She'd have to take our word for it.

I looked out the smudged bus window. The day had brightened and the sun threw buttery splotches on the sides of houses. Wasn't that just like my mother, to come up with a way to pretend things were fine. Except this time she was doing it for me. I leaned my head back against the blue upholstered seat and closed my eyes, a slice of sun warm on my face, when I heard a musical laugh behind me that sounded like Shirley Metzger. I turned and spotted three girls wearing sloppy joe sweaters and bright faces, talking with a confidence that told you they knew where they were going in life. Facing front again, I thought I could understand how a fatherless girl with a scatterbrained mom could go bad but I wasn't convinced it had to be that way. Maybe you just needed something or someone to coax you along.

I squinted out into the sun. There was a lot I still had to learn, but one thing I knew for sure. I wasn't going to waste any more energy trying to be a small-town hot-shot like Shirley Metzger. Another thing I knew was that I wasn't meant to be the kind of girl who'd one day put on a satin gown and take a solemn oath to be a Worthy Advisor in the Order of the Rainbow at the Marysville Elks Club and I wasn't the kind of girl who'd be content crocheting afghans, bragging about her Kelvinator and her Hotpoint.

I closed my eyes and watched the sequins flash. Rhonda. She bent and twisted, hair swinging, muscles stretching, air crackling with the energy she gave off. I'd been thinking a lot about her lately. I hadn't figured out why yet but there was something about her that seemed to carry the secret I was looking for about life. Maybe it was however tightly Rhona twisted and turned, she could always untangle herself and toss her hair. Rhonda was her own person.

I reached into my purse and fingered my Dorothy Parker book. I pulled out a sterling silver ballpoint pen Aunt Cora had given to me as a going-away present. A ballpoint pen was something new. You didn't have to dip it into ink, just flick it and write. I turned the pen this way and that, watching the silver catch the colors of the sunlight. I opened my notepad and wrote my name; the pen worked perfectly. No inky blobs, no chicken scratches, just firm, swirly indigo blue letters. A nice color of deep blue with a silvery edge to it that reminded me of the Delaware River early in the morning when the mist is rising and the sun is flirting with the water in little prickly flashes in the distance.